THE EMPTY PLACE AT THE TABLE

JOHN ELLSWORTH
JODE JURGENSEN

SUBJUDICA HOUSE PRESS

1

I t was just a sandwich I wanted, preferably egg salad but tuna salad would do as well. It was late at Belmont Hospital, and the cafeteria would close in ten minutes. I hadn't eaten since the night before and felt drained of all energy. Sweeping aside a lock of hair from Lisa's face and kissing her forehead, I left in search of a sandwich. As I came around the corner to the elevators, I could look straight ahead out the tall windows and see the lights of Chicago laced with drifting snowflakes. It was beautiful, but it didn't register, worried as I was for my daughter.

The cafeteria was on the first floor of the hospital. The elevator arrived, opening to discharge a man wearing scrubs. I remember thinking he looked nervous. I punched LOBBY on the bank of elevator buttons and leaned back against the wall as the doors closed. If only...I thought if only Lisa's fever would break and the sickness that had landed her in the hospital was brought under control. The doctors weren't sure what it was that was causing the frightening temperature spikes. Some thought it was an infection, the body's way of fighting a disease. Her general malaise over the last month, plus the temperature, led others to speculate it was possibly the onset of leukemia. Lisa was my first and only child; I alternated between praying for the best and expecting the worst. It's just how I react under stress.

The elevator stopped on 2, and a nurse entered. She lifted a travel cup and began taking long gulps, oblivious to the fact I was watching her.

I turned away. My eyes filled with tears. I loved that four-year-old of mine more than life itself. If it were possible, I would gladly trade places with my baby and crawl into bed and happily die, knowing that she was going to be well and healthy. But that wasn't how hospitals--and life--ever worked. Plus, it wasn't me lying there in the hospital bed, bathed in sweat, coming in and out of consciousness. It wasn't me: it was my first and only child, my precious Lisa of the *Frozen* videos and Barbie dolls. Lisa, my love.

The elevator whooshed open, and the lobby appeared before me. I knew the way to the cafeteria as I had been living in the chair beside Lisa's hospital bed for seventy-two hours. I had been down here four times for coffee and sustenance. While I hadn't wandered far from my daughter's side, I had made quick trips for machine coffee, too, and once to valet parking to check on my car. But other than these sprints, I had held my baby's hand all the way so far.

Yellow footprints were stenciled on the floor as a guide to the cafeteria. I, without much realizing what I was doing, began placing my feet on the footprints, navigating the hospital without raising my eyes. My OCD always managed to surface when I was stressed. A little bit OCD, a little bit clingy mother. I also refused to step on cracks outside on the sidewalk. *Step on a crack and break your mother's back.* A little bit OCD, for sure. Which explained why I had doted on my daughter for her first four years. I knew every wrinkle, every freckle, ever wisp of downy baby hair on my daughter's body. My baby was a map that I knew by heart. Didn't all mothers memorize their kids? I couldn't imagine any mother not doing it.

At precisely 9:56 p.m. I entered the cafeteria and hurried to the serving line where sandwiches were nicely displayed beneath cabinet lights; it didn't fool me: they looked much better than they actually were when eaten. Still, it was something to ingest. Who could tell--the cafeteria food might satisfy the food cravings that overcame me every twelve hours, forcing me back downstairs to the food place.

"Just the sandwich," I told the cashier, a sleepy-eyed woman with a paperback beside the cash register. I checked the cover upside-down and realized it was the third time that week I'd seen that book. Everyone was reading it. I wondered if the gift shop might be open so I could grab a copy too. I decided to check.

"Nothing to drink?" the cashier asked.

"Nope, just the sandwich."

"Three-ninety-nine, please."

"Here you go."

"Out of five. And here's your change. Have a good night, ma'am."

"Thank you."

Ma'am? Did I really look that old? I was all of thirty-two, which really wasn't ma'am territory. Or was it?

I was tired, thinking like that, and I knew it. Maybe tonight I'd get an hour or two of sleep between nursing rattles and clatters when Lisa was checked. Maybe.

The gift shop was closed, so no novel.

I punched 8 and waited as the elevator caught its breath and began lifting me upstairs.

The nurses acknowledged me as I passed by their station on my way to Lisa's room. But no one called me ma'am, which was a good thing. I just wasn't ready to be a ma'am yet. And why was that word bothering me so much anyway?

Into Lisa's room I turned, only to find my daughter's bed empty. For just a moment I stood there at her bedside, bewildered and uncertain. I knew I was tired from lack of sleep; had I misunderstood one of Lisa's caregivers? Had someone told me she would be going for another scan?

I backed out of the room and checked the number beside the door. Sure enough, 811. I went back inside and, leaning across my daughter's bed, pressed the nurse call button. I counted slowly while waiting for a member of the nursing staff to materialize and tell me that Lisa had been taken to radiology for another CT scan. The scans were routine; once a day, at least, so I wasn't freaking out. But I also realized I was fighting against freaking out; no one had told me another scan was scheduled that night. Wouldn't they have mentioned it at the nurses' station when I passed by on my way to the cafeteria? Or coming back? They certainly should have.

A nurse appeared, a night-shift beauty queen whom I knew as Sensa. Sensa was tall, dark-skinned, flashed a quick smile at tense moments, and was all business. She hurried up to Lisa's bedside, across from me.

"Did you see the nurses or radiology take her?" Sensa asked before I could ask the same question myself.

"No, that' s why I buzzed you. I'm assuming that's who has her, right?"

"Let me check her chart."

Sensa proceeded to the keyboard at the head of the bed and began tapping keys. As she did, I realized the nurse was just as mystified as I was. My pulse rate suddenly doubled. I felt the fear down deep in my bowels and fought to control it. There had to be some explanation. Sensa would turn around at any second and smile and report Lisa's whereabouts.

But she wasn't smiling when she finally turned.

"There's no CT order. Or any other order that would remove her from her room. I'm calling security."

Sensa pressed a large red button on the electronics panel and said into a mesh-covered microphone, "Security to eight-one-one stat. A patient is missing."

A patient is missing? It sunk into my brain like a roof caving in on me. First came the panic, then came the tears, then came a struggle to remain calm and collected so that I could help hospital security think through the predicament.

"Call down and tell them not to allow any cars to leave the

parking lot, please!" I ordered Sensa. Sensa made the call and nodded.

"Smart. Thanks."

"Good. Oh, my sweet God, what do we do now?"

Without waiting for an answer, I trotted into the hallway and looked both directions. There wasn't a soul around except at the nurses' station. I ran in the opposite direction, down to the end of the hall where the family waiting room was usually occupied by one or two souls waiting for loved ones. In I ran, only to find the place deserted. The restroom door was closed. I knocked once and entered. It was a small room with just one toilet and one sink. Empty. I ran back into the hallway and began trotting toward Lisa's room.

Just as I arrived, I saw security coming my way. Two men and one woman. She was wearing a gun on her belt. Holding it against her side, she was the first to run up to me. The men followed close after.

"Shouldn't we be checking all the other rooms on the floor first?" I cried out.

"Let's go back inside the room, ma'am," said the burly security guard in the blue shirt and pants. He was oldish--maybe sixty--and wore his hair in a flat top and his glasses halfway down his nose. I followed his instructions and entered my daughter's room.

The bed was still empty. It hadn't been just a bad dream.

"Oh, oh, oh!" I cried, "For the love of God, somebody do something!" I was in full panic mode now, tears streaming down my face, with an urgency pressing down on my chest demanding I do something. However, for the first time in a long time, I had no idea what it was I should do to place angels around my baby. I closed my eyes, weeping, clenching and unclenching my fists. Quickly, however, I realized I was no help to anyone like that, so I forced the tears from my eyes and took several deep breaths. *Do these people have any idea how I'm feeling? Do they have any idea where Lisa was taken?*

"You okay?" Sensa asked.

"I'm trying!" I cried.

The second and third security officers were on their shoulder mics giving orders to other guards in the hospital and, I hoped, at all parking lot exits.

"All right," said flat top, "we have the exits blockaded. Nobody leaves here until we find your child. Now, give me a description."

"Please," I begged, "shouldn't you be searching every room so they can't hurt her?"

"That's underway, ma'am. Now please describe her for the bulletin I'm about to issue."

I didn't hesitate. "Age four, forty inches tall, medium-length blond hair, pale blue eyes, a small pout when she smiles. On her lower left back, almost closer to her hip, there's a small birthmark in the shape of a sailboat. My pet name for her is 'Sailor,' in fact. She also has something like cradle cap, although she's too old for that. Probably from being in bed so long."

"Answers to?"

"Lisa. Last name Sellars."

The security officer updated all hands with his shoulder mic, broadcasting the patient's physical description and name and room number.

"Everybody in the hospital is alerted, all floors, all parking lot exits, police were called and are arriving downstairs even as we speak. Now tell me, is there a relative--an ex-husband, maybe?--who might snatch your child?"

"No one like that. Her father was killed in Afghanistan, and my sisters don't live here. One's in Poughkeepsie, one's in Merced, California. My parents are in London with the State Department. I have no enemies, and I'm not wealthy. It wouldn't be anything like that. At least I don't think it could be."

At just that moment, the officer's shoulder mic squawked. He repeated something back and then turned to me.

"They think they've found her just down the hall. There's a family waiting area and a little girl answering Lisa's description has been found sleeping on a couch."

"Take me there, please!" I said as coolly as I could, though I was unable to totally fight down the apprehension and my words came out more like a command than a request for help.

"Follow me, ma'am."

Our entourage burst out of Lisa's room and hurried the other direction from the family room I had searched. We trotted past the nurses' station, down to the end of the hall, where we charged into a family waiting area. There we found two other security guards, talking gently to a child maybe twice Lisa's age.

"Not her!" I cried. "Now what?"

We headed back toward Lisa's room just as several police officers turned the corner at the far end down by the elevator bank. I began trotting toward them.

They went into Lisa's hospital room. We met them there. Then came the questions. Pretty much the same questions the security officers had asked. They seemed to focus a little more on potential enemies or family members with an agenda who might swoop in and grab my daughter. Again, however, I could offer nothing unusual to support that theory. A young police officer returned from the nurses' station with the news that two nurses had seen a patient wheeled by on the way to radiology. Mics were keyed, and staccato conversations batted back and forth: security reported no female child showing up in radiology since seven o'clock. Radiology's complete patient log was produced, and security reviewed it. Sure enough, no Lisa Sellars on the list.

Then a plainclothes officer arrived, a no-nonsense-looking woman wearing her hair pulled back in a ponytail, a large firearm riding high on her hip beside a gold detective's star. She stuck out her hand and introduced herself to me as Detective Kendra McMann. It was now her investigation, she said; she was from Chicago PD, and missing children was where she put in her eighty hours weekly.

She took over the search of the hospital and hospital grounds. Police opened every door in the entire complex, looked inside every restroom, supply closet and laundry room, and talked to all security staff. This process took an hour. While it progressed, I sat in my chair beside Lisa's bed and willed her return. It became apparent to me that I wasn't going to leave there without my daughter. They would have to drag me out.

I crossed my arms and sat back. Just then, Detective McMann caught my eye.

"What I would suggest right now," the detective said to me, "is that you let me take you home. I'll ask some questions along the way. Then let's set up a command center in your home. That way you'll know what's going on every minute. It will also give us a chance to view your daughter's room, collect DNA, and plan our investigation."

"Go home? I can't leave here, not without my daughter," I insisted. *Do these people not understand you cannot leave your child?*

"Ma'am," said Detective McMann, "I'm of the opinion your daughter is no longer in the hospital."

"What do you mean, no longer in the hospital?"

The detective reached to lay a hand on my forearm. She squeezed gently, and her calm brown eyes fixed my own with a caring stare.

"I mean your daughter has been kidnapped. That's where I come in."

"Kidnapped like--"

"Yes, ma'am. Your daughter has been stolen from the hospital. The next step is to sit down and teach me everything you can about your child, your family, your friends, and possible enemies."

"All--all right." I turned to Sensa, the nurse. "You'll call me if she shows up if she was taken for testing or something?"

"Of course. We have your cell number."

I felt the floor sliding out from under me. The reality was that my connection to my daughter was slipping away and there was nothing to grab or hold onto. At that moment, I slumped down in the visitor's chair and broke down, sobbing and wiping at my eyes. Sensa passed me a tissue.

The others left the room to wait outside in the hallway.

It was always the same, I would learn. The parent needed several minutes to say farewell to their love, their cherished one, their dreams. But another part of me didn't believe any of this, not a damn bit. This other part of me knew without a doubt that my little girl would be located at any moment and that I needed to be here to see her.

"We should go now," McMann said. "The sooner we get a command center set up, the better our search will be. Organization is everything. Let's go set up in your kitchen right now, Mrs. Sellars. You'll be in touch with the entire effort every minute of the day and night."

Without fully trusting what she was saying—yet liking the command center idea—I did what she wanted and stood to leave.

When I finally emerged from Lisa's room, Detective McMann took my elbow and guided me to the elevators. It was time to face whatever reality I was facing; her touch told me that she would be there for me regardless. My mind raced over the TV shows I'd seen about child abductions. I remembered that the first twenty-four hours were critical because if Lisa wasn't located during that window of time, the chances slipped to less than ten percent of her ever being found. It was a statistic I knew the detective would never share with me. At least not yet.

From Detective McMann's point of view, I guessed such statistics would just have to wait while the twenty-four-hour race against the clock began.

At 10:42 p.m. in 2004 that clock started ticking at Belmont Hospital in Chicago.

Lisa was born to a woman I knew all too well. Lisa was then adopted by me shortly after her birth. The birth mother and I were not friends. But we both knew I should have the child. At one time I hated her, but, with time, that had given way to a righteous disgust. She wasn't a terrible person, but she was a cheat. The baby's father was my fiancé. He made sure we named the baby Lisa, a nod to my name of Melissa, which I likened to a small honorarium for not leaving him.

The birth mother had been out dancing at Cicero's All Saints Club on New Year's Eve--if you can call elephantine lumbering a style of dance—when ordinary abdominal pangs morphed into labor pains. Someone took her to the hospital where she was prepaid by Mark, my fiancé. Everything was arranged ahead of time.

Mark and I had been an item almost since our freshman year when we met at a football game between Illinois and Northwestern. I was enrolled at Northwestern, Mark at the University of Illinois. We went to a party at my friend's home and later bundled up and walked along the shore of Lake Michigan in the pre-dawn light. After that night--and next day--we were inseparable on weekends. During the week, he was downstate and I was in Evanston. Which meant it was FaceTime and texting, which really wasn't a bad way to go to college, because we both were eager students and worked hard at keeping Honors GPA's.

He loved my looks, which all young women love to hear. I was five-eight, about one-hundred-thirty, with blond hair and eyes that alternated between blue and gray. My hair was usually chopped short because I didn't like to waste time on it in college days. At one point I actually made the Northwestern Cheerleading Squad but quit after two weeks when I saw what a time-sink it was going to be. Good grades were my siren call; I didn't have time to travel and rah-rah I had found out.

Mark loved my family. My sisters were much older than me but Mark hit it off with them right away. But the problem was, my parents were never in the U.S. just about the entire time I was in high school and college. My dad worked for the State Department but could never talk about his work. To this day, I still think he's a CIA spook, but he would never admit it even to me. So we aren't that close, in parent-child terms, although financially they've always supported all my dreams. I tell them I love them when we talk on the phone, and they say they love me, but I knew early on that I was going to do family differently when it came to my turn.

Mark was the father of the baby. Maybe some women would have thrown him over when he got their roommate pregnant, but I didn't. I had my reasons, not the least of which was I loved this man with all my heart and I wanted all the parts of him that I could have. The baby was born during our final semester, and my lawyer immediately filed the adoption papers. We went to court that same week, and the judge signed the papers. Lisa and I celebrated with a meal out. Lisa didn't cry through any of this, which I took as a positive sign.

The early days were hard. Mark and I were very different. I was a Chicago native who had attended Northwestern University and earned a degree in journalism. He was all about hunting and fishing and NFL football. But he wasn't a chauvinist and he didn't abuse the animals he hunted and fished. He took only what he could eat and shared that with his welfare grandparents who'd raised him.

Mark had been in Army ROTC at the University of Illinois, and he was overseas when Lisa came into the world. We hadn't wanted it that way, of course, but the Army orders came, and Mark had no choice. He was gone a week after the orders came, before Lisa's birth. It left me with a very whiny birth mother whose legs and feet were swollen, whose back ached, who couldn't sleep with all the kicking inside her womb, and who had just screwed up her final exams at Northwestern because the symptoms and pains ran her to the ground. She basically just gave up on everything.

Three years later, he had been stateside once and had seen our daughter. Upon his return to combat, two weeks later the helicopter he was piloting during a firefight outside Kandahar crashed. The plane was so hopelessly incinerated there wasn't enough left to positively ID the pilot and co-pilot. What human remains could be found were blindly divided between two body bags. The funeral was closed casket; I had seen the last of my husband when I said goodbye to him just after Thanksgiving. With Mark's death, my OCD relented. There was no longer anything to hold together with my obsession glue.

When he was killed, I was working as an associate producer on *Laura in Chicago,* the worldwide TV talk show watched almost exclusively by women. The money was good enough that we'd managed to purchase a condo in the Loop. Mark's parents helped with the down payment. Still, I earned enough to keep current after the purchase. When the news was delivered to me at work that Mark had been killed in action, I left the Laura Studios and went straight home on the L train. I paid the babysitter up to the minute and told her she wouldn't be needed for two weeks. I then went into withdrawal with Lisa by my side. I refused everyone who wanted to come see me and help me through the tragic time. It wasn't until the next day that I let anyone close, and that happened to be Mark's parents. They hadn't been told about Mark's fatherhood. Still, they needed to see Lisa, who they regarded as Mark's offspring. They told me Lisa represented their last living connection to their son.

Which was when I let his parents in on the secret: Mark *was* Lisa's bio father. I explained the birth mother was actually my college roommate who'd had a fling with Mark one night. She admitted to me that she had seduced my boyfriend just to see if she could. Surprisingly--even to me-- I didn't move right out of the dorm and allow my love for my roomie to turn to hatred. I didn't because I was impossibly in love with Mark and wouldn't risk driving him away. Plus, I could parlay this into a win for everyone.

I strategized what came next—I've always been good at

chess because I can see moves at least three ahead. Truth be told, I didn't scratch out my roommate's eyes, because I knew her career path wouldn't allow for a baby in her life. She was a BSN student and, as soon as she graduated that May she was scheduled to begin a summer program in California before entering medical school in August. A baby just wasn't going to work in her life, but she was Catholic, so abortion was out. So I made her a proposal: I would adopt the baby. No need for Mark to adopt; he was going to be named on the birth certificate as the father anyway.

My roommate agreed. There was talk between us to the effect that I would allow her to visit Lisa anytime she ever wanted, but, like much sentimental talk, it didn't happen. Once the roomie was in med school at Stanford, she never returned to Chicago again, that I knew of. And if she had come back, she hadn't bothered to contact me. Nor did I call her. Better left alone, I decided. Up to the day Lisa was abducted, my roomie had never seen her offspring. Because of this, I never harbored a thought that the person who stole Lisa out of the hospital might be her birth mother. It just wasn't like that.

When I shared the story with Mark's parents, they were speechless. Then, in a sudden rush of competing emotions, they began crying and laughing: they were ecstatic that their granddaughter carried their son's genes. She really represented their son now that he was gone, and she was a part of him, something tangible that they could still hold and cuddle and kiss. So a special bond was formed the day I told them.

Mark's parents were wealthy--living in Glencoe, second in average income only to Hollywood. They made it clear that they would do anything they could do to help us in the years ahead. The kind of financial help they had in mind never was needed, though. Eighteen months after Mark's death, I was promoted to Executive Producer of *Laura in Chicago*, and my salary with bonuses shot into the seven figures. Our cramped condo was sold; the proceeds were used as a down payment for a horse farm outside Schaumburg. Now we had a pond and geese out of one window in our family room and a sunny woods out the other.

After Mark's death, there were other men, and dates and parties, but no one even began to equal the love I had shared with Mark. I knew what real love felt like and I wasn't going to settle for less now in my new life. So I pretty much lived alone with Lisa and concentrated on giving my baby the best environment and parenting possible.

Then this sudden spiking fever put Lisa in the hospital. The doctors had not decided on a diagnosis by the time she was abducted, though they tended toward thinking it was some form of meningitis. But the night of the kidnapping—after Lisa had disappeared—lab reports indicated she had turned a corner. She would be well enough to go home soon. I was heartbroken by the irony: Lisa was to have been discharged to go home the next day. It was just all too much to comprehend.

DETECTIVE MCMANN GUIDED me out of the hospital. Her car was parked in ER parking. Six inches of new snow had to be scraped from her windshield. I pulled the hood of my parka back off my head once we were inside the car and the heater was putting out warm air.

We followed behind a uniformed officer driving my Subaru SUV. Kendra handled the black Impala easily and nosed out into traffic, heading west toward Schaumburg. Twenty minutes later, we exited at the Schaumburg exit, passed by the mall, and headed west on Golf Road. It was lightly snowing that January night and previous snows were plowed into the median.

As we drove home, I alternated between calm and contemplative then frantic with outbursts of tears and sobbing. Plus there were self-recriminations for leaving her alone in her room. I wracked my mind trying to think of someone who might wish to steal my daughter. I wondered whether my being listed in the TV show's credits had anything to do with Lisa's abduction. Might someone out there have decided I was an earner able to pay a fortune in ransom? It was very possible, Detective McMann said.

Only time would tell. And that would come in the form of a demand for ransom. The detective felt but didn't say to me that night that she would have preferred a ransom note to silence. Ransom was a hope of getting the child returned. No note meant that the child was taken for other reasons. Usually, those other reasons were sexual assault and homicide or a selling of the child into the slave trade. I pulled out my phone and brought up Lisa's most recent snapshot. Detective McMann shuddered and her slack jaw clenched. She was the exact model of the child the sex trades were seeking. Blond. Blue-eyed. Beautiful.

"She's a beautiful child," the detective said as she drove us into the horse farm neighborhood.

"Yes," I said. "She is perfect."

"I've got good feelings about this one."

"Do you have good feelings about all of them?"

"Never."

D etective McMann's tone turned light and chatty.

"Where did you grow up?" she asked me.

"Evanston. I went to high school and then college in my hometown."

I told her about Mark and how Lisa came into our lives. As I talked, I would catch myself about to refer to Lisa in the past tense, and I would freeze up. Then there would be a pause while my brain tried to rephrase my comments as if Lisa were still with me. No past tense. Past tense meant you were acknowledging something was *then* and not *now*. I wasn't ready to do that--nor would I ever be. As we drove along snow-covered streets, I was thinking maybe some of what I told her was useful and maybe some of it was just her way of keeping me occupied.

She asked about my parents. *Is there some thought my parents might be involved in Lisa's disappearance?* The thought would never have occurred to me. She asked about their closeness to Lisa. I told her they had only seen Lisa one time in her first four years. But they had been that way with me and my sisters, too: remote, always traveling, fantastic providers of goods and services but falling way short of meeting our emotional needs. It just never seemed to occur to them that you owed kids more than the economies of childhood; I had sworn to myself even before Lisa was born that she was going to get all of me, not just the bank account parts.

By the time we arrived at my house, Detective McMann had a pretty decent idea who I was. The uniformed officer driving my car pulled in first. We waited while the garage door rolled up, triggered by the unit in my car. Then we rolled inside the four-car garage and parked beside my car. We three went inside my house through the mud room door. Then the uniformed officer flicked a wall switch, bringing the articulating door back down. He followed us into the kitchen.

We gathered around the large kitchen table with its seating for eight. Detective McMann opened her laptop and turned it on. I disappeared into a back room and emerged a few minutes later with Isaac, my teenage nephew. Was I having uncomfortable feelings about Isaac at that point? Evidently something was bothering me; I wanted him to be interviewed then and there.

"Detective McMann, this is my sister's son, Isaac. Isaac lives with us while he's attending Roosevelt here in Schaumburg. I thought you'd probably want to talk to him, too."

McMann looked up from her laptop and shot a tight smile Isaac's way. "Sure, Isaac. Grab a seat and let's take your statement. Officer Rhodes," she said to the policeman who had driven my car back from the hospital, "why don't you have

Ms. Sellars show you how to brew up a pot of coffee on her machine? It's going to be an all-nighter."

Taking the cue, I made coffee while the uniformed officer watched. Isaac took a seat across from Kendra and pulled out a box of cigarettes.

"May I?" he asked.

"Not my house," Detective McMann said. "Ask your aunt."

"She doesn't care."

He produced a BIC lighter and fired up. Just when he was settled and getting relaxed, the detective began.

"Okay, my tape recorder is rolling, so let's jump right in. Tell us your name, please."

"Isaac Toms. My aunt is Melissa Sellars."

"Your aunt has told you what happened tonight?"

"Jesus, why aren't you all out looking for her?" Isaac complained. "She's only four years old, probably scared shit-less right now."

"Isaac!" I shouted from the coffee pot. "Enough!" But he was right and my sharp tone only meant I couldn't handle the truth just then. At least not yet.

"Well, I'm just saying."

"I know what you're saying. We already know that. The police, for your information, *are* out looking for your cousin. These officers are assigned to setting up a command post in our house. That's why we're all here and not out looking for Lisa, as you put it. Please save the criticism for later, all right?"

It was rhetorical. Detective McMann continued.

"What is your age?"

"Twenty-three."

"How long have you lived here with your aunt?"

"This is my second year. I just started the second half of my sophomore year in school."

"What are you studying?"

"Languages. I want to work for the CIA."

"What are your parents' names?"

"Robert and Ina Toms. Stanleyville, Missouri."

"Why are you in school here in Chicago?"

"I--I got in trouble in Missouri. I was ordered to either remain gainfully employed or stay in school. College or trade school, he didn't care. But it had to be one of them."

"Who didn't care?"

"The judge."

"What kind of trouble?"

"I got someone pregnant. Then she told her dad I had raped her. But we were a couple, I didn't rape her. But it was my word against hers, and I had been in trouble before, so they took her word."

"What kind of trouble before?"

"No big deal. Shoplifting."

"No big deal? That's a crime of moral turpitude."

"If you say so."

At that point, I came to Isaac's rescue by interrupting to take drink orders. My mind had overruled my initial bad feelings. I remember thinking, *Why am I feeling unsure? Isaac had nothing to do with Lisa's disappearance. He is the definition of the good cousin who plays with his cousin, takes her to movies and to the park, and generally treats her like a little princess. Move along.*

I passed out cups and filled them. Soon, everyone was nursing a coffee, including the uniformed officer.

"So am I done?" Isaac asked me.

"Ask me," said the detective. "And no, you're not done. I want to ask about your relationship with Lisa. Tell me about you and your cousin."

"Well, she lives here, and I live here. We don't see much of each other because she's in bed by the time I get home from Mickey D's."

"You work at McDonald's?"

"I do. And I've got the greasy shirts to prove it."

"Do you ever spend time with Lisa?"

"Weekends I'll see her more. I might pull her around in the wagon when the weather's good. Two weeks ago we went tubing in the snow. She loved it. But then she got sick."

"Did the tubing make her sick?"

"Hey, officer, did you hear me? My major is Arabic, not medicine. How would I know what made her sick?"

"Good point, Isaac. I'll withdraw the question."

"You should. Don't try to trip me up, please. Last time I talked to the cops, I went to Juvie for a year. Never again."

"No, you won't go to Juvie if you get in trouble again. You'll go to adult prison. Or jail. Now, Isaac, I want you to think carefully about this next question. And I want you to reflect on how serious it is to lie to the police before you answer. Here it is: Did you have anything to do with Lisa being taken from the hospital tonight?"

"Oh, shit! Aunt Mel, can't you stop this crap? You know me better than that. Tell her, please!"

"Just answer the questions," I muttered. My attention was focused on him. My feelings were all over the map, and I was again wondering about Isaac's honesty that night. I was seeing Isaac in a whole new light. "You know what?" I continued, this time to the detective, "I had no idea about the rape charge against Isaac. I thought it was domestic violence since Isaac was living in the girl's basement when it happened. I didn't know about the rape. Why didn't you tell me, Isaac? Why didn't my own sister tell me? I'm feeling pretty stupid right about now."

"Hey, it was no big deal. I didn't do what they said, Aunt Mel. You know me better."

"I don't know that part of you, Isaac. You lied to me. You had me believe it was something else."

"Now you know the bad story, Aunt Mel. Do I have to move?"

"You know what? I'm thinking about that."

"All right," said McMann, "the recorder is still spinning, so let's get back to my questions, please. Isaac, did you want to do harm to your cousin, Lisa Sellars?"

"What, are you on something? Hell no! She's my cousin, Dude."

"Did you help anyone kidnap your cousin? Maybe tell someone where she was tonight?"

"Hell no!"

"Did you ever want to have sex with her?"

"Aunt Mel, do I have to answer this crap?"

"Go ahead, Isaac. Just give your answers, and we'll soon be up to speed."

"I never wanted to have sex with any little kid."

"How about Lisa?"

"Hell no!"

"Did you ever touch her inappropriately?"

"Not on my mother's life!"

"Do you know where Lisa is right now?"

"No."

"Do you know who has her?"

"No way."

"Do you know who took her?"

"It wasn't me, lady."

"Do you know who took her?"

"Oh, hell no."

"Mr.Toms--Isaac--I think that's all for now. But you stay

around the house tonight and tomorrow in case there are more. Understand?"

"Yes. Except I gotta hit school tomorrow."

"Not tomorrow. Your aunt needs you around here."

"If you say."

"I do say."

Isaac looked around the room, avoiding eye contact with any of the people who'd been watching and listening.

"What can I do?" he finally asked me.

"About?"

"Can I help find her somehow?"

The detective spoke up. "You can make a list of everyone you've had contact with over the last two days. Names and numbers, please."

"What for?"

"Because I said," McMann replied. Her voice was still even and objective. I admired that. The woman hadn't given any response or signal about how she felt about any of Isaac's answers. She was professional, and that made me feel better, at least momentarily.

People have asked me since that night: weren't you panicked and running in circles crying and screaming? There was one point when suddenly, with no warning whatsoever, the floor fell out from under me again, and the room started spinning. It was like an other-worldly feeling, the thought that Lisa had been taken. I wanted to jump to my feet and run around the house screaming at that moment. But I knew that would do precisely nothing to get my baby back. By every bit of will I had deep down inside, I was forcing myself to remain calm and calculating. I could fall apart later, on my own time. For now, the police needed me, and I was going to take a deep breath and be there for my daughter. Lisa deserved no less.

"All right," McMann said, turning back to me after Isaac had left the room, "Do you have a list of people to call?"

I replied by sliding a piece of notebook paper to McMann. "Eleven people. All family except the last two. They're work friends who should at least be notified I'm not going to be at work tomorrow."

"You said work was busy. But you took off this week when Lisa was hospitalized."

"Yes, she went from bad to much worse in an hour. I called 911, and they took her in. I followed in my car. Regulations-- they wouldn't allow me in the EMT truck."

"Sure. Now I know you work for the *Laura* show. You're the Executive Producer, and you're moving the studios?"

"We're starting the move of Laura Studios from Chicago to L.A. soon now. I'm going to be hammered at work. But now with Lisa, I may have to hand in my resignation. I'm definitely not going to Los Angeles while my baby's missing in Chicago."

"Which brings up a point. There's a chance Lisa isn't even in the Midwest anymore. It happens. I don't want to frighten you any more than you already are, but we've had a series of kiddie grabs where the children were taken out of the country."

"Oh, God, don't tell me that!"

"I'm sorry. I just want you to start thinking much bigger as we go along here."

"I'll try to."

"Good. Now, you make a good living. I think you told me seven figures?"

"With my bonus, I made one-point-five last year. I'll do more this year. For all that matters."

"It might. Whoever took Lisa might have gotten your name off the TV credits for the show. It's been known to happen. We might get a ransom call or letter."

"Oh, my God."

Just then, McMann took a call on her phone. The call went for a minute, so I got up and refilled everyone's coffee cup, including my own. I slowly stirred in half-and-half while the phone call droned on. My thoughts were coming in jagged fragments unrelated from one to the next. I shut my eyes and felt a sudden rush of tears. It couldn't be helped. I pulled out my handkerchief. Just then, Detective McMann reached over and patted me on the back while she was still on the phone. My shoulders shook as the tears flowed.

"So much for staying calm," I said to Officer Rhodes.

"Don't worry about it," he said. "This is the hardest thing any human ever has to go through. I've seen it before."

"Really? How did it turn out?"

"Not good."

My face fell.

The cop continued, "I mean they finally found the little boy and everything. Found his body. God, why am I telling you about that? I'm sorry, Mrs. Sellars. Please forgive my stupidity."

"It's all right."

"Now you know why I'm in a uniform and not in a suit. Mr. Duh."

"It's all right, really," I said with a forced laugh at the man's humor about his brain power.

Just then, the detective put her phone back inside her coat. "Well, the FBI is now on the case. They're reviewing all CCTV at the hospital as we speak."

"Video?"

"Yes, they're studying all the exits from the hospital. They will have everything studied by midnight and get back to us here."

"That's great. So I hold my breath until then?"

"Why do you say that?"

"I mean, wouldn't you? I'm praying we can see the face of who took her. Isn't that what we're doing here?"

"Yes, exactly. That's right."

"I need to call my sister and some other people. They're on the list."

"Please do," said Detective McMann. "How about I start at the bottom with your staff? I can let them know you won't be in until further notice."

"God. I guess that's right. Absolutely then."

While Detective McMann remained at the kitchen table with her phone, I went into the family room, stepped down into the conversation pit, and choose a plush purple couch where I'd make my calls. The numbers were already in the phone. It wouldn't take long.

First up was my oldest sister. That call wouldn't take five minutes. She carefully chose her words as she asked about Isaac and whether the cops had questioned him. I reported that they had and that Isaac had been very cooperative.

"Did he tell them about--about his conviction for sexual assault."

"You mean the rape charge? He did. I feel like someone grossly misled me about that. I thought it was domestic violence when we talked about him living here. I asked about domestic violence and you said yes."

"Well, it was domestic violence too. But they dismissed that when he said he was guilty of sexual assault. It was all very confusing."

I wasn't confused. But I finally let it go. It was neither the time nor the place to push the issue. So I backed off. But my sister--her voice quavering--sounded terribly upset. I considered the situation and decided that I'd be nervous and scared if my son, with a prior conviction for rape, had been in the vicinity of a young girl who'd disappeared. I understood and tried without much enthusiasm to put my sister's mind at ease.

Several more calls, short and sweet. And then came the most difficult call, the call to Mark's parents. They were happily involved with Lisa, even attending the adoption hearing in court. After that, they made a practice out of showing up at least once a week to spend an afternoon or a night or a weekend day with their granddaughter. They had come to the hospital every day while she was ill and would spend hours just sitting and watching her with me. I loved them but still could hardly stand to look at my father-in-law, so much of Mark's face was visible there. And his mother's eyes were his own eyes. So it was hard, but I knew how important grandparents were, especially to kids in a single-parent household.

It was like turning hounds loose on those poor people to have to tell them their granddaughter had been abducted from the hospital. They cried and settled down then cried again, all the while asking how they could help. I didn't want them in my home just then so I asked them to sit tight, please. I promised updates twice a day and said I would be the one calling so they would know what I knew. Mark's father was weeping when we hung up. Charlie Sellars was not the type of man who would cry openly. I didn't think anything about it at the time. Later, however, I wondered if maybe he hadn't overreacted to the news. I thought it odd but pushed it from my mind.

Mark's mother was resolute and angry at whoever had kidnapped their grandchild. Given the opportunity, I had no doubt the woman would have shot the kidnapper. She had a temper and had always had a penchant for lashing out at those who wronged her. She was a force to be reckoned with in her own right, and because of that, she was just too much for me to handle right then. I could not allow her to hear about Isaac's criminal history, that much was clear.

Then my mother-in-law said, in a very calm voice, "Call me when they catch him. I promise I will see that he never does this again."

I let it slide. I was too tired and too distraught to do anything else but let it slide.

Still, I had no doubt that Rebecca Sellars would shoot first and ask questions later.

At around two in the morning, the FBI called. The CCTV videos were inconclusive. Computerized face matching was going on as we spoke. McMann hung up from the call and explained it all to me. The FBI gathered together all the video of all hospital entrances and exits between pertinent hours and studied the faces of the people coming and going. The agents looked closely at bundles and packages they might be carrying as well. This was done with eyeballs, and it was done with computers, she explained. They were thorough like the FBI is always thorough. So far, nothing--that was about how far we'd gotten.

Early the morning after the abduction, I heard McMann call the Missouri District Attorney who had prosecuted my nephew, Isaac. She put the call on speakerphone.

"This is Golden Robinson. My secretary said this was a Chicago detective?"

"Yes, this is Detective Kendra McMann, CPD. I'm calling

reference one Isaac Toms. I am told you prosecuted him awhile back."

"I did. Good old Isaac. Anyway, how can I help?"

"What was the result of his case?"

"He pled no contest to second-degree statutory rape. That's intercourse with a person under seventeen years."

"Where the actor is over--"

"Right, where the actor was twenty-one or older."

"How old was the vic?"

"Let's see. She was fifteen. They had been dating for several months without her parents knowing. Then she became pregnant. Evidently, her folks found out, and she told her dad that Toms had raped her."

"The parents believed this? Even after she's dating the guy for several months?"

"Well, the grand jury believed it. She made an excellent witness, as I recall. She was honor roll, 4-H, band, student government--all the things grand juries love in a kid."

"Been there, done that, for sure. So the original charge was what?"

"First degree. Which we didn't have. I wanted a plea to second and got it."

"Now here's what I'm actually calling about," said McMann. "Did Isaac Toms ever display any predilection toward much younger girls? Was there ever any talk about that?

"Here are my case notes. Yes, the notes reflect that our

victim's younger sister once spent an entire day away with Toms without her parents' consent."

"Good grief! What happened?"

"Our assault counselor questioned the child, did the play dolls, but it was all inconclusive. No charges ever filed or even considered, actually."

"How old was this girl?"

"Four.

Long silence. McMann looked at me, and I met her gaze. This stuff was all new to me, and I realized it made him a person of interest. McMann thanked the DA and hung up the phone.

"Well?" she looked at me.

"I didn't know. Nobody had told me that."

"In all fairness, neither Isaac nor your sister might even have known the little girl was questioned for possible abuse. So maybe that's why you haven't been told."

"My sister's pretty aggressive about these things. I'm pretty sure she would have had a face-to-face with the victim's parents before it was all over. I'd be surprised if they didn't mention to her that Isaac took off with their four-year-old for a whole day."

"Very possible, if that's your sister's M.O."

"It is. She doesn't leave stones unturned, particularly when her kids are concerned."

"So here's what we have. Your nephew got a fifteen-year-old

pregnant when he was twenty-one. What twenty-one-year-old male wants to get it on with a fifteen-year-old?"

"A sexual deviant," I said.

"That's my thinking. Of course, we have no proof of deviant behavior, just--"

"The hell we don't. Screwing a fifteen-year-old is deviant behavior in my book."

My own words hit me like a freight train. Lisa was missing. She was female. She would eventually catch some man's eye. Maybe even at her present age. My mind veered off. I couldn't deal with that line of thinking any further. I needed to change the subject or get up and run out of the room or scream at the top of my lungs for a full minute. Whatever, I needed to pass this fear out of me.

But I couldn't see how to do that. It was just starting to settle over me, the whole rape scenario that's always lurking. Men rape. Men--probably--had my daughter and were going to demand money for her. There was nothing else for me to do just then except pray.

"So what do we do with this info about Isaac?"

"I think I'm going to need to have a much more extensive conversation with him. Right now he's a person of interest."

"Poor Isaac."

"Poor Isaac? Why's that?"

"I mean if he's--"

"Melissa, let's get something right up front. If this grown man had anything to do with your daughter's disappearance he's not poor Isaac anymore. Until we know for sure he's clean he's not poor Isaac. Can we agree on that?"

"Yes."

"And while we're on the topic, do you have any other family members I need to be concerned about?"

"No."

"What about your husband?"

"I thought I told you."

"Probably you did."

"My husband died in Afghanistan. I haven't remarried."

"Any buddies of his ever come around?"

"Never."

"What about other men? Have you been active?"

"That's a one-hundred-percent 'no.' Never even thought of anyone else."

"Have any men put a move on you? Asked for your phone number? Slipped you a card and said to call them?"

"Not one."

"I know you work for a hugely popular TV show that's seen around the world. Is there anyone from that part of your life who has shown extra interest in you from the norm? Any admirers or followers of Laura?"

"Sure, I mean we get all kinds of crazy emails and telegrams and letters with pictures of men's privates--everyone gets that stuff. But none has singled me out. If they single out

Laura, she has a team of ex-FBI agents who investigate all that stuff coming her way. The deviant pictures, the threats, the marriage proposals. These guys keep track of all of that."

"What's the name of their company?"

"XFBI."

"Ex as in ex-wife?"

"No, just the letter 'X' followed by FBI."

"Oh, XFBI."

"Yes, they're worldwide. I deal with them regularly on my security tasking."

"You're in charge of security?"

"Maybe I haven't been clear. I'm in charge of everything. I'm the executive producer. The buck stops with me. As well as the deviants, crazies, Casanovas, weirdos--I get them all."

"So XFBI is on the payroll?"

"Sure. All hit shows use someone like them."

"Did not know. Okay. If I asked you, 'Melissa, who do you think might have taken Lisa?' what would your answer be?"

"Some crazy sicko. Only a sicko would take a very ill girl from her hospital bed and run off with her."

"Agreed. But do any names, any faces come to mind?"

"Well, you've made a big thing out of Isaac and maybe rightly so. He's the only one."

"Fine. We'll definitely interview him much more thoroughly and retrace his steps yesterday and last night."

"Question, Detective McMann. Would it make any sense for me to call in XFBI at this point and ask them to help?"

"It wouldn't hurt on down the road--if we get that far. But for right now I'd prefer not to have any potential witnesses or leads messed up. Please give me at least the first forty-eight hours and then we'll talk."

"All right."

I decided then and there that in forty-eight hours I would call Klamath, my contact at XFBI, unless I had Lisa back.

5

Reports were called into the command HQ in my kitchen all morning. However, each call was even more of a letdown than the last, as far as I was concerned. This was because each call was negative, a zero, a goose-egg. Nothing about Lisa's abduction was known even twelve hours later.

Nothing the CPD and FBI tried had turned up offered even a whiff of information about a little girl being kidnapped from her hospital bed. The nurses at the nurses' station had seen someone wheeled by headed to radiology--they had assumed. When pressed, they admitted they didn't actually know they were going to radiology. They might even have been sneaking out of the hospital, they added when they were questioned the second time around.

Detective McMann knew the procedures at most hospitals, so none of what was being reported back was a huge surprise. For example, people who come to take patients to radiology wear scrubs and athletic shoes. This only happens when a doctor orders radiology, but, as far as the nurses are concerned on the floor, who was being taken where was really not their concern. Patient movement was all just too much to keep track of, so it wasn't part of their job description.

"Let's consider what we do know," the detective said to me just after the sun peeked over the horizon. "One, it's clear to me that someone has been watching you."

"That infuriates me. But you're right. How else would they know when to snatch my baby?"

"Exactly. They were watching, and that means they were nearby. Maybe one of them was even a nurse or some other hospital employee. Even someone just wearing the garb to make it look like they were an employee handling a routine matter in case anyone should stop them and ask."

"So now I have to try to analyze who might be watching me? But why me? I'm not wealthy."

"Really? The executive producer on Laura doesn't have a large stash somewhere? How about money in the Caymans? You up for that, Melissa? Think hard, now. Where's the money, how much is it, and who knows it's there?"

"Okay. When Mark was killed, I got a cash settlement. Insurance money. Plus, for the past several years I've received five-hundred-thousand-dollar bonuses from my job."

"Now you're getting somewhere, Mrs. Sellars. Who knows about the money you've got squirreled away?"

"My bank? The people with access to my account records?"

"Which means the bank's entire IT department, accounting department, and an assortment of assistant vice-presidents that all banks keep around. We've got a lot of questions for a lot of people just at your bank. Now, has anyone there, in particular, ever said anything about your money or how much money you have?"

"Not that I can recall. Someone different always waits on me. And mostly I do the drive-through, but those people change all the time. It's never the same individual in the window."

"What about inside? Have you taken out a loan where you've met with a loan officer, for example?"

"No, not that I can think of. But I did put a large chunk of money in Overland Fidelity and Trust."

"What's that?"

"They have mutual funds. A finance guy who works on my production staff recommended them. He said even Laura keeps money there, so I thought: why not?"

"You have a contact there?"

"Ed Springer. He's my investment adviser, and he's really sharp. But I don't think Ed's who you're looking for. He's very outdoorsy. I can't see him wanting a kid. Especially a kidnapped one."

"What kinds of things has he said?"

"Really, he just encourages me to keep saving and investing. He wants me financially independent by the time I'm forty. So I do what he says."

"All right. Now, you know what? This is your neighborhood, and these are your neighbors. We're going to canvass them with uniformed officers, but real quick I'd like you to go around. Ask them if they've seen anyone or any unusual vehicles in the past few weeks. Vehicles that caught their eye for any reason. Can you do that?"

"It's still early."

"By the time you have another coffee, it should be fine. Please handle that for me."

"Of course I will," I told the detective. "More coffee?"

"No, but I would like some scrambled eggs if you have any. I can fix them myself."

"Not as long as I'm here you won't. It would be my pleasure to make breakfast for you and one-Adam-twelve in there." I was referring to the uniformed officer who at that moment was catching a catnap on my family room sofa. The gas log was going, and he had kicked his shoes off and curled up on the purple couch. I had thrown a comforter over him that my grandmother made. Between the warm and the blanket and the sleep deprivation, the officer hadn't lasted five minutes. Which was when I started calling him one-Adam-twelve after the TV cops I used to watch.

"Scrambled, no bacon or sausage. I'm almost vegetarian."

I had to stop and smile at her words. "That's like being a little bit pregnant, isn't it?"

Suddenly it hit me again, roaring back like a midnight freight train: my daughter was missing. I had been up for three nights in the hospital, where I had barely caught even a few winks, and now all night with the police coming and going and calling in and out, and I was exhausted. I was so far gone that I found myself suddenly sitting down on the floor, placing my face in my hands, and weeping. I kicked out my legs and kicked my heels against the floor. "Give her back, bastards!" I screamed. "Give me my baby!"

AN HOUR LATER, after showering and changing, I was feeling better when I slipped on my parka and headed out the front door. Snow was skittering sideways in the brisk wind. A pale disk of sun tried without success to pierce the gloom of clouds hanging overhead. Another Chicago winter, I thought as I eased down the porch steps onto the sidewalk.

I decided I would start my canvass next door and work my way out. We lived on five acres and so did most of the others in my neighborhood, so the houses were far enough apart that I had to walk a good football field to get next door. Cutting across the frozen grass of my front yard to get out to the road, I pulled the zipper on my parka all the way up to my chin. I shivered beneath the goose down, but it was more than just the cold. The shiver was about my daughter, a fact I still couldn't fully comprehend through my emotional fog. But it was there: my precious Lisa was gone, and even the cops were running into brick walls. So far that morning there had been nothing but negative reports from all districts and all police agencies. The case was now almost twelve hours old. Another twelve hours and the cops would fold up their tents and go home because the next case would demand their attention and because Lisa's case was looking futile. Sure, they would keep looking, but the fervor would be nothing like the first twenty-four hours. So it was probably now or never. I found myself wiping stinging tears from my eyes. And they weren't just about the blowing snow and the wind. I was hurting beyond anything I'd ever felt. Even the loss of Mark paled in comparison to my loss of Lisa. It was inconceivable how much it hurt and how frightened I was. So I stepped up onto the porch of my next door neighbor and rang the bell.

Thelma Lee was the heir of a local pastry manufacturer. She was also a no-nonsense member of the neighborhood who was always on the lookout for unwanted visitors to our streets. In one era she would have been called a snoop. But in today's world, she was a concerned citizen and just then I was so happy she was. She treated the public streets like private ones, belonging to the people who lived along them, and woe to the stranger in the suspicious looking van who drove up her street because Thelma was just as apt to call the police on them as not. If anyone had seen anything, I predicted, it would be Thelma Lee.

The older woman opened the inside door, saw it was me, and pushed open the storm door.

"Come in, dear. You must tell me about the police cars at your house. They've been there all night? Is it about that nephew of yours, that Isaac? Is he in trouble? I can't say I've ever had very good feelings about that one. Here, sit down."

I sat on a white sofa already populated with four tabby cats. I made sure to position myself as far from the herd as possible, as I was deadly allergic to cat dander.

"I'm not here about Isaac, Thelma. I'm here about Lisa. She was in the hospital, and someone took her. She's been kidnapped."

"Jesus H. Christ!" the older woman exclaimed. "Excuse my language, excuse me, Lord. What horrible news. Well, how can I help? You want to know have I seen anything suspicious in the neighborhood? I'm sad--well, happy--to report that I have not. Nothing for several weeks now, ever since it turned so cold."

"No strange man or woman sitting out watching my house?"

"Nothing like that, dear girl. No, and I would know if there had been someone like that lurking. I would be the first to know, and I would call the police anyway. Of course, I did spend part of last week at my daughter's."

We talked on for several minutes, but then I stood up and excused myself, explaining that I had several neighbors to get to before people left their homes that morning for work. Thelma entirely understood but requested a hug. I hugged my friend and then, with new tears stinging my eyes, stepped back outside into the wind chill. Stuffing my hands into my coat pockets, I made my way out to the road and on to the next neighbor's house. There was no answer at the door, so I went one more house—the Katzenja's re-done Victorian that was the pride the neighborhood, stately and as accurately recreated in the style of the original as possible. Up onto the porch and then ringing the bell while I dabbed my eyes with a damp clump of tissue.

Henry Katzenja opened the door. "Melissa, come in, neighbor. It's too cold to stand out there to talk."

I went inside and unzipped my coat. "I can only stay a minute, Mr. Katzenja."

"Sure, sure, what is it?"

"My daughter is missing, taken from the hospital. I'm here to--"

"My God, you can't be serious, Melissa?"

"I'm definitely serious. Someone took my Lisa from the hospital last night. The police have asked me to knock on doors and see whether anyone's seen anything suspicious in our neighborhood."

"That would be affirmative, for me."

"What? Affirmative, as in you have seen something suspicious?"

"Sure. There's been a black SUV parked halfway down to Thelma's every night for a week. I've called the cops, but they say it's a free country. They won't even come by and talk to the driver. I see him out there, parked facing the wrong way. So maybe he was watching your house since his car was pointed that way."

"Oh, my God! Did you get a license plate by any chance?"

"I did, let me see if I can find where I put that. Wait here please, Melissa."

Mr. Katzenja disappeared in the direction of the kitchen--I knew the layout of the front of the house from Christmas Eve drinks the Katzenja's always offered, an open invitation to stop and say hello. He returned minutes later, his face crestfallen.

"Sorry, I cannot turn it up. But I'll keep looking."

"Oh, my God, please do, Mr. K. That could be the break we're looking for."

"I will. And I'll come right over when I find it. Now let me suggest you check with the Washingtons across from me. They might have seen it and written down the license too."

"Yes, I'll hurry over there right now before Doris goes off to work."

We said our goodbyes and I crossed the street with a new burst of energy. If only someone wrote down the license, I was thinking. If only--

I rang the bell on the Washington's friendly old Victorian, which looked like it had been designed and built by the same builder as the Katzenja's place.

Immediately the door was opened, and Doris was pulling me inside out of the cold.

"Dear girl, you're going to catch--"

"Doris, Mr. K says there was a black car down from his house recently. Did you by any chance get the license number?"

"I did," said the stout, pale-skinned woman. "Wait one minute, please."

She returned with a piece of notepad paper that said across the top FROM THE DESK OF D. WASHINGTON. Below, in a fine hand, was written KLM-044J. The plate was noted to be an Illinois plate.

"What's this about, Mel?"

"Lisa was taken from the hospital last night. The police are looking for anything suspicious."

"Dear God, what's this world coming to? Was she very sick?"

"She was. That's what is so terrifying, in addition to the kidnapping. God love her, I'm praying she isn't dying by now." Again the tears burst forth, and I collapsed against

Doris Washington, who took me in her arms and began patting my back.

"There, there, there. Let it out, honey. I know it's horrible."

"Oh my God!"

"I know, I know. Now you take this license plate number and hurry back to the police. They'll find Lisa before ten o'clock with this. I'm certain of it."

"Thank you, Doris. Oh, my God, thank you!"

Then I was outside, crossing the porch, down the snow-packed steps, and heading into a run for my house.

Ten minutes later, there was an APB out on the black SUV. Thirty minutes after that, it was reported found. But the news wasn't conclusive. The vehicle had been abandoned behind a 7-Eleven in West Chicago, a very tough part of town. McMann explained to me that it had been towed to the police yard and already the police technicians were dusting for prints and searching every surface before they vacuumed. Then the hair and fiber analysis would begin and comparisons made of hairs from the vehicle to hair from Lisa's brush.

"Guardedly optimistic," was how Detective McMann told me she was feeling. "Hopeful, but not celebrating. Not yet, Mrs. Sellars."

"Melissa. Please call me Melissa."

"Sure, Melissa."

"So what do we do now?"

"Wait while the CSI and lab techs do their studies. Then, if we're lucky, we'll know whether Lisa was ever inside that vehicle. It might be our first break. Start praying."

"You kidding? I've been praying all the way since last night. Not that I'm a believer or anything. But finding the SUV is starting to make me one."

"All right, then."

Tears of hopeful relief came again, and I headed for the guest bathroom and new tissues. Then it was time to wait for news from the crime lab. So we sipped coffee at the table without speaking.

The words had all been said. This was it, the time when we got our break or didn't.

My hands were shaking so bad it took both to return my cup to the saucer. Detective McMann pretended not to notice.

She started to say something to me then caught herself. I could read her mind: what good would it do at this point to give solace for the umpteenth time? I was beyond that.

Now we needed answers.

And fast.

6

The name of the black SUV's registered owner was Grant Baedeker. The title search provided Detective McMann and her partner Jerry O'Reilly the address of Grant Baedeker. At eleven the morning after Lisa's disappearance, Detectives McMann and O'Reilly met for coffee downtown on the Loop; afterward they began driving west on the Eisenhower and got off on First Avenue in Maywood. They weren't far from the Cook County Courthouse; the area was very familiar to them. Baedeker lived west and a bit north of the court, so McMann headed off into the neighborhoods. Every corner was either a liquor store or a neighborhood grocery or a combination of the two. Finally, they came to a Jif-Lube next door to GiGi's Nails. They parked and headed inside.

There were three bays with lifts inside the small garage, and an office off to the side. They tried the office first, where a matronly woman was sitting on a stool behind a mechanical cash register, filing her nails. She hardly looked up when the two detectives entered; but then they displayed their badges--their stars--, and the woman was all ears.

"Grant Baedeker," said Kendra McMann. "He work here?"

"If you call cleaning out the registers and heading for the girlie shows every afternoon working, then I guess he does. Grant owns the place. And four more just like it."

"Does he drive a black SUV?"

"He did. It's been sold."

"To who, if you know?"

"Lady, I ain't the DMV. Don't them computers in you all's cars tell you who owns what?"

McMann ignored the comment.

"Where might we find Mr. Baedeker?"

"His home's in Maywood, but I don't know where."

"What times does he come in?"

"Around four, five, something like that. Don't ask me about his phone number. The mailbox is full, and he don't answer. Not ever."

McMann turned to her partner. "Jerry?"

He spread his hands. "I guess we wait. I'm game."

"I'll leave you here. One of us needs to keep moving. Sharks die if they don't move."

"So you're leaving me. Nice."

"I'm senior, so you're staying here."

Her partner smiled. "No problem, Mac. I'll keep an eye on Ms. Birdsong here so she can't make a quick call to Baedeker and warn him off."

"Who's Ms. Birdsong?" the cashier asked in a querulous tone.

"That would be you, Birdie," said O'Reilly. "As in 'a little bird told me.' You're not warning anyone about anything, especially your boss. You and I are glued at the hip. No calls to dear old Grant, you read me?"

"I do. I wouldn't call him anyway."

"Sure you wouldn't. If you were my mother, I might believe you. But you're not, and I don't."

"All right," said McMann, "I'll call in and get updated. I'll let you know where I'm off to."

"Fair enough," said Jerry O'Reilly. "Talk soon."

"Roger that."

Detective McMann sprinted out through the new snow storm to her unmarked Impala. The windshield had frozen over, so she scraped the ice away with her gloved hands then climbed inside. Within seconds she was on the radio to dispatch for an update.

There was a new development, probably unrelated. It seemed a second little girl went missing from a second hospital last night, too. Same routine: taken from her room and wheeled right down to the elevators and out of the hospital. Another team had that one.

Detective McMann signed off and sat back against the seat

of the car. She folded her arms and studied the flakes collecting on her windshield.

Strange. Another kid grabbed. What were the chances of that happening? Had the same gang grabbed both Lisa and the other child? Why would anyone do that? Unless they were selling the girls into sex slavery in Dubai. That was always a possibility, and it was an all-too-common scenario. Some Saudi prince might have placed an order for two female children of a certain hair color and race. You never knew about such things. What often appeared as a mystery on first look quite often turned out to be explained in the most obvious way on the second look. Oil money meant child trafficking. It always had. Not to mention the rest of it. Then there was also electronics money in the Far East. Japan and Hong Kong were horrible, evil places where cute blonde American and Scandinavian kids were sold into an all-too-willing market for pre-adolescent flesh.

McMann shook her head and then slowly reached out and turned on the windshield wipers. The defrost had melted the collecting snow and ice, and the first sweep of the wiper blades undid all of nature's handiwork from McMann's windshield.

She cursed and pulled the shifter down into reverse, backing out of the parking slot and heading back onto 7th Avenue.

Time was running out. Both girls could be airborne and headed out of the country at that very moment. But if they weren't then there was still hope. McMann gunned it and swept across two lanes to get headed back out to the Eisenhower. It was time to return to Schaumburg and get updated by the uniforms who were following-up with a canvass of their own of Melissa Sellars' neighborhood.

She couldn't get there fast enough as the thoughts of Dubai hotel rooms plagued her mind.

Just then her radio crackled again.

"Be advised a female child has reached the Cook County Morgue. Officers have your victim's mother en route. Proceed to M.E.'s office and meet her there to view the body. There is a match in the general description. Repeat, there is a match."

"Oh, shit," McMann whispered under her breath. She jumped back onto the Eisenhower and began racing east. She had to be there ahead of Melissa in case there was positive ID. She didn't want her to go through it without a strong female presence at her side.

That thought prompted her to hit the siren and lights.

The waters parted, and she was flying along the 290 ready to do the unthinkable with a woman she hardly knew.

She prayed that the trip solved nothing, a strange prayer for a detective.

7

K endra McMann was the daughter of a retired Chicago Police Department sergeant who had done his twenty on the streets and then launched his own detective agency. She was the granddaughter of a New York City police officer who had walked a beat in Brooklyn his entire career. Both men had stories that kept the family up late at night on a Saturday, usually loosened up with plenty of bourbon and beer.

She was married to a man who worked as a county computer programmer, a man who was working on his master's in software engineering at an online school. Matt was gentle and loving; one of his hobbies was repairing old pianos and organs. He excelled at this and over the past year had talked about starting his own company doing nothing but keyboard repairs.

They were a happy, childless couple. McMann herself had seen enough on the streets of Chicago and from the front seat of an unmarked vehicle that she had decided against having children of her own. As it was, her sister in Elm

Grove had two kids that McMann doted on. That was close enough to the fire for her. She refused to venture any nearer.

Her supervisor was Denny Lambert, a black man with an eye on becoming chief someday. Lambert was very political, which meant that too many of McMann's cases were suddenly pulled away from her and disposed of without explanation. In those times she knew that someone with juice had approached Lambert and asked for a favor or made a threat that could have political ramifications, so he had dropped an investigation to turn the heat back down.

McMann's partner, Sherry Escanaba, was stay-at-home sick when Lisa Sellars was abducted. McMann was handling their cases herself. Some days she would have a temp join her: usually a uniform who'd been pulled off the street and told to come to work wearing a suit. These helpers were usually over-eager and grasping at the small window of time during which they might solve an important case and get considered for detective school.

As McMann drove to the Medical Examiner's building, she considered what Melissa Sellars was actually up against. For one, she hadn't told the woman that the way the case was developing—or, rather, not developing—she'd probably never see her daughter again until some hikers or hunters found a shallow grave giving up the bones of a four-year-old female. That was the usual result in these cases where the victim wasn't located in the first twenty-four hours. It was a result that the police department had to let parents experience for themselves because they forever believed their child would be one of the lucky ones. Even after a positive ID, some hope remained. It was human nature, and Melissa Sellars would be no different, McMann was sure.

Driving along, her windshield wipers beating the snow away, she could feel the old familiar tightening in her chest as the day drew inexorably closer to that moment when she'd have to tell Melissa that she'd been assigned a new case and would have to move on. She usually tempered that by saying the new case wouldn't be given the same priority by her as Melissa's case. That would help assuage the mother's panic and fright, but it was also untrue. The fact was, these grab-and-run cases were the stuff of daily reports and were so constant that new files were being opened by CPD at a rate that kept the investigators "knee deep in files," as one investigative reporter had put it.

She pulled her Impala into the M.E.'s parking lot and the constant sorrow she would forever feel when she came here suddenly washed over her. No police officer looked forward to views. It was heartbreaking, of course, to be there when family or friends ID'd a loved one. But it was part of the job, and McMann was determined she would be there with victims' loved ones whenever possible as the sheets were peeled back from the frozen faces.

She pocketed her keys and hurried inside.

8

Detective McMann had me ride to the M.E.'s office with two uniformed officers. She was going to be driving in a different direction when we finished so the officers would take me back home. Later that day, she told me she'd pulled into the M.E.'s parking lot and run inside. Her goal was to beat me there. She badged the clerk and found, to her enormous relief, that I hadn't arrived. She told the clerk to hold me at the front desk when I arrived. Meanwhile, she went off in search of coffee.

I was alone in the backseat of the squad car with two uniformed officers in the front. They were talking together as they proceeded down the 294 and then rejoined the 290 for the last leg of the trip to the morgue on Harrison Street. At the parking lot, they pulled in beside Detective McMann's ride, and everybody got out. The police officers took their places on either side of me, and we began the long walk inside. Honestly, at that moment I knew how prisoners felt when they were being walked to the electric chair.

At any moment, I feared, I would just collapse and turn into a black spot on the parking lot.

I felt my heart pounding in my chest by the time we reached the entrance. Then we walked through the small lobby and up to the reception window. The woman behind the glass slid it open. "You Ms. Sellars?"

"I am."

"Detective McMann will be right back. She asked that you wait here in the lobby for her."

The officers escorted me to a waiting area and remained standing until I was seated. Then they sat down close by and said nothing. I was too numb to even speak. Besides, words were useless in this place.

Five minutes and here came Detective McMann, a cup of coffee in hand. She nodded to us and we stood then followed her through a hospital-style door marked PRIVATE.

Down the hall to a second desk.

The morgue clerk nodded as we approached his desk. "Yes?"

"Unidentified white female child. Arrived sometime this morning?"

"Sure. Let me get an attendant." He lifted the phone and paged someone to his desk. Minutes later, a young Asian man wearing a white lab coat and a look of deep concern came for us. We followed.

Inside was a huge wall of cadaver drawers. The attendant checked his clipboard against a date and time entry and then motioned us down to the far end where the more recent bodies were stored. He reached and drew open a drawer at waist level. The body was covered head-to-toe by a sheet.

I felt like I was about to black out. I saw spots, and I almost lost my footing. I would have fallen if the officers hadn't steadied me. I drew a deep breath and nodded.

The attendant peeled back one corner of the coverlet. I leaned across his arm and peered down at the face.

"Jesus," I said in the shakiest voice. "Jesus, thank you."

"Not?" McMann said.

"No, not her," I said. With that, I erupted into a sobbing hulk that the two officers had to help out of the morgue. They half-carried me back to their car and lowered me inside.

"No, change of plans," called McMann across the parking lot when she had finished with the front desk and caught up. "Put her in my car."

The transfer was made. Detective McMann leaned in through the passenger's door and buckled my seatbelt. I looked in the outside mirror and was shocked at my white face and dilated eyes that were wide and staring. There were no words to help; McMann didn't even try. She hurried around to the driver's side and climbed in.

My head flopped back against the headrest. I was crying softly, shaking my head from side-to-side.

"Did you see that baby's face?" I whispered. "Jesus, what a beautiful little girl. And no one has claimed her yet?"

"It happens. Usually, the parents haven't been notified by

the police that there's a possible match. It's early in the day yet. Someone will be in by nightfall to claim her body."

"Oh, my God. My baby, my precious Lisa, where are you?"

"Look, I'm going to drive you home, and then we'll meet with the officers who've been out in your neighborhood. Then I need to head back downtown."

"Downtown? Does that mean you're moving onto the next case?"

"Well...it means a lot of things. There isn't much I can do until I have leads. Right now my partner, Jerry O'Reilly, is waiting to talk to the man who owns the black SUV from your neighborhood. That could be huge. And of course I'll be there when those questions get asked. Jerry'll call me."

"So until then, we're kind of stuck?"

"I don't know that I'd call it stuck--"

"Come on, Detective McMann, you're going to have to level with me. We're at a dead end here if this black SUV guy isn't a lead, am I right?"

I heard the air whoosh out of McMann's lungs. What was the sense in dancing around it?

"You're right. We have nothing if the black SUV doesn't take us to a new understanding."

"What about the hospital? You're sure they've searched every room?"

"Yes, every room and every closet."

"What about the hospital morgue?"

"That too. I wasn't going to bring it up."

"Well, leave it to me."

"Yes."

~

FOUR POLICE OFFICERS from the citywide search of bus stations and airports had assembled around my kitchen table. One-by-one they recited what efforts they had made and what results--or lack of results-- they had to report. The whole purpose of this exercise, I was told, was to see whether other vehicles had been seen in the area that were perhaps lurking close by my house or whether other neighbors had actually seen faces or had descriptions of people and so forth. But so far, nothing.

But then McMann's phone chimed, and she pulled it out. She spoke for almost a minute. Then she listened before speaking again. She finally hung up.

"Well?" I whispered, afraid to say it out loud.

"Joplin, Missouri. Another body that fits Lisa's general description."

"Oh, my God!"

"They're sending photographs."

"Oh, my God."

"So how do you want to handle these, because there will be more. Should they come directly to your phone or do you want them to come to my phone and then we meet and go over them all at one sitting?"

"Send them to me. I can't wait between."

"Can do. But call me just in case."

"In case of what?"

"You know. In case one is Lisa. Call me before you do anything else, and I will be here in ten minutes from anyplace in the city. Okay with that?"

"Okay."

"Now, for the other officers here, let's go around the table, and everybody give three minutes on your morning up and down the block. We good?"

Nods and grunts of assent.

"Good. Michaels, let's start with you."

The uniformed officer with the silver name tag that said ROBIN MICHAELS began nodding. "I had the next block north, south side. Out of eleven homes, six had somebody home. All six invited me inside to talk. What I found out was that most of the people don't pay much attention to local traffic. I think that's because their road makes a T-intersection into a very busy secondary road with traffic that constantly turns and comes up their road to go back and go the other direction. In other words, their road is the next best thing to a U-Turn out on Abbott Expressway."

"Did anyone have anything?" McMann pressed.

"Nothing actionable. Sorry."

"Officer Periwinkle?"

"Yes, Sergeant. I had the north side of the victim's road. A dozen houses, seven invites. Three of them noticed the black SUV hanging around, but nobody thought to write anything down. They all said the same thing: by the time they realized it had come back two more times, it was too late, the thing was gone and didn't come back again. So nobody got a license plate except one older lady who thought it began with an 'S' because her first granddaughter is 'Stephanie' and it made her think of that name."

"Nothing actionable, fine. Next?"

The round-table continued much the same way, and I was struck by how little people actually noticed what was going on in their neighborhood--hell, even on their own street.

My face and chest were suddenly hot. My thoughts darted back to Lisa, and my heart began crying out for my missing daughter. The proceedings around the table dissolved in my mind and all I could imagine was the man who had come into Lisa's hospital room and how swiftly he had made off with her. I hadn't been gone from the room for ten minutes, and Lisa went missing. I kicked myself for leaving my daughter alone, and I wondered whether all hospital security was so lax that just anyone could come and go on hospital floors and take people out of their rooms under the guise of a hospital orderly taking someone to radiology or to PT or whatever.

I came out of my daze--for a moment. I checked my watch. 1:07 p.m. Then a cold hand gripped me as I realized that very soon all the people gathered around me would be gone on other assignments. Time was running out; even Detective McMann had other cases that would take away her time and attention.

I found myself wanting to cry out, to insist that enough

wasn't being done, to demand that everyone stay another full day and help. But I didn't. I knew this was routine to the lot of them, this coming together and canvassing after a child went missing. I also knew that after their shifts they would all go home to their families and say a silent prayer of thanks that it wasn't one of theirs that was gone.

When the updates concluded, I looked up and realized I had actually heard very little of what had been said. But that was okay; no new action was planned as a result of the canvass. Everyone was leaving on other assignments now. Even Detective McMann was gathering her things together although she wasn't actually unplugging her laptop and folding it away. So I got up and made another pot of coffee in hopes of impliedly inviting the detective to stay on and continue with her work.

It wasn't necessary. McMann explained that she would be remaining with me until it was time to go and confront Grant Baedeker. She had many questions for the man in the black SUV who just might have been staking out my house before Lisa disappeared. Her intensity sparked new hope inside me; maybe this was, in fact, the break that would crack the case. I began praying the same beseeching prayer over and over, crying out for help and praying for my daughter's well-being and safety.

The rest of that afternoon was spent fielding calls from my staff who were calling with offers of help and prayers for a quick recovery of Lisa. Then even the star of the TV show herself called to wish me well and to tell me that others were covering my job. Of course, they weren't covering as well, which made me feel good knowing my job was safe and that my boss missed me.

Calls from family were intermingled. Along with those I also called Mark's parents and let them know what was going on. Mark's father insisted they were driving in to help and this time around I didn't resist. I actually thought it would be good to have them around my first night home alone. So I agreed that it would be best if Rebecca and Charlie drove into town and stayed with me. Who could say? They might even have ideas to offer, to follow up. Additionally, Rebecca was a force to be reckoned with--the woman who wouldn't hesitate to shoot the kidnapper who had taken their granddaughter. She would have to be restrained if it ever came to court appearances or that sort of thing. But I decided their presence far outweighed the negatives. In the end, I couldn't help it and broke into tears and admitted I needed all the help I could get and that they should come without delay.

I then called my parents in London. My father was a diplomat specializing in trade policies between the U.S. and the U.K.—so he claimed. My mother worked as a buyer for Macy's, chasing down the latest in fall, spring, and summer fashions for the U.S. market. It was a job she loved; I doubted that my parents would ever return to the U.S. to live, they so thoroughly enjoyed England.

The terrible news was shared with all relatives and close friends. When it was done, I sat down in the family room conversation pit. I was testing what it felt like to be alone in the house without my daughter.

Then I abruptly stood and went back into the kitchen, where McMann was typing rapidly on her laptop. I filled a coffee cup and sat down across from the detective.

That "being all alone" feeling was too much.

I didn't think I'd ever be able to do that--not after having my daughter and then losing her. Being alone was one thing. But being alone during a tragedy-in-the-making was more than any human being should ever have to face.

It felt good to be near the detective.

I hoped she would stay around-the-clock until Lisa was found.

9

Detective McMann left Melissa's at three-thirty that first afternoon. She was off to interview Grant Baedeker, the man whose name was on the registration of the black SUV. She began driving east on the Eisenhower and got off on First Avenue in Maywood. Five minutes later she came to the Jif-Lube next door to Gigi's Nails. She parked and headed inside.

Her partner, Jerry O'Reilly was still waiting in the office. With him was the same cashier, but this time a new face had arrived. McMann knew he was Baedeker before they were even introduced.

"Is there an office where we can talk?" McMann asked.

O'Reilly answered. "No office. Can we do this in your car?"

"Surely." It was snowing and blowing outside, so the trio hurried into McMann's still-warm automobile, and she started it up and switched the heater on. McMann was behind the wheel, Baedeker had been directed into the passenger seat by O'Reilly, and O'Reilly now occupied the backseat right behind Baedeker so the subject couldn't see him. McMann half-turned in the seat, drawing her leg up and across the leatherette seat cover. She knew that O'Reilly had already patted the guy down; that was SOP with them. So she launched right in.

"Mr. Baedeker--"

"I go by Grant, Miss."

"Grant, we're here about a black Escalade titled in your name. Do you know which vehicle I'm talking about?"

"Yes. I don't have it now."

"You mean you've loaned it out? Or did you transfer the title?"

"Sold it. Title transfer is pending until the buyer's check clears."

"And when did this happen?"

"Saturday."

"Just this past Saturday?"

"That's right."

"Mr. Baedeker, your vehicle was seen parked several days in a row in the vicinity of Abbott and Oakland. Does that location ring a bell?"

"No. I wasn't in that vicinity, don't even know what town you're talking about."

"We're talking Schaumburg. Not far from Golf Road."

"I haven't been to Schaumburg in--oh, I don't know, a year? Two years?"

"Did you leave the vehicle behind a 7-Eleven?"

"Are you kidding? I'd never do that with a Caddy."

"Are you married?"

"Divorced."

"Kids?"

"One grown daughter in East Moline. We don't talk except for a call at Christmas. Long gone."

"Have you loaned your Escalade to anyone in the past week?"

"Nope. That car is my pride and joy. Nobody drove it except me."

"Why did you sell?"

Baedeker slowly nodded. "Yes. Down-sizing. But don't mention it around my people inside. Things have been very slow since Christmas. Cash flow problems so I couldn't keep up the payments. Figured it was better to sell and get something for myself rather than just turn it back."

"Turn it back?"

"You know, give it back to the dealer."

"Mr. Baedeker," O'Reilly said from just behind the subject's ear, "how do you explain your vehicle being seen in the Schaumburg area over the past several days?"

"I don't."

"You don't what?"

"I don't explain it. I wasn't there, so I don't know what some-body saw. Who says they saw my car there anyway?"

"That's confidential, and there's an investigation underway, so we can't say," McMann came back. "Do you know a woman by the name of Sellars? Melissa Sellars?"

"Melissa Sellars? Not that I know of. I mean, she might have been a customer, but I wouldn't remember that. I'm usually not even around the shop."

"Yes, we understand you usually come in once a day, hit the drawer, then disappear to a titty bar," McMann said smoothly. "Does that sound like you?"

Baedeker laughed. "No law against tits is there, officer?"

O'Reilly leaned his face up just behind the subject's ear. "Talk nice, ducky. You're outnumbered here."

"Sorry. I just don't think it's CPD's business where I spend my time."

"Maybe not, but when your vehicle was seen three days running in the vicinity of a crime victim's home, we're sure as hell going to ask any and all questions we damn well need to ask. No law against that, is there?"

"No, ma'am. I didn't mean--"

"Forget it. Have you been to Belmont hospital recently?"

"No. I've never even set foot in Belmont."

"You didn't go to the pediatrics floor in the past week?"

"Is this about a kidnapping? Jesus, you've really got the wrong guy."

"How do you know it was a kidnapping?"

"Well, I--I--"

"Mr. Baedeker, my partner in the back seat, has a DNA collection kit. Will you give us permission just to take a sample of your hair from the back of your head?"

"Sure, just don't make a huge mess, that's all."

O'Reilly immediately plucked several hairs and tucked them inside a sample jar before the subject could change his mind.

"What's it all about?"

"Just being cautious, Mr. Baedeker. Now, would you mind taking us to your home and letting us look around?"

"Yes, I mind. Get a warrant."

Baedeker's face had suddenly clouded over, and his voice dropped an octave. Clearly, he was no longer the innocent, cooperative owner of a lube shop. His entire demeanor had changed with McMann's request.

"We can do that. We can get that warrant."

"Good. Just let me out of here."

"No, I think I'll keep you right here with me, Mr. Baedeker, while Detective O'Reilly obtains the warrant. Or do I need to lock you up for my own safety while we execute the warrant?"

"Hey, I won't be a problem. How about letting me hang around my shop while you do this."

"Fair enough. You still living in the 1800 block of Howard in Niles?"

"Yes."

"I'm going to have an officer posted outside your home in about five minutes. Do not go there or attempt to go there until we have executed our search warrant. Do you understand me?"

"I'll just stay here at the shop until you say so. I've got paperwork to catch up."

"Really? Where do you do that paperwork?"

"Usually in my car."

"Where is your car?"

"Out front."

"What are you driving?"

"A Toyota. Where's my Escalade?"

"Police yard. Why do you ask?"

"I'd like to drive it."

"But you told us you sold it."

"Not until the check clears, officer."

"So you're still driving it, the title's still in your name, but you want us to believe you've sold it?"

"That's why I haven't been driving it the past several days. The new owner was testing it out."

"Wait. Why didn't you tell me you haven't been driving it the past several days?"

Baedeker spread his hands. All color was drained from his face.

"Because you didn't ask."

"And who is this purchaser of your vehicle?"

"A woman I know. She works at the Kit-Kat Klub on Ina Road."

"She's a stripper?"

"A dancer. She would prefer 'dancer'."

"Well, I can appreciate that. So, 'dancer' it is. What's her name?"

"She goes by Hermione. That's her name around the Kat."

"Do you know her real name?"

"Nancy Callender."

"Where is she now?"

"Probably at the Kat working the pole. She makes two grand a night there."

"What is she to you?"

"She's going to be my wife. I hope."

McMann leaned back against the door on her side. She studied Grant Baedeker for several minutes.

Then, "Let me take a wild-ass guess here, Mr. Baedeker. Does your friend Nancy Callender know Melissa Sellars?"

"Who's she?"

"The victim's mother."

"Where does she work?"

"Executive producer on *Laura in Chicago*."

"That must be it. Hermione was a guest on *Laura* about a month ago. They did a thing on exotic dancers, and Hermione demonstrated her pole technique. She was dressed, of course."

"And that's where she met Melissa Sellars?"

"Hey, you said that, not me."

"Damn right I said that. O'Reilly?"

"I'm on my way."

"Mr. Baedeker. You know what' s expected? If you leave the premises before I tell you it's okay, you will be immediately arrested and thrown in jail. Are we clear?"

"Totally clear."

With that, Baedeker and O'Reilly climbed out of McMann's Impala and O'Reilly climbed into the next car over and headed for the Kit-Kat Klub and a conversation with Nancy Callender aka Hermione. McMann watched as Baedeker hurried back inside his lube shop. Then she backed out and hit her sirens and lights.

She had an appointment with a judge who didn't know it yet.

A warrant was needed. A warrant followed by a search of Baedeker's home.

Then a conversation with Melissa Sellars.

If Hermione remembered Melissa, then Melissa would very likely remember Hermione aka Nancy Callender.

McMann felt like she had just fit one piece of a vast puzzle to another.

Then she was running Code 3 eastbound on the 290. Dispatch had a judge waiting with an Assistant State's Attorney.

The warrant was waiting for her testimony.

10

I welcomed my in-laws at 4:35 p.m. Charlie Sellars was a strapping ox of a man whose company built steel boilers. His wife, Rebecca, was a fiery woman with a sharp tongue and penchant for shopping on Michigan Avenue too much. They lived in Glencoe, a North Shore Chicago suburb of about nine thousand people, located north of Evanston, north of Winnetka, in a kind of isolation close to the beach and heart-stopping restaurants. Coming to my home represented a huge drop in home prices but Charlie, an old-school Democrat, and a man of the people felt right at home.

Their driver brought their bags into my guest bedroom and then returned to the family Rolls. He was told to find someplace nearby to put himself up for the night. The man always carried a change of clothes and toiletries in his bag; such requests for overnight stopovers were more and more frequent now that Charlie Sellars was semi-retired and had taken to a little more traveling around.

They were on their second lemonade in my kitchen when the front doorbell rang.

"That should be Colonel Eustice," Charlie said. "Let me get it."

He returned minutes later with a white-haired, closely shaved, neat-as-a-pin man who walked like a soldier on review.

"This is Colonel Johns V. Eustice, Melissa. The Colonel is a friend of mine. He's retired Army Intelligence with a stint in the Corps of Engineers as well. He's helped me out several times with internal security matters. The Colonel will be taking over the search for my granddaughter. The police department has been notified. They retain custody of the case, of course, but they are on notice the Colonel is running a parallel investigation."

"What--what--" I stuttered. "You should have asked me about this, Charlie. No offense, Colonel, but I'm not sure I'm comfortable with this."

"Hell, daughter," cried Charlie Sellars, "nobody's comfortable! But our baby girl is missing, and that calls for doubling-down. It's the only way to handle these things."

"Really? How many missing-persons cases have you handled, Charles?" asked Rebecca. "You talk like a goddam war hero yourself. That hoo-rah crap is what got our boy killed, and I want it stopped immediately. Melissa, we didn't come here to interfere. I'm going to ask the Colonel to back out politely and leave this to the police."

"No can do, ma'am," said the Colonel. "With all due respect, my men are already fanned out through the city giving this case everything we've got. Besides, Charlie hired me, not you."

Rebecca's eyes narrowed at the Colonel. "But Charlie answers to me, got it?"

Colonel Eustice's eyes shifted between the Mrs. and the Mr. He wasn't sure which way to jump.

"You know what?" I suddenly interjected, "I kind of like the idea of a parallel investigation. I'm glad the Colonel is here to help. You may stay, Colonel and thank you for coming. Thanks to you, too, Charlie, for making this happen. Rebecca, the decision is mine as I'm Lisa's mother. Please respect me in this."

Rebecca turned her head away in a huff. I knew that she was going to be difficult. I had forgotten since their last visit just how difficult my mother-in-law actually was. Now I remembered why they weren't invited for overnights all that often.

"First thing I want to do is view your daughter's room, Mrs. Sellars," the Colonel said, already far down the road on stay or go. "I need a sense of who she is."

"Are you serious?" I asked. "She's just four years old, Colonel. She really isn't somebody yet."

"Don't get me wrong, Mrs. Sellars, but I have a special sixth sense about these cases. Please humor me."

I couldn't hide my confusion. Was the man serious that he had a special sixth sense? Or was that just a manner of speaking? I honestly didn't know, but I decided that his viewing Lisa's room couldn't hurt anything. Who could tell, it might even help. At least he said it would, and right then I was so terrified about news that could come any minute about my daughter that the Colonel's request was a very minor sidelight. I showed him back to Lisa's bedroom and left him there. His request.

Returning to the kitchen, I picked up my phone and noticed a new message. My heart jumped, and I shakily sank back down into the chair I'd occupied since last night. My hands jittered and jumped as I worked the icons to bring up the message. Rye, New York, Coroner's Office, said the sender's ID. I knew I was about to see the picture of a dead girl when I punched the jpg icon. With a deep breath and a silent prayer, I opened the file.

The picture wasn't all that clear, and the girl's face was severely bruised. But I studied it and then passed the phone silently across the table to Charlie. He took one look, looked away, and passed the phone to Rebecca. She was able to give the photograph more consideration, turning the phone this way and that. Then, "This isn't Lisa. No way it could be."

"Concur," said Charlie.

"I agree," I said. "Pass it back, and I'll message them."

Rebecca handed over the phone, and I typed a message that was half condolences and half commentary about the child not being mine. I sent it off and hung my head as tears came into my eyes, and I shook with relief. "My God," I muttered. "Dear my God."

Five minutes passed in silence, followed by the doorbell chiming again. I excused myself.

Bundled in a heavy parka was McMann, who had left her car running, lights on, at the top of the circle drive.

"Come in!" I greeted her and stood aside.

"Only got a minute."

"Would you like to come in and meet Lisa's grandparents?"

"Nope. Can't stay. Just have a question."

"Okay. We can talk right here."

"About a month ago a stripper appeared on your show. Her professional name is Hermione, and her real name is Nancy Callender. Does that ring a bell?"

"The show with the strippers, yes. It was a very popular show, and everyone in the audience received swag from Victoria's Secret. Even the men."

"The woman I'm talking about was a pole dancer. Remember any such thing?"

"Yes, I do. She gave us a demonstration of her art. Dressed in shorts and a shirt."

"She was driving the black SUV that was spotted in this neighborhood. I'm not saying she was driving it in this area, I'm saying she had access or custody of the vehicle about that same time."

"How do we know this?"

"Grant Baedeker. Turns out he's selling the Escalade to this pole dancer. She works at the Kit-Kat Klub."

"Why would a pole dancer be in my neighborhood?"

"Why? Because she learned about you while she was on the TV show. You're the show's executive producer, she put two-and-two together and decided you'd be hot to pay top dollar to get your daughter back. This is total conjecture, but it's my conjecture, and I'm feeling pretty good about it compared to all else we have to go on. So you do remember the incident, the woman on the show? But you don't remember her especially. Is that fair?"

"Yes, that's exactly fair. It's making more sense. But one thing. Why haven't I got a call about ransom or a note or demand or something?"

"It's still early in the case. That will come."

"I don't know how much longer I can wait."

"I have a feeling we'll hear from the perp before you turn out the lights tonight. Just keep your phone lines open like I asked. And keep the faith, Melissa. I've got a good feeling about this one."

"Honestly, you do? You're not just saying that again?"

"No, I'm not just saying that. I really believe we'll get Lisa back all safe and sound. You develop instincts after awhile in my job."

"Well, the first day is almost over."

"Let's just ignore that. We're going to come out of this on top regardless of those old sayings about the first twenty-four hours and all that. Let's just stick to the script. Stay by the phone, answer and agree to anything he demands, call me immediately."

"I'll do that."

"Okay, gotta run. I'm going to Baedeker's place with a search warrant. I'll call you when we're done."

"Thank you. So much."

"Okay, so long."

"Goodbye for now."

I watched my detective plod off through the ankle-deep snow. I wondered where my sidewalk man was. It wasn't like him not to come and clear the walks and driveway at least a couple of times that day. But so far, nothing. I hoped he was all right and just running late.

Just as I was thinking about him, who should come through the front gate but the familiar SUV that my driveway man drove. A black SUV. With a snowplow on the front end.

I shook my head and closed the door.

I couldn't make everyone a suspect.

11

K endra McMann ran lights and sirens full-on all the way out to Niles, the home of Grant Baedeker. While the man with the black SUV cooled his heels back at his lube shop, Detective McMann and three members of the CPD crime lab were set to go through every square inch of his residence in search of any trace of Lisa Sellars, now missing twenty hours.

She pulled up in front of the address, a duplex--side-by-side--and waited for the crime lab van to arrive. When everybody was there and assembled, the head CSI took out his lock picks and had them inside the premises in thirty seconds.

It was dark and smelled faintly of cannabis and damp. McMann was told to wait just inside while photographs were taken and the first round of vacuuming was performed. So, she did as she was told.

When the photos were all snapped, and the vacuums turned off, McMann had her first look around. She then pulled on latex gloves. First stop, the refrigerator, and freezer where perps often hid money and drugs. If Baedeker had received money for his part in the kidnapping, McMann was determined to find out. She pulled open the doors and peered around inside. Then she opened the meat drawer and then the produce drawer. The man must not eat at home very much, she thought. Nothing in here but brown mold on the back reefer wall and a fifth of vodka in the freezer.

She then located his bedroom. Up with the mattress and looked beneath. Then to the closet, where she dug her hands into the pockets of his trousers and windbreaker, another common hiding place. The CSI's would already have been inside the toilet tank, normally her third stop. Then something caught her eye. A *Holy Bible*, on the table next to his bed.

No way, she thought. Not a *Bible*, not this guy. She bent down and opened the book. A Perfect rectangle was cut out of the book's pages from top to bottom, exactly the size of the stack of hundred-dollar bills that now occupied the space. The detective didn't touch the money, always a great source for fingerprints. Perps will wear gloves for everything else, but when it came to cash money, they needed to lay their skin on that. Fingerprints grew on hundreds like mushrooms in springtime. She called to a tech to come get the *Bible* and bag it.

She found shoes under the bed and ran her latex-gloved hands inside, feeling around for any contraband.

Nothing there.

The techs had already removed all vent covers and vacuumed lint, hair and fiber from the openings and the mouth of the pipes. So that was done, she noted to her satisfaction. She looked at the ceiling. The overhead light fixture was unscrewed and hanging loose. Again, vacuumed and searched.

The en-suite bathroom proved tricky, as the bathtub itself was actually a new shell dropped over the original tub. She again called on the techs to remove the shell and look inside the skin. Same with the medicine cabinet: they were to remove it from the wall and check behind. Satisfied that she had made about as big a mess in the man's bathroom as possible--which wasn't actually her intent at all--she next went into the second bedroom. It had been furnished with a reclining loveseat, a fifty-inch flatscreen, small fridge, and a daybed. Just for giggles, she switched on the flatscreen. First, to see if it worked or whether it needed its case removed; second, to see what the subject might have been watching. You never knew what surprises that might yield. But this time it was futile: MSNBC came on the air, and a replay of *Rachel Maddow* sprang to life. MSNBC, the detective thought, seriously? She thought this over for a moment, then clicked the TV control's recall button. Now she found she was on an adult channel with an invitation to watch 180 minutes of college girls making out, all for just $9.99. According to the sub-text, the owner of the set had already purchased the video and could watch it for another eleven hours until the clock turned over and he'd have to move along. Or pay again, if it was really all that satisfying.

She dropped the remote in disgust then looked around before extending the footrests on both segments of the love seat. Then she dropped to her knees and peered underneath. Freshly vacuumed; good, the techs were a crackerjack team, and she was glad. Satisfied that all was under control, she stood and searched out the head CSI. She told her that she was leaving the premises. Two uniforms were waiting outside the door if the techs needed anything.

DETECTIVE JERRY O'REILLY found the Kit-Kat Klub was every mother's nightmare: naked young women everywhere, lecherous men of dubious mating value, plus the usual muscle, larcenous bartenders, and bedraggled women to keep an eye on things. The Klub offered three dance poles for enjoyment, one of which was occupied continuously from ten in the morning until two the next morning. Dead air clung in the corners and close spaces, while the bar smelled of disinfectant. O'Reilly wasted no time tracking down Hermione, who was found in a small stall down a dim hallway, giving a private dance to a man whose wife would be disappointed in him. O'Reilly watched through the curtain and then burst inside. The man froze in mid-stroke, immediately stuffing his semi-erect member back into his Dockers. O'Reilly badged Hermione, and her customer fled.

Hermione shrugged into a negligee.

"I'm over eighteen," she smiled through a thick lip gloss. She looked like forty years reached through an alley.

"Still, Daddy would be so disappointed."

"Who do you think that man was? That was Daddy."

"A black SUV you're buying was seen in a neighborhood of police interest. Why were you there?"

Hermione was blotting her lipstick with tissue plucked from a box on the single table in the stall.

"Why do you think I was driving? I'm not the only one interested."

"According to your BFF Baedeker, you're the only prospect who's been driving the Caddy. Again, why were you in Schaumburg?"

"Oh, there's a law against going to Schaumburg now? Is that it? Sheeesh!"

"Tell me what you know about the little girl you were watching in Schaumburg. I want to know where she is."

The dancer shook her head and made a zipper mime at her mouth.

O'Reilly took a step forward and seized the woman's wrist. He twisted it outward as one twisting the throttle on a motorcycle.

"Ow! Ow! What the hell's the matter with you?"

"We need to know about the little girl, Nancy. I'm not leaving here, and I'm not going to stop hurting you until you give me something!"

"I...don't...ow!"

"Uh-huh. Let's try that again." He twisted even harder, and she plunged down onto her knees from the torque.

"She's--she's--I don't know. A customer gave me a thousand dollars."

"To do what?"

"To find out about her. Her mom's habits."

"Did you find out anything?"

"When the mom comes and goes."

O'Reilly shook his head violently. "That's not enough. Tell me what you did!"

"I followed them to the hospital. Then I made a call. I got to keep the five thousand dollars."

"Oh, now it's five thousand?"

"For all of it, yes. You're hurting me, please stop!"

O'Reilly responded by twisting even harder. "I want this person's name."

"I don't know it. Twice I've given him a private dance. Then he asked me if I'd like to earn five thousand."

"And you jumped at it, am I right?"

"I did. I've got bills like everyone."

"Tell me how you got in touch with this person."

She was on her knees wincing. Cries of pains punctuated her loud breathing.

"He gave me a phone. I called him on that. Then I threw it in the Chicago River like he told me. That's all I know."

"You called and told him which hospital the little girl was in?"

"Uh-huh. That was it!"

"Stand up. We're going downtown."

"What for?"

"I'm charging you with conspiracy to kidnap. It could get even worse, depending."

"Mister, I've got two kids of my own. They're with their sitter. I can't just leave them."

"Not to worry. Our team is on its way to your house as we speak. The kids will be taken care of."

"Please tell Miss Sellars I'm sorry. I didn't know--"

"Sure you knew. Save the bullshit excuses for someone who cares. Where's your coat?"

"In my cubby in the back office."

"Let's go get it. You're done for the night. Maybe done for the next twenty years."

"Jesus."

"Yes, praying is a good idea for you."

They left the stall, and he followed her into the back office, shoving a man aside as he shoved his star in the guy's face. She grabbed her coat and purse out of the cubby. She asked about getting dressed, and he only told her to bring her clothes. She looped the clothes bag over her wrist and followed him out of the club. At the car, she was still shrugging into her coat.

"My nipples are so hard," she said with a smile at him.

"So put your fucking coat on. Nobody ever taught you?"

"You're so mean."

"Lady, you don't know mean. You'd best be praying nothing happens to that little girl. If something bad happens, you won't live to see your next birthday. I fucking promise you."

"So cold."

"Zip your fucking coat and get in!"

As O'Reilly headed for the California Avenue Jail, Hermione rocked up and back in the seat beside him. He hadn't cuffed her and thrown her in back. He hadn't needed to.

He owned her.

12

This time, McMann waited out front of Hermione's building while the technical services team searched the dancer's apartment. She wanted a pristine scene with no suggestion she had gone inside and contaminated the scene with hair or fibers tracked in by her from Lisa's house. She was very smart and very careful--her style at all times.

While she waited, McMann went online and checked her emails. Then she logged into the CPD dashboard and went over inter-departmental messages. There was one from her captain, and she clicked it open.

Just great. Another case assignment. She was going to have to leave Hermione's and travel to take down another missing person report. The uniforms had been there, and now it was her turn. She sighed and closed up her laptop. She advised dispatch that she was proceeding to the nursing home where an elderly gentleman had gone missing. She asked that dispatch advise CSI she'd had to leave. A uniform was with them upstairs in Hermione's, and that was sufficient police presence, so she could safely leave.

As she backed out of her parking slot a pang of regret cut through her chest. She was abandoning Melissa and her search for baby girl Lisa. She felt horrible and found herself gasping for air just for a moment or two. Then she collected herself together and dropped the Impala into drive and headed downtown.

Well, she knew she was going to have to call Melissa and advise her she'd been called to a newer case. She dreaded making that call. So she switched on the FM radio and drummed her fingers on the steering wheel as she picked her way eastbound.

Halfway in, she decided she had to call and putting it off any longer wasn't fair to Melissa. She punched the number with the saved contact on her phone.

I COULDN'T STAND WAITING while they searched the stripper's house. But I had no choice. Finally my cell rang.

I picked up and said hello. My voice sounded like someone at the bottom of a well.

"Melissa? Detective McMann calling. How you holding up?"

"That's not why you're calling, is it? You're going off to another case. I just knew it would happen tonight."

"I have no choice. While we wait for the results of the search of Hermione's apartment I have to take a call downtown. It will take all of an hour."

Sure, I thought, plus two hours writing up the report.

But I couldn't say all that. "It's all right. My in-laws are here, and they have Colonel Eustice helping us now."

"Colonel who? What jurisdiction is he from?"

"He's not. He's Army Intelligence, retired."

"OMG. You have got to be kidding. Please call him off."

"I figured they'd already told you by now."

"Not yet. But now I know, and I want this Colonel Eustice guy out of my case."

"Your case? You're leaving my case as we speak."

It was the first disagreement we'd had in almost twenty-four hours. We both hated it. I did, and I'm sure she did, too.

"I'm sorry you feel that way, Melissa. But believe me, I'm still on your case. I'll be back to you tonight yet."

"Promise?"

"I swear it. Even while I'm working something else I'll still have a close eye on your case. I guarantee it."

"Well--"

"I promise to check in at least twice tomorrow, too."

Long pause. Then, "That's it? You'll be checking in? Will you be doing actual work on my case tomorrow?"

"If we receive an actionable lead, yes. Otherwise, I'll be waiting, just like you."

"The FBI called me tonight," I stated glumly. "They're deferring to your jurisdiction."

"That's SOP. They always defer unless it's a case of known interstate flight. Then they hang onto it."

"How do we know it isn't?"

"Isn't interstate? Actually, we don't, I guess. It's all just speculation right now. You sleep with your phone tonight in case that ransom call comes in, all right? Remember, agree to whatever they say. Then call me immediately. And leave the colonel out of it. Are you listening to me?"

"I am. No more colonel. He won't listen to me, though. My father-in-law hired him. He says he's already got a team on the street following up leads."

"I don't even know what that means. We have no other leads except Baedeker and Nancy Callender at this point. I sincerely don't know what else he might be following up. I mean it, do what you need to do, but call him off."

"I'll try. But at least he's doing something."

Long silence.

"Melissa, we're doing everything that's indicated so far on your case."

"Really? Tell me about Nancy Callender, please."

"I've only been able to speak to Detective O'Reilly for just one minute because he's with her right now. But what we know is that someone paid Nancy Callender--or Hermione if you prefer her stage name--, to spy on you."

"What?"

"That's right. She was the one driving the black SUV. Or, rather, parked along your street in the SUV. She was establishing your daily habits, when you come and go. Then she followed you and Lisa to the hospital. She made a call to a man who gave her five thousand dollars. That's what we know so far."

"Did she tell you his name?"

"Not yet. She claims she doesn't know his name."

"Where did she meet him? How can we track him down? I'm sure he has Lisa, McMann!"

"We don't know anything other than he paid her to watch you and she did that."

"Is she being charged with a crime?"

"O'Reilly will be offering her ways to reduce the seriousness of her case. By giving us names, for one thing. That's what we really need right now."

"Dear Lord, let my baby be safe from these animals!'

"As soon as O'Reilly is finished up with her, I'll call you. I promise. No delays, I'll call immediately. O'Reilly knows this and Jerry's a good guy. He'll stay on it and keep me up to the minute. That about does it for now. Okay?"

"If you say so. I've got a mother-in-law that could get those answers out of Nancy-whatever in about five seconds. Can she talk to her?"

"You know she can't. Okay, I have to go now. But I'll be back to you very soon. Probably within the hour."

We hung up. I was left with a silent phone and the crushing news that the taking of my child had been planned out and the groundwork laid in a very systematic fashion. I

wondered if this was just another child slavery ring operating in Chicago. There were others; the papers were full of
stuff like this lately.

I went back into the kitchen and sat down next to Charlie,
my dear, brusque father-in-law. I leaned over and rested my
head on his shoulder. He reached around and patted the
side of my head. "What'd she say?"

"They have someone who followed me to the hospital the
night I took Lisa."

"Names? Addresses?"

"Not yet. They're working on it."

"Colonel? Anything you can jump into here?"

"Definitely. I'm calling this McMann right now this second."

I looked up. Sure enough, the man had his phone out and
his reading glasses down on his nose as he dialed the
detective.

"No!" I cried out, holding up my hand. "Don't call. Please. I
want the police to do this. I appreciate everything you and
the Colonel have done, Charlie, but that's enough. At least
for now. She's going to call me back within one hour."

"Fine," said my father-in-law. "And if she doesn't then I turn
the Colonel loose."

"All right. Whatever. Rebecca, would you be a dear and get
me some orange juice? There's a big jug in the fridge."

"Sure enough, darling."

Orange juice was served. I took two swallows and fell asleep
sitting up.

I woke up as they were tucking me under a blanket on the couch.

"My phone."

Charlie held it up. "Right here beside you on the table."

"Night."

"Get whatever sleep you can. I'll wake you when your phone rings, just in case."

"Thank you, Charlie. Charlie?"

"Yes?"

"I wish Mark was here. I miss him with all my heart."

"Me too. He was the best of the best."

"The best."

"Good night."

Twenty minutes later, my phone played its tone.

I awoke, instantly frightened. "What? Tell me, Kendra."

"We have a name."

13

U p and down, up and down. The little girl was quiet while on the swing set. But that was the only time.

It was warm and sunny outside at ten-thirty in the morning. Parrots could be heard squawking and screeching in the jungle just a hundred yards away. The place was alive with them, but the little girl was oblivious.

"I love my mommy," she sang to clouds as she swung up and back. "I love my mommy."

Twenty yards the other direction from the jungle sat a single story house with a porch across the front and a patio on the roof. The little girl could see two men with guns sitting on the porch closest to her, watching her swing and talking in low tones. She didn't know the language. Whatever they were saying was funny, because they laughed and swatted each other with their hats. Just then, a rotund, very dark woman wearing a red and white print dress and a white apron came out onto the porch, clapping her hands together. The little girl looked up. It was time.

She ambled up onto the porch, and the men stopped talking. The woman draped an arm across her shoulders and helped her inside. They went into the kitchen.

"Are Luis and Raoul bothering you?" the woman asked the girl.

"No. When do I see my mommy?"

"Maybe today, maybe tomorrow. You are going to a very special house today when the airplane comes for you."

"Who lives there? Is my mommy there?"

"Two weeks and she's still on the mommy," the woman said in Spanish to a younger woman who was chopping onions on a cutting board.

"The doctor says she can fly now."

"She's all well. They took good care."

The younger woman looked up from her chopping. "Tell me, Poquita, what is your name?"

"Angelina."

"Very good!" both women exclaimed. "Your father will be so happy. So will your mommy."

"Doesn't mommy like my other name?"

"She likes your new name. She told me on the phone."

"Can I call her?"

"She will be there this afternoon. That's Esma's promise to you."

"Esma, can I feed the goats?"

"First we feed the chickens. You can help me feed the chickens."

The little girl shouted a merry, "Yes!"

"All right. You go out and tell the chickens to get ready. You tell them Esma's coming."

"Okay."

Her blue eyes sparkled in the sunlight as she danced across the grass to the chicken pen. She had to move a bucket over to reach the sliding wooden clasp that kept the pen door closed. But she made it, climbed down, and stepped inside.

But now what? No sooner was she inside than realized she couldn't reach back up to lock the door again. So she stood there, chickens flowing around her feet as they scrambled out the door and jumped and flitted across the grass, headed for the jungle and the fruit they knew was there. It was always there, flavoring the air, beckoning, and the flock was on its way.

The little girl stepped outside of the pen, moved the bucket back, and relocked the gate.

"There," she said to no one. Then she went back inside the house.

"Well?" said Esma as she took off her apron. "Did you tell them?"

"There's no one there."

"What you mean, no one there?"

"The chickens aren't home."

"What?"

Esma hit the door at a trot. Señor Ignacio Velasquez would be furious if his chickens were gone. They were prize-winners, all of them, added to his collection from around the world. When she reached the pen, she threw up her arms and yelled, "¡*Caramba!* All gone!"

She turned and looked for the girl with the blue eyes. There she was, near the jungle, staring into the green maze with her hands raised. "Come back," she cried again and again.

By the time Esma caught up to her, the little girl was weeping and wouldn't stop.

"There, there, I'm in trouble, not you, Poquita. I let you out of my sight. Esma knows better with one so young."

"I want my mommy."

It must have been the hundredth time that day. Esma, flabbergasted and frightened, couldn't hold back.

"Your mommy is dead, and she isn't coming back!"

"No!" the girl little turned to the woman's body and began flailing her with fists and kicking with her feet. At a total loss as to how to react, Esma tried gripping the child firmly. But still, the flailing and screaming wouldn't stop. So, finally losing control, she drew back her arm and backhanded the girl across the side of the head. She staggered back, slumping, arms dropped to her sides, and sat down on the deep grass in a daze. As she sat there, she realized she couldn't see anything. Her eyes wouldn't focus. So the crying began again, but now it was more in the mode of wailing for something precious that's been lost. This went on for several minutes until Esma, who by now had snapped out of her rage and terror, realized what she had done and scooped the child up with her arms. She began crying over the child and patting her back and kissing her head, which prompted the child to respond in kind and now both were weeping as the woman carried the child to the porch. The two men who had been talking there were half-raised out of their chairs.

"If you hurt her and Iggy can't sell her he will kill you," said the darker of the two. He made the universal slicing sign across his throat.

"Did you damage her, Esma?" demanded the second man. "Let me look."

He stooped over and peered down into the child's face, studying her features with his own dark eyes.

"This one I might keep for myself if no one wants her now," the second man said. "She is perfect for my son."

"No way," said Esma. "She belongs to Señor Velasquez, and you don't want me to tell him what you said."

The second man's eyes grew opened wide. "You don't tell him nothing, Esma. Or I cut your throat."

Meanwhile, the blue-eyed child was hearing these words and becoming even more scared. Her crying peaked like never before, and all three adults stood there, watching and listening, without an idea between them of what they might do.

But then they heard the helicopter coming.

"Oh, it's your mommy!" Esma crooned to the child. The little girl replied by making fists and wiping furiously at her eyes until the tears were gone.

"Mommy? Coming for me? Yeah, Mommy!"

The helicopter spun down through the air, landing in the pasture between the jungle and house. While the props were yet spinning, a dark man in a navy suit and white shirt with red tie ducked down and trotted for the house. At the porch, he opened his arms and motioned the little girl to come to him. She didn't. She only stood and stared at him; her vision was back. Then she looked around behind him.

"Mommy?"

Ignacio Velasquez, the man in the suit, broke into peals of laughter. "Daddy, sweetheart! Come to Daddy!"

"You're my daddy?"

"I am, I am!"

"Do you have my mommy?"

"Yes, she's waiting for us at our new home."

"Do we have to go on that?" she said, pointing at the helicopter.

"We do. But guess what? You get to wear headphones and hear the pilot talking."

"I like headphones."

"Of course you do, sweetheart. How is she?" he then said to Esma.

"Doctor says she's fine now."

"What did she have?"

"I don't know. He didn't tell me. But I gave her the medicine he brought, and she opened her eyes in just one day. So she's fine now. Good as new, aren't you, Poquita?"

"Poquita? I think we'll call this one Maria. Would you like that name?" he asked the little girl.

"I like Lisa. That's my best name. Lisa."

"Well, we need a new name for you. We'll call you Angelina and save Lisa for special times. Is that all right?"

The girl ignored him. "I want to fly to see my mommy. Let's go now."

With that, Velasquez took the girl's hand and walked her out to the helicopter. Like any gentleman would, he pulled open the door and then lifted her up onto the seat. When the door closed, Esma could see the man talking and smiling at his newest venture. She knew he would keep her for a few years, teach her the language, and then sell her for at least one million dollars. Probably to Dubai. Dubai loved white women with blond hair and blue eyes.

The girl's future was guaranteed.

"Lisa," she said. "The world is yours."

14

CW3 Mark Sellars

"Mister Sellars, spool 'er up," shouted CW3 Mark Sellars' crew chief. Sellars tossed off a salute and turned to his controls. The AH-64 Apache out of Kandahar air base lifted into the air joined one other Apache and set off in the direction of a firefight with U.S. soldiers pinned down. Two men posing as maintenance workers on a mountaintop water reservoir near the Afghan village of Issa Quel had fed supper to the First Platoon of Charlie Company in the shadow of the highest water reservoir. But then, as the troops began making their way downhill, the repairmen began shooting at the troops with a Russian-made machine gun. Five troops were reported wounded when the call came in, with one U.S. staff sergeant on the verge of death. They needed air support and a medevac without delay.

Two medevac helos were already inbound from a base nearby. They would meet the Apaches midway when the heavily armed Apaches swooped ahead to provide covering fire.

The site of the attack wasn't hard to find--the Army already had a nearby observation post mapped out, and the reservoir was on the highest hilltop. No other villages or qalats were around it, so no civilians would be put in harm's way by the attack the Apache pilots had in mind. As they bore down on the water reservoir, CWO Sellars quickly shot two rockets at the south side of the water reservoir to suppress the insurgents. The platoon on the ground was "danger close" to the helicopter's fire, which indicated that friendly forces were within close proximity to the target. The soldiers were flattened down on the north side of the ridge, only fifty yards down the slope. Meanwhile, the horrendous fire from the Russian gun kept raining hellfire down on them. Sellars could see from the Apache that the First Platoon had an impossible angle to return fire. If they didn't get help from Sellars and CWO Ambrose in the companion Apache, all could very well perish before sunrise.

Later, Sellars would admit to the Taliban that he was a little bit nervous in a situation that required heavy gunfire that didn't hit friendlies. The Americans, at the pilots' direction, had scurried around to put down strobes to identify their position, which greatly relieved the pilots' nerves. Plus, Sellars and Ambrose had operated in that area many times before and, with their precise control of their guns, they were able to put the rounds where it counted. Nevertheless, the machine gun fire continued, and the troops were at a very high risk.

Sellars made a rocket pass and Ambrose swooped in from the north side of the ridge, spraying the insurgents' position with his .50-caliber machine gun. The pilots' night-vision goggles let them see the ghostly green infrared-targeting beams emanating from the troops' weapons. The beams crisscrossed the water reservoir. The pilots could also see an increasing spark and twinkle of bullets bouncing off the water reservoir's walls as the First Platoon was increasingly better able to return fire thanks to the pounding given the insurgents by the Apaches.

As the air assault continued, the Apaches took turns shooting at the insurgents. One aircraft would fire as the other maneuvered for a weapons run in the opposite direction of approach to the ridge.

"Can't imagine two Talis could create so much commotion with one gun," Sellars radioed to Ambrose.

"Roger that," came the reply crackling in Sellars' headset. The noise-canceling headset tempered the engine noise in his own cabin, but the noise from Ambrose's cabin heavily penetrated their exchanges and vice-versa.

When Sellars was out of position for a rocket shot, his "left seater," First Platoon commander Capt. William Yeats fired his M4 out of the open side of the aircraft to maintain suppression. As soon as they cleared the target, Ambrose swooped in and fired more .50-caliber machine-gun rounds, followed by two rockets from Sellars.

The flurry of explosions and bullets had the intended effect. First Platoon was no longer taking contact from the two insurgents, and the medevac birds had some breathing room to fly in and treat the wounded. A half-hour earlier, at 8 p.m., a pair of UH-60 Black Hawks had lifted off from the same FOB as the medevacs from the pitch-black airfield. "Dust Off Two-One" led the way as the chase bird responsible for navigation to the battle and radio comms. "Dust Off Two-Two" was the medical bird that would evacuate the priority casualties. Arriving on-site, the pilot of Two-Two held the aircraft steady as Staff Sgt. William Banister hooked a cable to the front of his extraction vest. The external hoist on the side the Black Hawk rapidly lowered the flight medic to the ground.

Chief Sellars continued pounding the area with rockets and machine-gun fire as the lift-offs of the wounded began with the hoist and cable. It was a moment of tense navigation and run-ups and all pilots were in constant visual contact as they worked around the others.

Without warning and never seeing the business end of the weapon, Sellars felt and heard the RPG rip into his aircraft as he was swooping in on a gun run at 150 feet over the target. The distinctive "Whump!" of the explosion and the jolt to the airframe threw him sideways in the seat. He felt the aircraft immediately fall out of control but activated emergency procedures reflexively as the Army had taught him. The Apache came down straddling a rocky outcrop, and it split crosswise, the tailpiece falling down the mountain and the front of the aircraft dumping the pilots in a nose-down position against the hilltop. Almost immediately, four insurgents stood and began running at the Blackhawk, their AK's blazing. When they received no return fire, the Taliban fighters ceased firing, knowing they either had KIA they could ignore or they had prisoners who could be tortured and made to give up important operational details.

Unconscious, CWO Sellars had no memory of being jerked viciously out of his seat and dragged off through the rocks and moon dust. His Left Seat was KIA. Sellars was wounded, suffering a broken leg and arm and disfiguring facial wounds that left him losing enough blood that he would soon bleed to death without help. The helicopter exploded and roared into searing flames when Sellars was but fifty feet away. Sellars saw none of this.

The T-Men dragged him all the way back to Issa Quel where he was unceremoniously dropped inside a mud-walled room inside a labyrinthine warren of rooms, all of which were encircled by a thick perimeter wall that small arms couldn't penetrate. He was left alone in the room for several hours, moaning and crying out deliriously for help. Fractures in his arms and legs and the pain they caused were switching him in and out of consciousness, and still, no help came. Just after dawn the next day, an old woman and her daughter came into the room. They gave him a drink of water, the first he'd had in fifteen hours. The daughter was a nurse. She examined his wounds and then went to the village chief and argued with him on the pilot's behalf. He needed a hospital, and he needed extensive medical treatment, she insisted. The village chief brushed her aside, telling her the pilot was the enemy and if he died, it made no difference.

The daughter and mother decided they could listen no more to the man's suffering. They bundled him up, commandeered one of the Taliban's pickup trucks from a friendly soldier, and dragged the pilot up into the bed of the Toyota. They then drove him for three hours over gravel and dirt roads before coming to a paved access road leading into Kandahar. Two hours later, Sellars was a patient at Kandahar General Hospital and received the treatment he required. Following two surgeries to pin a leg and his left arm, he was moved to recovery, where the daughter was waiting for him. She assisted the nursing staff with his care, refusing to leave his side, and refusing to allow the Taliban soldiers to take Sellars and torture him for information. At one point she threatened them with the reminder that her father was a high-ranking member of the Taliban and that she would enlist his help in allowing the man to heal. The Taliban soldiers left the recovery room and didn't return.

Why did she go to these lengths for the American pilot? Because her own brother was being held in captivity at the American base in Guantanamo. She hoped to make a trade when the American could travel--the pilot for her brother. Her mother--and eventually her father, when he was made aware--then took every step necessary to protect the pilot from his captors. But the day finally came: upon his discharge from the hospital the military took him to a filthy jail cell and cast him inside. He was without his post-discharge medications and physical therapy that was prescribed. The Taliban was going to allow him to starve and thirst for five days and then question him. They would see how cooperative he was.

But their questions fell on deaf ears. From the onset of the torture, the pilot drew a line in the sand and told them he would not cross over. He would not betray his country, would not betray his comrades, and he was prepared to die to protect them. A conference was held between the head of the camp and the father of the Guantanamo prisoner. A modified form of torture and starvation was applied. The jailers were restrained from killing their prisoner. They would be required to keep him alive until a trade could be made with the Americans for the Guantanamo prisoner.

Six months passed. At times, the pilot was caged inside a six-by-six foot steel contraption without running water and without a toilet and toilet paper. He suffered from severe chronic diarrhea, a condition that would plague him over the next ten years of his captivity.

Then a guard took pity on him and handed him a *Koran* and suggested he study it. Which he did. He studied and prayed and studied some more. He eventually converted to Islam and soon was attending prayers at the local mosque with other villagers and even his captors. Seeing this, his captors slowly began to assimilate the American into a more relaxed and less punitive degree of imprisonment. This went on for two years. Then he was assigned certain menial tasks around the prison. Another two years. Next, he was trusted with short errands into town, picking up items for the soldiers such as books and mail. Years and more years dragged by. In the end, he had been given enough freedom and found to be trustworthy to the point where his errands could take hours, and no one noticed. This was when the American vanished from the sight of the Taliban and hours later emerged at the American air base at Kandahar.

From there he was treated for a month for his residual disabilities and systemic diseases--namely the GI issues causing chronic diarrhea. Eventually, he was flown to Walter Reed Army Hospital in Bethesda, Maryland where he was debriefed and fitted with new uniforms and military items of clothing. His back pay was assessed, and a check was prepared for his pay. There was never a question about his captivity; his aircraft had been shot out of the sky during combat, and there was no evidence he'd ever cooperated with the enemy. The Army intelligence officers were concerned that he had converted to Islam and recommended an honorable discharge from the military.

But first, there would be a reconciliation with his wife,

Melissa Sellars. He had fantasized about seeing her again for too many years.

Now it was about to take place.

15

TWELVE YEARS LATER

Melissa

A dozen years ago, when I lost Lisa, I swore I'd never lose that entangled feeling that mothers have with their daughters. I'm talking about the feeling I always had that Lisa was still physically connected to me somehow, even though we were two. Call it what you will, our life juices flowed back and forth between us even to the extent that I always knew her mind and her feelings and she always knew mine. When she hurt, I hurt. When she was hungry, I fixed her something to eat. And we did our entangled dance without words between us. It was all here, in our hearts and our minds and we were, and we weren't one living, breathing organism.

I yearned for this feeling a dozen years later, but I couldn't quite re-create how it was. The feeling was gone; it was like music coming from another room where all you can hear is the bass guitar and an occasional painful lyric. That's what our entanglement had become. Just a memory laced randomly with pain.

We had a name, all right. The man's name was Ignacio Velasquez. Mark's parents and I hired everyone we could find who might be able to find him. The trouble is, there are thousands of people by that name in the U.S. There're even more in Mexico and Latin America, not to mention South America and Spain. We spent over two-hundred thousand dollars of our own money on investigators alone. Plus, the CPD and FBI went all out. But in the end, we had nothing substantial. Our people tracked down, surveilled, and interviewed over one-hundred-and-twenty-five men. It was a massive undertaking when I look back on it. Still, our investigation went nowhere.

I married a brilliant man named James. But I kept my last name of Sellars in the event Lisa ever came looking for me. She'd know me by Sellars, not by James' name.

James was tall but slight with long fingers and palms, the kind of hands you'd expect to see on a grand piano at Carnegie. He was a member of the law firm that kept Laura out of hot water and free from all the silly lawsuits people undertake against successful shows. James put a face on that law firm, and that's how I got to know him because I was still with the show. In fact, I hired his law firm myself. More than anyone before, James understood my constant sorrow. He'd seen me sob on Christmas Eve; he'd watched me go to bed on Mother's Day Eve and stay in bed with the curtains drawn and anxiety pills popped so that I could make it through what was always a very horrible day. At least that was how it was until we had Gladys, our first child--another girl.

Gladys was named after James' mother. Gladys was six years old--two years older than Lisa when she was stolen from me. She liked horses and sailboats and loved to play house, loved to watch Frozen and Moana and a zillion other videos. She also loved to spend hours with me cooking sumptuous meals on weekend nights. But there was one difference between my relationship with Gladys and that with Lisa: Gladys and I weren't entangled. Not at all. Maybe it was because I was healthier as an older mother and more able to give my child her space and let her be who she was rather than every day trying to create her in my image. Yes, that was probably it. I still had a sixth sense about things with Gladys, but there wasn't that automatic knowing like there was with Lisa.

Still, there was one thing with Gladys I tried to overcome that perhaps I never would. That was my hovering over her and keeping her within view at all times so that she couldn't be stolen. That was simply not an option for the universe to drop on my head and crush my spirit and destroy my life again.

My watchfulness compressed Gladys' life into segments where I was just outside her zone of activity--like when she was in her schoolroom--and segments where I was literally with her, which covered the rest of the time. If she wanted to walk next door to Sarah's house, I made up some excuse to accompany her outside and make sure she got there. She was still too young to notice that about her life and my omnipresence in it, but James noticed. And of course, I noticed, too.

For his part, James was a gem. He let me get away with heli-coptering. He understood. No doubt my attachment to

Gladys would become problematic in time. That was more likely sooner, not later, but I figured I'd handle it when necessary. In the meantime, I was right there, baby, right behind her, ready to murder anyone would try to make off with her. They wouldn't stand a chance. And yes, I had taken to carrying a gun, a silver .38 that I kept in my purse. I had one rule with Gladys that could not under any circumstances be broken, and that was my purse. Nothing could happen that would ever allow her to open my purse. She'd had that drummed into her since her second birthday, and she knew it was ironclad. Of course, my purse was never in plain sight around the house. I had cabinets where it was locked away until I was leaving the house. Then it went with me. If the hound of hell ever returned to steal another of my children, my gun made me feel more than capable of stopping him. I felt like I could meet force with force now, enough to prevent it from ever happening again. Shoot first and ask questions later: that's where I was at with any stranger who would ever try to walk my daughter away from a playground or pick her up in the school loading zone before me while I was waiting two cars back. I was a mother, and a mom and I was armed.

"Melissa, what would you think about arming hospital security officers?"

My head jerked upright. I had been lost in thoughts about loss and guns and love.

I was sitting in a small conference room at the JCAHO, a hospital accrediting agency in Oak Brook where the group I created was presenting a proposal for increased patient security at JCAHO-certified hospitals. My group was Patient Security Services, Inc. We were a non-profit whose sole aim was to raise consciousness about the lack of patient security in the hospital models of the Twentieth Century. Plus, we tried to see new standards adopted. We emphasized how this new day--this Twenty-First Century--had presented a new set of problems, what with sex trafficking of children and terrorism and vanilla kidnappings with ransom demands. So we had come to that room to present our views and, in the middle of it, I had lapsed into my continuing daydream about Lisa, loss, and the protection of Gladys.

I looked around and screwed up my face, so I looked edgy and involved.

"What do I think about arming hospital security personnel? I think we've made that clear in our written presentation to the JCAHO. Security personnel should be stationed at nurses' stations on all hospital floors. They should be armed. We already know about kidnappings of children and assaults on the aged and all the rest of the carnage that goes on against the infirm not just in hospitals but also nursing homes and pre-school facilities. We've witnessed the horrors of grade schools and high schools under attack by armed psychopaths. And now it's just a matter of time until one of those armed attacks happens at a hospital. So, yes, there should be armed security officers at every point of ingress and egress, and there should be security scans of encoded bracelets made as well."

"You're talking about bar codes for coming and going in our hospitals?"

"I am. And when an attack comes--and it will, God forbid-- I'm going to be available to plaintiffs' lawyers to testify that the JCAHO was forewarned by my group that the time was ripe for these attacks and abductions to happen in hospitals.

In other words, if you refuse to act, I'm going to become your worst nightmare."

Talk continued from there. I had made my point with those people, and it wasn't the first time. Maybe this time would be different; I was doing CNN that night, and that would produce a flood of emails, calls, and letters to the JCAHO. Ours was an idea and solution whose time had come round. I predicted the new requirements for armed security and encoded bracelet scans at ingress and egress would be in place before the new year. Maybe even earlier.

James and I lived in Glencoe, just like my in-laws Charlie and Rebecca. In fact, we weren't two miles apart. We lived there mainly for the schools and the police department. GPD profiled everyone passing through Glencoe. If you looked like you didn't belong in a community where the average home value was over one million, then chances were excellent you would be stopped and asked a few questions by the police. I needed that sense of additional security then with Gladys. One part of me said oh, this was the worst kind of elitism and another part of me said thank God I could afford to do it. Until you've lost one of your own, please don't judge me. That's what I told everyone.

After the JCAHO meeting, I drove home slowly and carefully. Gladys was in school, first grade at Warriner's Academy. The school had armed, uniformed security and armed, plainclothes security officers roaming the halls, so parents felt good about leaving kids there. There was a direct correlation, I'd learned, between the income one made and the need for extra security precautions where your kids were concerned. But that law didn't hold water in Lisa's case. Why? Because my earnings weren't the reason for her abduction. A ransom note never came. A call demanding millions never was received. Instead, she just disappeared from every place her grandparents, and I could think to look. And from everyplace the Chicago Police Department and the FBI could think to look. And from everyplace Colonel Eustice, USA (Ret.) could think to look. Not a day went by that I didn't regret not having received a ransom demand. At least I would have known there was another reason for my baby's abduction besides the alternatives.

My phone rang, and I told it to answer.

"Mrs. Sellars? We have received a young woman you should probably come look at."

It was the Cook County Morgue. I still got these calls; my name was on the list of parents of missing children who wanted to be notified if a dead body presented that no one could identify and no one claimed within ten days. This task would cost me untold pain and sorrow and regret for the dead girl's loved ones, but it was a task I felt like I owed Lisa, first, and, second, that I owed myself to perform. The thought of Lisa arriving in the morgue and being buried an unidentified pauper destroyed me; so, I went and looked when they called. The calls were based on race, age, identifying characteristics, and identifying marks. There hadn't been a body yet with the sailboat birthmark on her left lower back like Lisa's, but I went to look anyway. Who could tell? She might have had it removed, or it might have gone away on its own. I didn't know everything there was to know about such things, so I showed up at the Morgue maybe two or three times a month, and I had a look.

"I'll come by this evening yet. I'm on my way home now."

"We're only open until ten o'clock."

"I know that. I'll be there on time."

With that, I switched routes on my GPS and listened for new driving instructions.

Thirty minutes later, I was arriving at the morgue on Harrison Street. It was a dark December night--the sun went down at four o'clock--and the trees were glittering from last night's ice storm. It was a shimmering wonderland beneath the parking lot lights. You would think that such beauty would be saved for beautiful places and beautiful moments, but not so. Beauty that night was to be found in a horrible juxtaposition of the morgue parking lot to the morgue itself and its tortured corpses. I paused and had a look around before going inside. Anymore, I admired beauty in the world whenever and wherever it presented itself. I was not stupid. Not anymore.

They knew me inside, and the woman behind the Plexiglas partition spoke my name and motioned to the door marked PRIVATE. I passed through and was greeted by Amber Losse, one of three nighttime technicians servicing the public requests for views, as they were called.

"Mrs. Sellars," she smiled. "Thanks for coming."

"Thanks for calling me," I told her. "Please keep it up. I want to be here if--you know."

"We know, Mrs. Sellars. Well, we have a young woman tonight with a very disturbing gunshot wound. I hope you're up to it."

"Would it matter?" I said with a snap in my voice. Then I caught myself I didn't mean the flash of anger for Amber, so

I tried to soften what I'd said. "What I meant, Amber, is that I have to look no matter what condition they're in. As long as the face is still human, I prefer to be notified."

I couldn't be much clearer than that. Call me, I was confirming to her. Call me no matter what. Unless the face was missing altogether. Then don't call.

Amber looked up from her computer screen just then. "Oh, wait. We don't have one case. We have two you should view tonight. The second one came in just twenty minutes ago."

"What kind of shape is she in?"

"She was a pedestrian in a crosswalk, it says. But, good news, Mrs. Sellars, she's very viewable."

"Well, welcome to my lucky night, then."

She pulled the first body tray out of its refrigerated cell. The body was nude, without a cover. It was a very young woman, maybe all of seventeen. I turned sideways to view her face. It definitely wasn't Lisa, not unless Lisa had let someone tattoo a dragon on the side of her neck with flames shooting up onto her cheek. On the other hand, what did I actually know about the Lisa of the present day, how she would be, what she would and wouldn't do? So I looked again, more closely now.

"Can I see her lower left side?"

Amber complied, rolling the body onto its right side and pinning it there with both of her arms.

Putting my head very close to the kidney, I searched up and down for the telltale sailboat birthmark. There was none, nor was there any scarring to indicate it might have once been there but was later removed. Nothing like that.

"Okay, Amber. This one's a negative."

Amber lowered the body back down onto its back and then went to a table behind her and plucked off a nice, clean body sheet, which she shook out and settled down over the girl.

"Next time she'll be a little less traumatic for someone to see. I'm sorry she came that way for you."

"It's all right," I said, though it really wasn't. It was gruesome and gave me nightmares. I believed that I could remember the face of every girl I had ever viewed. Every last one. Maybe not, really, but my dreams were overflowing with faces. Many nights my dreams taunted me with face after face, wound after wound, until morning came and I could come awake and stop the show.

"Here's another," Amber said mundanely. She covered a yawn with her hand. "Sorry. Tonight it's early to bed."

The drawer opened.

This girl was maybe twenty-five--way too old to be my Lisa-- unless, again, she had aged precipitously due to drug use.

"May I see her teeth?" Her teeth would tell me a lot about any drug use.

Amber reached a gloved hand and peeled the girl's upper lip back and away. The teeth seemed clean and well-cared for, nothing like I'd learned to expect from a drug addict's mouth.

"Okay. Thank you. We might as well view the hip."

"Left side again?"

"Always the left side."

The body was rolled up onto its right side so I could again glance around for a birthmark. Any birthmark would interest me at this point, but, again, there was none. At which times I wondered, yet again, whether I'd made it up in my mind about Lisa's sailboat. But then I would carefully disengage from those doubts and reaffirm what I had always known: Lisa had a small sailboat-shaped birthmark on her lower left back/hip. That was it.

"Is that it?" I asked.

"Until next time," Amber said, intent on pleasing me with the implicit promise to call me yet again. She couldn't know, of course, how much I hated that there would be a next time. Or maybe she did know. Maybe it was stamped all over me, especially my face, which had aged twenty years in ten.

"Good night, Amber."

"Good night, Mrs. Sellars."

Outside, the ice crackled and snapped in the trees as a slight breeze had come up. The asphalt of the parking lot was slippery. I reminded myself yet again how foolish it was to wear heels on days like that. So I tiptoed one foot after another, taking care that one sole or the other was in touch with the ground at all times. The thought of that thing--one sole or the other--could have launched me into an existential cant at that moment, but I was too tired to play that sole/soul game and let it go.

Forty-five minutes later I was home.

16

J ames was waiting for me just inside the kitchen door from the garage. He looked desperate, frantic even. "Come in," he said grimly. "I'm afraid I've got some very upsetting news."

So. This was it. They had found ; then, and she was dead. Deep down I had always known it would eventually come to this. It was only my hope that had been keeping her alive up to that point. Reality didn't care about my hope; reality was about to tell me she was dead and gone.

"What is it?" I said, barely able to choke out the words.

"Come into the kitchen. I've got coffee. Let's sit down and talk."

"Your hands are shaking," I said to James. "I'm sorry you have to go through this, poor man." Anything to get the focus off what was coming, if only for a moment.

We went into the kitchen, and I removed my coat and laid it on the table. Then I sat down and folded my hands on the table. James returned with two coffees and sat down at the head of the table--his place--just at my left.

"There are two men waiting to talk to you in the living room. They're not what you're thinking. They're from the Army."

"What? What's the Army want to talk to me about?"

James rose slowly to his feet. "I'm going to go in with you to support you. But you can just as easily pretend I'm not there."

Now I was confused. Support me but pretend he wasn't there? What in the world could he be talking about?

He helped me up, and we balanced our coffee as he led me into the living room. Sure enough, two soldiers were waiting there, both in uniform and both looking very grim. The taller one introduced himself to me first.

"I'm Captain Roger McMillan. This is Lieutenant Winkler."

We shook hands all around.

"You'd better take a seat, Mrs. Sellars. This is going to be difficult."

Probably protocol in how these things are done: telling me to take a seat first. Then it dawned on me: Army-Colonel Eustice; Colonel Eustice-Army. Charlie's bosom buddy Colonel Eustice had turned up something through his Army contacts, and Lisa had been found. I swallowed hard and found I was already fighting to hold back my tears.

"All right," I said when I was seated. "What is it?"

"Chief Warrant Officer Mark Sellars has been found."

I was stunned. Did he just say what I think he said? Mark, my Mark? Found?

Chills traveled down my spine, and my breath caught in my throat. Then I was overwhelmed with a sense of guilt like I'd never felt before, guilt that I'd done something horribly wrong. I didn't have far to look to understand where it was coming from. I had abandoned my husband and married another man. I had failed my husband. My heart was gripped by fear, and I felt myself gasping for air.

"Your husband has been held by enemy forces nearly ten years, Mrs. Sellars. He is well--though he's down a hundred pounds. He's now in Maryland, where our doctors and intel-ligence are working with him. It'll be a week before he gets to come home."

I could only look at James. Tears had welled up in his eyes, but he forced a tremulous smile at me, and I knew, in that instant, that he was freeing me to make the most difficult decision of my life.

Mark Sellars was my boyfriend from college and my first-ever lover. He's the one your mind returns to when you're fifteen years older and thinking back. He's the one you've always known you want to spend your life with. That's who Mark was--even now.

"Wait a minute, Captain. How sure are you it's Mark?"

"Dental records have already confirmed it's Mark. It's your husband, Mrs. Sellars." The captain then looked at James. "Sorry, sir."

James waved him off. "Hey, I'm only a bystander at this point. It's all good."

I turned to James. "Please, James, you're much more to me than a bystander. You're my husband now."

Then I turned back to the captain, and he smiled tightly at me. I spoke directly to him, "Well, James is my husband now. Don't you see?"

"Ma'am," said the captain, rising to his feet, "I'm sorry we've complicated your life but I'm also happy Chief Sellars has been found. We're going to leave you two now so you can talk. Here's my card. I'm assigned to the Joint Personnel Recovery Agency out of Virginia. I'm the base Special Operations Officer, and I'm always nearby. Please call me if you want. Anytime. And if you need to come by and talk with me or with any military staff, please call me, and I'll make arrangements. Good night, ma'am. Good night, sir. We'll see ourselves out."

Just like that, they were gone, slipped off into the night and leaving me with the worst and most fantastic news I'd ever received. My personality immediately split: one part of me couldn't wait to see Mark; another part of me was already swearing I would remain faithful to James. Heart versus head, I guess, is what I was really feeling.

I turned in my chair and looked at James.

"Is Gladys in bed?"

"She is. She's been up there almost an hour. I can still hear her singing, though. Maybe you can tell her goodnight."

With a calming inhalation of air, I climbed to my feet. On the way upright I had to steady myself with the arm of my chair. "Whoa!" I said as I nearly fell over. James was at my side in an instant, and it came to me: he is always there for me. He loves me, and I love him.

Upstairs I found Gladys sitting up in her bed, three dolls spread across her bedspread. They were in various stages of undress as I came in. She leaped from her bed and ran to me. "Mommy!"

My arms opened wide, and I swept her up and began spinning around. She held on, and peals of laughter erupted as we made one circle after another--our usual nighttime routine when I came home from work late. Then I slowed down, stopped, and hugged her tightly against me. "Love you, Pumpkin," I whispered in her ear.

"Love you, Mommy. I love Daddy, too."

"Yes, I love Daddy, too."

"Mommy, who was downstairs?"

"Just some men."

"Why were they wearing uniforms?"

"They're in the Army."

"Oh."

"Yes."

"Am I going in the Army?"

"No, sweetheart, you're never going in the Army. Mommy and Daddy are too old to go. So none of us is going in the Army."

"Then why were they here?"

I didn't lie to Gladys. She had a right to the truth, I believed, no matter how hard or upsetting it was. That's what life is about, I always thought, learning how to deal with the truth. Not learning how to live without fantasy. So she got the truth from me that night.

"The Army found Mommy's first husband, Mark Sellars."

"Oh. Was he lost?"

"He was. He was a prisoner of war."

"Oh. Will he be coming to live with us?"

"No, Mark won't be living with us."

"Do you still love him?"

"Mommy still loves him," James said, suddenly appearing behind me. "Mommy still loves Mark, and that's a good thing. We can love other people in our house. It's safe to do that here."

My eyes welled up at his words. I hung my head almost in shame as if I'd been caught doing something wrong, something I wanted to hide from James.

He came up behind me and encircled my waist with his arms.

"Come here, Gladys, you get in on this family hug too," James said to our little girl.

Then it was just the three of us, a unit, a family I knew I could never let go.

But what of Mark? How would that work? I began crying then, my head tossed back as I silently wept.

Gladys didn't see my tears. Honesty was one thing.

Honesty overlaid with screaming pain--that was something else. She didn't need to see that. With any luck, she wouldn't ever experience that, either. At least not until she was grown.

One thing was clear to me. I wasn't going to forsake James, and I wasn't going to forsake Gladys. Neither one of them deserved to share in the hell I felt settle down over me that night as my mind went wild.

It came to me then, a hard, bitter truth: I hadn't thought about Lisa for the past half-hour. My loss of Lisa had been overshadowed by my finding of Mark. Which could only make me wonder: would my reunion with Lisa be just as fraught with such conflict as I now felt with Mark returned? Or would it be pure love, both ways, no regrets?

I had to find out. More than ever, I had to find out.

With Mark back--the father of my missing child--I was that much closer to those answers.

If anyone could find her, it would be Mark.

LATER THAT NIGHT, after James and I had made love, we lay beside each other. Neither of us was sleepy. Our lovemaking had been fast and clumsy as we had tried to prove with our bodies just how secure our marriage was and just how much each one of us wanted to keep it that way. I needed desperately to be able to say something to James to guarantee my fidelity. I felt like I wouldn't ever leave him and, after a few hours had passed since the Army visit, I had begun feeling put upon, like an outside force was trying to saddle me with an overwhelming burden, and I was fighting to stay clear of it.

How do you choose between the husband you love and the husband you love? There should be a song or a poem or a book or something that gives some guidance to people like me. I was certain I wasn't the first military wife whose husband returned after years of captivity. Surely there were others.

James dropped off to sleep, and I tiptoed downstairs to my office. My laptop came on instantly, and I was unthinkingly reviewing my email. Then I saw it: an email from Captain McMillan. Evidently, he hadn't wasted much time getting from my house back to his office, where he emailed me. He said that he'd just received word that Mark had been transferred to Walter Reed Army Hospital in Bethesda, Maryland. He also said that Mark was anxious to see Lisa and me. Nobody had told him anything yet, evidently.

I emailed Captain McMillan in reply. Who would tell Mark of my remarriage and the disappearance of our daughter? I asked. I told him that on the one hand, I thought the Army doctors should do that but on the other hand I, as his wife, felt like I should be the one to break the news to him.

It appeared that Captain McMillan lived at his office because he emailed me back not five minutes later. They would update him on his family--if I requested--or they would leave that to me. It was my choice.

I closed my laptop and sat back. This had shaken me to my core. When I saw the official Army emails my heart had jumped, I had to admit. Just the notion that I could have my Mark back if I only said the word made my husband upstairs look like he was on the moon. How had he ever come between us? I wondered. Then I kicked myself. Stupid girl, he didn't come between you, you picked him out from any number of interested men, seduced him, and created an easy path into your life. Unlike with Mark who'd done all the pursuing and wooing, with James, it was different. I was the predator, for want of a better word. Plus, predator was pretty accurate. I had found him and devoured him once we fell in love. Poor James never had a chance.

Into the kitchen I crept, intent on pouring a late-night glass of wine, only to find James there at the table ready to talk.

"Look," he said, "I've been thinking about it. I think you should have the freedom to go to your husband and do what you need to do with him. Then decide. Make a decision and make it last forever. We all deserve peace about this, and nobody wants it dragged out over time, least of all me. I'll wait here with Gladys while you're gone and I'll be here with her when you come back. If you don't come back, Gladys will live with both of us, one week with you, one week with me. It'll be awkward for her and uncomfortable, but life isn't always perfect, and she knows that. Is this what you need to hear from me? I could tell I wasn't getting through to you upstairs and I don't like to leave things hanging. So talk to me, Melissa, please."

My hand shook as I poured a tall glass of wine. "You want?" I asked. He declined, saying he had work tomorrow.

Taking my seat, I brushed imaginary crumbs from the table as I sat there thinking and feeling my way into whatever it was I was about to say.

Then I began. "We're in a situation that's nobody's fault. It's not Mark's fault, not your fault, and not my fault. Remember, James, I buried my husband before I met you. He was gone, and in the ground, the Army told me. The only thing was, the service and funeral preparations were closed-casket, so I didn't get to ID my husband. I can't imagine the horrors someone else is going to face when her husband is found in my husband's burial plot. Just devastating for her."

"What do you need to do, Mel?"

"I need to see Mark and tell him. It needs to come from me."

"And then?"

"Well, he'll have Charlie and Rebecca. They won't leave his side. I'll call them in the morning and give them the news. They'll probably beat me back to Bethesda."

"So you're going to Maryland?"

I looked at him. "Do I have a choice."

He looked at me. He shook his head. "No, Mel, you really don't have a choice. And just let me say this. If I were in your shoes, I'd do the same thing. I'd need to go tell my spouse and be there when they fall apart."

"I'm not looking forward to it. Thanks for being understanding, James. You always come through for me."

"This one's a no-brainer, Mel. You have to be there for him. He deserves to know. What will you tell him about Lisa?"

"What do you mean? I'll tell him she was abducted from the hospital years ago. What else is there to say?"

"He'll want to talk to your detective. He'll want to do something."

"You know Mark pretty well. Yes, he'll want to do something, and you know what? I'm going to be right there egging him on. I'm in his corner on that one."

"When are you leaving?"

"Friday. The show needs me the next couple of days, then I'll go."

"Like I said before, Gladys and I will be right here. We're not going anywhere."

"Neither am I, James. I'm just going to deliver a message and some bad news, see what I can do to help lessen his pain; then I'll be home. I expect I'll leave here Friday and be home Sunday. That's all it should take."

"Good. We'll pick you up at the airport. Just let us know."

"Would you mind if we went back to bed and tried again? I really need to be held," I said. The wine wasn't helping, just making me feel sour and heavy-legged. I poured most of it down the sink.

Then James followed me back upstairs, and we went into our bedroom and closed the door.

An hour later, I fell asleep about the same time as my husband.

For the first time in weeks, I slept all the way through to the alarm.

Heavenly.

17

C hicago to Washington via Dulles Airport took right at two hours. Then a cab to Bethesda and I was in place late Friday night. I called the hospital. Tomorrow morning at ten I could see Mark.

The next morning at exactly ten a.m. I was allowed to go up to his room. His "quarters" they called it. Upstairs on the elevator I went, then stopped at the nurses' station. I introduced myself.

"I'm Chief Sellars' wife, and I have a question."

The rather buxom, flaxen-haired nurse close by looked up at me. "Sure, hon. What can I tell you?"

"My husband has been gone over ten years. We thought he was dead."

"Ma'am we know all about the Mr. Sellars. Skip to your question, please."

"How is he? I mean, how do I treat him? He knows where he is and he's oriented by now, I'm sure, but what should I expect that'll be different from how it was all those years ago?"

"He'll be more nervous than you. He frets terribly that he looks sixty years old now. He says you're going to leave him over the lines in his face. When he arrived here, his hair was very long. We've had the barber over here twice to fiddle with his hair. Plus they wanted to shave his beard. He fought them but the military won, and he had to shave it off."

"Wait, the barber came here?"

"Yes, he did."

"Why here?"

"Ma'am, Mr. Sellars is confined to quarters. He can't leave his room. Against orders."

"Whose orders?"

"The Army's orders. Does it matter who?"

"I'd like to know just in case I need to contact them."

"Well, the Joint Personnel Recovery Agency is who actually has orders for him presently. I can get you their number."

"No, not necessary. So what I do, just go down to his room and walk in?"

"Why not? He knows you're coming. He got the message you sent to the nurses' station."

With that, I shrugged and began walking toward Mark's room. It felt otherworldly to me like I was operating in a dream. My stomach was clenched up with fear of what I had to tell him, and another part of me was excited to see this man. The last time we were together, he was my husband.

Now he doesn't know that he's not my husband anymore. No one's told him, my request which the Army has allowed me. Just outside his door I took a deep breath and blew it out slowly. Just breathe normally, I told myself. Breathe.

At first, I didn't recognize the man. He was lying on the bed, wearing khaki shorts and a blue-striped bathrobe over a T-shirt that said ARMY STRONG. But he was the only man in the room, so it had to be him. His hair was clipped short, military-neat, and he was clean-shaven. I smiled and walked toward him, arms outstretched. In my mind's eye, I thought this was how a wife separated from her husband should look when approaching the man she loved.

He stood up from the bed, took a step toward me, and stumbled. Then I saw: his foot was curved in at the ankle so that when he tried to stand, he was standing on the outside edge.

"Broke some bones when I crashed," he said with an endearing smile. He picked himself up from the floor and, as he was struggling to come upright, I grasped his upper arms to help lift. Immediately I felt the difference: this man's arms and shoulders were rock-hard. I didn't remember the Mark I knew feeling like that. Then he was upright and holding out his arms, and I fell into his embrace. We stood like that for what seemed like hours, unspeaking but weeping.

Then, "Oh, my God," he whispered. "You're actually you, and you're actually here with me."

"I thought--I thought--"

"You thought I was dead. I know, Mel. The goddam Army told you I was dead. Bastards. I'm sorry about that. It must have killed you."

"It did. It killed me."

He looked over my shoulder. "Is Lisa here? I thought she'd be with you."

"Uh, can we go someplace and talk?"

"Can't leave my room. Let's sit on my bed. Here."

He smoothed the bedspread and helped me up onto the rather high mattress. I sat with my back to the foot of the bed, and he sat opposite me.

"Well? My daughter?"

I took a deep breath. "It was about two years after you left us. She was in the hospital with meningitis, and somebody stole her!"

Then I was weeping and looking for a box of tissues. I cried long and hard. It was the first time I'd been able to mourn the loss of my daughter with her father and the feeling just overwhelmed me. He reached and took my hands in his.

Then he said, "And you got her back? Or what?"

"We never got her back. She's been gone ever since."

His back stiffened and he released my hands.

"What have you done to find her?"

"Everything. Your parents and I spent hundreds of thousands of dollars on private eyes and surveillance and everything trying to find her."

"Where do the police think my daughter is?"

"Honestly? They don't know. There's a man's name we got from one woman who helped him watch us and plan the abduction. Her name is Nancy Callender. The man's name is Ignacio Velasquez."

"Good. Now I know how I'm going to spend my back pay. Every last dime of it goes to finding our girl."

"Oh, Mark!"

He stood up again and limped back and forth beside the bed. Finally, he stopped.

"What about you? Did you wait for me?"

I burst into tears again. "I tried, darling. Honest to God, I tried!"

"But there's someone else now. I understand. I get that. You can tell me."

"I'm married to a nice man named James."

"Okay. What's he do? Is he good to you?"

"He's a lawyer, and yes, he treats me wonderfully. You'd like him, Mark, he's--"

"I know. I know. Now let me tell you about me. There have been changes on my side of the street, too, Mel."

"I know."

"No, you don't know. While I was captured, I converted to Islam. That's why I insisted on keeping my beard. I told the Army the beard was religious, but they finally decided they could cut it off, that it would be legal to deny a soldier his religious beliefs."

"Islam? How does that work?"

"We have a mosque, we have prayers, we have church,

though not like you'd expect, probably. We have religious holidays, and we have the book. That's what got me through all those years, my faith."

"The holy book of Islam."

"Yes. And there's lots more about it too. I'll teach you if you'd like."

"That would be good," I said, though I couldn't imagine how we'd ever be together long enough for him to teach me anything. Not if I had to go back to James.

Wait. Had to go back to James? Was that had like it was my duty? Or did I want to go back to James? The longer I looked at Mark, the more my inner reservoir of devotion to James was trickling away. Then definitely washing away, then it was gone.

I wanted my husband back. I was sure of it.

"Listen," I said. "I need you to listen to me for a minute, okay?"

"Okay."

"I want to be with you. I've loved you since we were teenagers in college and I still love you now. Just seeing you has turned my world inside out. That's how I really, honestly feel."

He was shaking his head. "Melissa, listen to you. You're talking about leaving your husband for me. I'll bet there are kids?"

"One, a girl. Gladys. But she'll be with us, you and me. James won't fight me on this."

"No, no, no, she's James' daughter. I already have a daughter. Now listen to this very carefully. Before there are any decisions made about the you-me-and-James stuff, I am going to find my daughter and bring her home. Home to you and home to me. That is my mission at this point. Whatever happens between you and me--that's for later."

"Okay." With a rush of new air pouring into my lungs I could breathe freely again. Mark was much wiser that I remembered. He was right, actually, first things first.

"Every single day my daughter isn't with me or you she's a prisoner. I've done that prisoner thing. You and I cannot even begin to imagine what's she's been through and what it's turned her into. But that's all right. Water washes us all clean in the end. Do you have a laptop along, by the way?"

"Back in my hotel. I didn't bring it here. Didn't think I'd need it." I laughed.

"We need it. Okay, Mel. You go get your computer, please. I'll order some pizza brought in and we'll re-open the investigation into the disappearance of Lisa Sellars. You ready for this?"

It wasn't at all what I'd gone there expecting. Nothing of the sort. I'd thought there would be flowing tears, priests, and pastors, psychologists and philosophers, but no. It was just two parents who loved their daughter.

And who were going to get her back, come hell or high water.

Mark's words.

18

That was Saturday morning. By mid-afternoon Saturday, with my laptop open on Mark's bed, we had managed to cobble together everything I knew about Lisa's disappearance. Mark said we should brainstorm then, so we did. His theory was that Lisa had been abducted into sex trafficking. He told me that from what he'd seen in Afghanistan, it fit the sex traffic paradigm correctly. The staking out of my house and the hospital by Nancy Callender. The precisely timed taking of Lisa from the hospital when I was away from her room just briefly. The fact of no ransom note or demand for payment for her return. The fact we hadn't heard from her even though she was in her middle-teen years now and even though she had been old enough when taken to know her last name and where she lived. It was all right there, he said. She was someone's sex toy at this point--a reality that I hadn't been able to admit to myself. But now, with Mark at my side, I could coherently think about such things, and I was amazed at how it broadened my thinking about Lisa and where she might be today.

Which was anywhere in the world. Mark said he guessed someplace like Dubai, where blue-eyed, blond girls are highly valued and where top dollar is paid. So should we start looking in Dubai? Not so fast, Mark said. We needed to trace her movements--if possible--and see where that led, rather than just jetting off somewhere and hoping we were on the right continent.

So we began with the name, Ignacio Velasquez. We decided that Zone 1 would be Mexico. Zone 2 would be Latin America. Zone 3 would be South America. Mark said we would focus first on Zone 1, Mexico. Why? Because there were kidnappers roaming all over Mexico looking for inventory, as Mark put it.

We were making plans for our assault on Mexico when a young man in uniform entered Mark's room with an envelope. "Orders, sir," he said and abruptly left.

"Oh my God," Mark said as he tore open the envelope, "let's hope this is what I think it is."

It was. The Joint Personnel Recovery Agency--the DoD arm that had placed Mark in Walter Reed Army Hospital--had determined that Mark's capture in Afghanistan was legitimate and that his time in captivity was involuntary and that his time in the service of his country had come to an end. He was discharged effective immediately from any further military service, back pay to arrive by the end of next week.

We stood there looking at each other, dumbfounded. Then the news hit us, and we were in tears.

"You don't know, Mel, how much interrogation and corroboration I've been through to convince the powers-that-be that my captivity was legitimate and that I wasn't someone who had abandoned his post."

"But the helicopter you were flying crashed. Weren't you shot down?"

"I was. But the military is always suspicious because even crashes of aircraft can be faked. Even where a passenger died, like my case. They're a very suspicious bunch."

"Okay," I said, "but as of right now, it's time to celebrate. Let's get you out of here and someplace comfortable. I think that for tonight you should come to my hotel room and take the extra bed and sleep there. We can have room service, you can enjoy the view out of my suite, and we can spread out and work at an actual table."

"Maybe that's a good idea, Mel. But you and I have a history of winding up in bed together. You're married now, and that can't happen at this point."

I had the feeling he saw where I was with this. He needed confirmation that I would stay on my own side of the room, so to speak. I totally agreed with what he was saying, that we couldn't afford to sleep together, not if we were going to be able to focus on Lisa.

"Simple," I said, "we just don't go down that path. What we're doing to find Lisa is much bigger than all that. We don't need marital drama in the middle of it to screw things up. You'll have your space in my room, and I'll have mine. Or, I can get you your own room, and we can work from there if you think you can't resist my stunning beauty."

He laughed. "Actually, with my religious beliefs being what they are now, you're safe with me. There are certain lines I can't and won't cross. Illicit sex is one of them. As much as I'd like to jump your bones, I won't be doing that. Shacking up in the same room is totally safe with me."

Despite my circumspect intentions, at that moment an immense feeling of disappointment swept over me. I had my husband back but not really. It was very confusing as I reset in my mind where I was, who I was with, who was waiting back in my home, and what I was doing. I knew at that moment that I'd make a terrible mistress because I'd be so destroyed by guilt and self-hatred. Plus, Lisa overrode all of it. Nothing could be decided until we had our daughter back. Assuming she was even still alive.

On the taxi ride to my hotel, we discussed that third possibility--that she might have been taken and killed right away. That her body was moldering in the ground somewhere or at the bottom of Lake Michigan. Mark was able to put these things into words, and I listened and agreed out loud to what I'd already known inside but couldn't bring myself to admitting. Our daughter could already be dead, and we were beaten before we even started.

Nevertheless, when we got inside my room, we took up right where we left off in Mark's hospital room: from the assumption that Lisa was still very much alive and that she had probably been taken to Mexico at first.

"Now, who in Mexico would take her?" he said.

I said, "The cartels. That's who I believe took her. One of the cartels."

"Which cartel?"

"Well, I've done some reading. There are three main cartels.

One is in Tijuana, the other is in Culiacán in Sinaloa. There's also the Gulf Cartel. They are all terrible gangs. So let's do some looking online and see if anything jumps out at us."

I set up my computer on the dining table in my suite and called down to room service for coffee and sandwiches.

Then we began.

Tijuana was of course almost straddling the U.S. border. From what we could turn up on the Internet, Tijuana, of the three cartels, was most heavily involved with U.S.-Mexico border crimes other than drugs. Prostitution on both sides of the border. Illegal firearms. And a steady flow of coyote vans and trucks moving undocumented souls into the U.S. That--along with the drugs--was the biggest moneymaker for the Tijuana Cartel. We rated it number one on our short list of probable kidnappers.

Next, we moved east and south and found out what we could about the Sinaloa Cartel.

The Sinaloa Cartel operated primarily within the Golden Triangle, an area in north central Mexico, and was considered by the U.S. Intelligence agencies to be the most powerful drug cartel in the world. Due to its greater distance from the border, it had a much smaller presence in human trafficking and human smuggling than the Tijuana Cartel. We rated it number two.

The Gulf Cartel seemed distant and remote. A not-very-interesting number three.

All in all, we decided that Tijuana should be our first stop. It seemed percentage-wise to have the highest number of crimes against people of any of the three Mexican Cartels.

Next, we began planning our assault.

We decided to pinpoint the leader of the Tijuana Cartel and to infiltrate his base of operations and see what we could learn. How to do that? We talked for several hours, with Mark taking the wheel on this part of it. He had participated in hundreds of covert raids in Taliban country in Afghanistan, and he knew everything there was to know about gaining a foothold and working from there.

So we asked ourselves, what profile would stand the greatest chance of coming into the zone of influence of the leader of the Cartel? We thought about enlisting the help of a Mexican private investigator to infiltrate the cartel.

"Someone like that would need to be very brave and steady in the boat," Mark said.

"Plus I don't know how much I could really trust someone else. It just seems to me that the cartels have so much power and influence that they can buy off anyone. The added danger to a Mexican national would be trying to resume his life after we grab Lisa. When Lisa disappears, he'll be the first one they come for. No one's signing up for that, I don't care how much money we offer them."

We sat and quietly stared at each other. Neither of us had anything further to offer as far as using outside resources. It had all been said. So we said the inevitable. Mark was going to go undercover in Tijuana as a player in the drug business. We talked for hours, afraid we'd maybe missed something. Like maybe we were overlooking a key feature of Tijuana and the cartel there that could instantly get Mark killed. We were getting very close physically by now at the table, and our hands would inadvertently touch, or our legs would touch under the table, and I found I liked the closeness, that I yearned for my husband Mark's touch. Of course, he wasn't my husband--I knew that. But in a way, he was because he had done nothing to be dislodged from that position in our lives. I had done it. I had done it with the help of the U.S. Army. But none of that matters when you're in the now, and you're at last able to touch the person you thought you lost. Things get very jumbled after that, I found. So I did the next indicated thing.

"I can't do this," I told him. "I want you too much."

Leaving Mark with my Amex Platinum card, I grabbed my purse and a small bag and headed downstairs. From there, Dulles International was a stone's throw. I took a taxi there and went from airline counter to airline counter until I found a nine p.m. flight to Chicago. Then I called Mark.

"I know I left abruptly. I did it because of the feelings I was having for you."

"I figured it was something like that. I was feeling the same way despite my strong religious aversion to infidelity. Only the infidels do that stuff."

"So here's what I propose. Tomorrow you go to the airport and catch a plane to Chicago. I'll meet you and we'll put you up in an executive hotel with long-term stay. Someplace furnished and roomy where you'll be comfortable and where we can get together easily and plan the mission."

"Sounds perfect. I'll have some money by Friday, and I can pay you back then."

"I'm not even going there. I sold our house years ago, and you got none of that. I owe you a big fat check for your half."

"No, you don't. Besides, I would've wanted you and Lisa to have the house and leverage it into what you have now. We're going to call us even at this time."

"We'll never be even. I didn't wait for you."

"Hey! Melissa, snap out of that! You relied on some information that twelve years later you found out was false. Nobody's holding your feet to the fire over something like that. It was what anyone would've done. Besides, let me cut right to the chase with you. If I ever get involved again, it will be with a Muslim woman. I've changed, and maybe you don't get that right now, but over time you'll see what I mean. We live in two different worlds, but we both happen to have one foot in a very exclusive world of our own, one where Lisa exists. Let's leave it at that, all right?"

"All right," I sniffed through my tears. "This is just very, very hard. Because I still love you."

I whispered that last part into the phone as if someone might hear me. But in the Captain's Lounge at the airline, there was no one else around to hear. Just the opposite: I was totally alone in more ways than one. I had the feelings; Mark no longer did. End of story. Get over yourself, girl. You're a married woman, and even the man you adore has moved on. Time for you to do likewise.

When I hung up, I found I was relieved. I could move on now without guilt.

At least until the next time our hands or legs touched.

A young woman dressed in the airline's hostess garb came

around passing out flight bags. She gave me one that said "Captain's Club" and I stuck my purse inside and went out and bought a book to read on the plane. Into the bag it went.

Where it remained until I unpacked it the next day at home.

19

J ames and Gladys were ecstatic to have me home. I don't know which one missed me the most. But it was reciprocal; I had missed them terribly too. I always did when I had to travel.

And nothing will ever match the look in James' eye when he saw we were still married, loyal, and that we would remain that way. He was suddenly brighter around me than possibly he'd ever been. Which made me happier and which made Gladys happier by default.

We took Gladys to Fuddruckers for burgers the next day at lunch. She loved the long tables of hamburger condiments and vegetables, loved getting to be a big girl and make her own, and lived for the strawberry shakes. We sat at the Beatles table and ate slowly, each of us happier than maybe we'd ever been.

It was like a storm had been weathered. The toughest possible temptation had been tossed in my path, and I had overcome. In a way, I felt very proud. But I also had to remind myself to remain cautious and guarded around Mark. Simple lapses could escalate into full-scale love-making between us regardless of our predilections, just like when we'd been young and at first didn't much care for each other. One night together ended all that, no further questions necessary, thank you.

That night after Gladys was asleep I curled up beside James on the couch in the family room. It was Saturday night, and he was watching Saturday Night Live. Intermittent outbursts and laughter shook and regaled him. I put my head in his lap and closed my eyes. Then I started dreaming about James and having another baby. I swear it: I saw her in my mind. She was unlike either Lisa or Gladys but, in my dream, looked very sad. She was riding a pony, and the pony refused to go where she wanted. So she climbed off and went around and scolded him with her finger. Believe it or not, that dream pony nodded and swung around to face the other direction. I remember calling out to her in that dream, asking her to tell me what she said to him. I knew it was important: I memorized the glade and the distant house in the place where this girl rode her pony.

Later that night, James made slow, gentle love to me. I kept my eyes closed and inhaled him and allowed my mind to see all the men I'd ever been with and James became them all. With a jolt, then, I realized in the next moment that I felt Mark's hands on me, felt Mark inside of me, whispering my name, giving me a new baby, a new child that looked exactly like the girl on the pony. With my arms stretched back over my head, I whispered Mark's name into the dark.

"What?" said James.

"What?" I said, coming out of my fantasy.

"You said 'Mark.'"

"No, I didn't. I didn't say anything."

"Oh, yes, darling, you said your dead husband's name who isn't so dead anymore."

He rolled over off of me and pushed away.

"Did you two make love?"

"No, definitely not!"

"How can I know that for sure?"

Always the lawyer; the question was seeking evidence because I knew James and knew that was how he operated.

"You just have to take my word."

"Your word is shaky right now. You said Mark's name while I was making love to you."

"If I did, I'm sorry. It was inadvertent. I was thinking only of you."

"And just happened to get my name mixed up with his. Shit, Melissa. What have you done?"

"James, he was my husband, for the love of God. My mind is very confused about it all. I'm the first to admit it."

"I don't like this at all. It doesn't make sense that you would say his name while I'm inside of you."

"Well stop trying to make sense for once. Feel the feeling instead of thinking. Don't I feel like I love you? Isn't my body responding to you?"

It was an old issue with us. He was a lawyer, and he thought life. I felt life. We were very different. We'd even been to see a counselor. We came away knowing that we were very different people with very different ways of being in the world.

"Are we off on that again? That I don't feel things enough, that I'm too cerebral?"

"No, there are just times I wish you could go with the feelings rather than the thoughts."

He stood up on his side of the bed and began pulling on his jeans. "This is bullshit. You never complained about my feelings before Mark came back. Now I'm not feeling enough? Well, feel this: I feel like you're comparing me to your real husband and you're sorry you ever married me!"

"Jesus, James, settle down. You'll wake Gladys up. Now come back to bed."

"No, you take the bed. I'm taking the guest room."

"Please don't do this," I whispered, "the whole thing is ridiculous."

"So now my feelings are ridiculous? I've gone along with you every step of the way since he came home. Now I need to protect myself if you're going to be thinking of him when I'm making love to you. You know what I feel? You want to know my feelings?"

"Yes, James. What are you feeling?"

"I'm feeling embarrassed. Embarrassed that I was so into you and so stupid for it while you were thinking about your real husband."

"Please stop calling him that. Please come back to bed."

"No!"

With that, he turned and stamped out of our room, slamming the door behind him.

It was no use. I had said Mark's name. I had been thinking about Mark.

What kind of wife was I turning out to be, forsaking my husband for--for my other husband?

It was all too much. I cried myself to sleep that night. Tears for James, tears for Mark, tears for Lisa, and tears for Gladys.

And tears for the sad girl on the pony.

Now I knew who she was.

She was me.

20

Ignacio Velasquez was a fearsome mortal who settled all disputes with a MAC 10. That gun in the hands of that man was madness, but nobody objected in all of Mexico because all of Mexico was terrified of him. But with his own people, he was kind. He called the girl *Pollo Loco* because she let his prize chickens flee into the jungle. When he came home that day and saw what she had done, he gathered her up in his arms and took her inside the house. He set her down at the kitchen table and ordered the women to feed her anything but chicken. She no longer got to eat chicken. Which suited the girl just fine. She'd seen a chicken killed for food before and she'd sworn she'd never eat another one. And she knew Iggy was right about her: she had purposely let those chickens escape. She loved the chickens, and hated Velasquez no matter how nice to her he was. She hated him because he wouldn't take her to Mommy when she was little and after. All of those years, all of that hatred. It had added up, and now Velasquez was ready to sell the girl to Sheik Omar Ilbrayami and be done with her.

Velasquez traveled with the girl to Riyadh in Saudi Arabia. As his 757 circled the high plateau upon which Riyadh was set, he wished for her sake the girl would open up to her new owner and be what she had been raised to be.

The Sheik put them up in his palatial home and viewed the girl that first evening.

"She is a virgin?" he asked Velasquez from across the dining table.

"Oh, yes. You may have your doctor examine her."

The girl stopped with her fork halfway to her mouth when she heard this. "No one will examine me," she hissed at Velasquez. "I am not some prop for sale."

Her English was good, her metaphor adept. She had been trained in Spanish and English and Arabian for this exact moment. But what her captor hadn't been able to do was break her spirit. His guest had a terrible way of refusing whatever request he made of her and of even going out of her way to thwart him. One time she had taken the .30-06 rifle, she was learning to shoot and suddenly turned around with it pointed at Velasquez's mid-section. The gun was loaded, and she had a look of determination fixed on her face. He spoke to her gently and slowly, at the same time ordering her to put down the gun. She looked around. Her captor's own bodyguards were pointing automatic weapons at her. With a small smile and a nod, the girl turned around and centered five of her next six shots. Then Velasquez came up behind her and said, "Very good for a dead girl." She had looked confused. He continued, "Had you raised that muzzle even one more inch you would now be dead, and we would be burning your body with fuel oil." At that moment she first realized how uneven the odds were of her ever escaping. He owned her, literally.

"I am not some prop for sale by you," the girl repeated to Velasquez at the sheik's table. Velasquez's eyes narrowed. He made no reply, keeping his eyes on his host, Sheik Ilbrayami. He was acting as if she hadn't spoken a word. And it was true, she hadn't, not where the two men were concerned. She was a plaything, and they would do with her as they pleased now and forever.

The sheik clapped his hands three times, and his secretary appeared. "Call for the doctor," he told the man. "We have a girl for him to see."

The secretary bowed low and left the dining room.

"What is her name?"

"We call her *Pollo Loco*. It's a pet name," Velasquez said with a laugh.

The sheik got up from the table and came around and stood behind the girl.

"Remove your blouse," he told the girl. "Let me see what I'm bidding on."

"Do it," Velasquez ordered. "Let our guest see half of the surprise you are."

The girl continued eating the vegetarian meal she had requested.

"Please," said the sheik, dropping one hand onto her shoulder.

Without warning the girl suddenly sprung from her chair,

swirled around to face the host, and pointed the blade of her table knife at his heart. "You'll never sleep again if you bring me here," she hissed. "Don't close your eyes with me in your home, Mr. Ilbrayami. It won't be safe!"

The Sheik took a step backward. "Out! Out of my house!" The battle was over, at that moment. He had cowered, and she had overcome the two men in an instant.

Velasquez couldn't apologize enough.

"Take her from my home!" the host cried. "This instant!"

The girl smiled. "Here's a man who wants to wake up tomorrow. A smart man."

Velasquez raised his hand at the girl but then stopped. If she were marked or her delicate, thin nose broken it would reduce her value by ninety percent. While he was an angry man, he was also a smarter one, and he lowered his hand.

"We will talk later," he said to her under his breath. "Mr. Ilbrayami," Velasquez said, "I have others. This one is only one of many. This one I have been saving for you and she has never been used."

The sheik waved off Velasquez.

"Take her away. Send me pictures. Go, now!"

Velasquez gathered up his bodyguards and the girl, and they left the sheik's country estate.

Rumbling back into Riyadh in the Land Rover, Velasquez watched the girl beside him in the back seat.

"Tonight I make you mine."

"You don't dare," she said. "It will be a million-dollar orgasm, and you can't afford that. Not even you."

He smiled wanly at her.

"Who said anything about an orgasm, child? And who said anything about how I will break you. There are many entrances into your soul that you don't even know yet."

She smiled in the dark, and he saw in the light of the dashboard the glint in her eye.

"Who said you would be the first? You would have been very disappointed tonight at the doctor's report."

With that, she burst out laughing and slammed her elbow into Velasquez' chest. He caught her arm and squeezed.

"Then taking you by force costs me nothing. Thank you for the invitation."

He threw her arm forward and pushed her hard on the back. She flew into the side of her door and slumped crazily in her seat.

Was she marked and ruined?

For the first time in her short life, the Mexican no longer cared.

She was no longer for sale.

21

M ark moved into a long-term Exec-U-Stay, and together we located the Colonel. It turned out he had moved from Chicago to warmer parts and settled in Scottsdale, where his daughter was living. Mark called him and introduced himself. I could tell from the phone call that as soon as Mark told the Colonel that he was Army, they were old friends. Could we come and meet with him? Tomorrow would be perfect, said the Colonel. Just call when you touch down.

So we did. On the flight to Sky Harbor in Phoenix, Mark and I had seats six rows apart. He hadn't thought it a good idea for us to be sitting that close together for three hours. I had to hand it to him, he was making every effort to keep his distance from me. And I was distancing myself from him, too. After that last night with James when I stupidly muttered Mark's name, I had become resolute that there would be no more slip-ups like that again. My husband and daughter meant too much to me to jeopardize even in unintended ways. So I read my Kindle on the flight, keeping myself busy and away from nagging thoughts of first James and then Mark and how it would be with them when the search for Lisa was all over. I was sick of the same thing playing over and over in my head. It was then I realized just how much I was missing Lisa. The two men were secondary to her and my need to have her back home. I vowed from then on to keep my focus on the Lisa plan and to give up the nonsense about Mark and James. I was married to James, and that was the end of that. Mark was going to bring Lisa home, and that was that.

We landed and drove into Scottsdale along Scottsdale Road. How the city had changed since five years ago when I came here to set up an interview with Charles Barkley. It was much larger, the traffic heavier, and many of the old-West indigenous stores were gone, replaced by expensive chain stores and high-end shops.

The Colonel's house was actually a condo that overlooked a man-made lake. It was on the second floor. Neither Mark nor I said a word as we made our way from the parking lot into the elevator and then upstairs. My guess was that he was going to spend the rest of our mission avoiding being alone with me and avoiding all small talk. Which was all right with me.

It was the Colonel himself who answered the door and took us inside. Refreshments followed--sun tea brewed in a gallon jug on his porch in the bright, hot Arizona sun. He was a widower and lived alone. He said he served on the Scottsdale Rodeo Committee and that kept him busy. With a wink at Mark, he added it also kept him in the company of a flock of beautiful women. I ignored this part. I was anxious to get down to our mission.

When we were gathered around the table, the Colonel asked what kind of mission we had in mind.

"We believe our daughter is being held in Tijuana by the cartel."

"Hmm. That's Ignacio Velasquez country. Very dangerous place. What are you planning?"

"We are going to locate his home and overwhelm him with armed gunmen we bring in by helicopter."

"Who are these men?"

"I've been contacting some old friends from my Afghanistan unit. Many of them are retired or moved on. But all of them volunteered to go in with me."

The Colonel turned to me. "What about you, young lady? What is your role?"

"I'll be going through the front door. I'm the only one with a fairly good chance of identifying Lisa."

"How old was she when taken?"

"Four, going on five."

"So your task is to visualize how she has changed over the past dozen years and be sure you kidnap the right person?"

"I wouldn't say 'kidnap.' More like recovery."

"Recovery, that fits better. All right, these men live in armed camps. They are surrounded by dozens and dozens of armed guards. How does your small force deal with all those men?"

"Well," said Mark, "that's where you come in, Colonel. I am

projecting those armed forces will be living apart from the Velasquez *finca*. We will identify that location, and you will infiltrate and blow them all to hell. Weren't you with the Corps of Engineers?"

"I was. And I know explosives forward and backward thanks to one of my Army schools and much experience. We blasted out the airfield at Bagram Air Base, for example."

"I flew in and out of Bagram."

"Everybody does."

"So, Colonel, let me ask the sixty-four-dollar question. Are you in or out?"

He sat back in his chair and laced his fingers behind his head. He sat in that position, rocking up and back for a long minute. Finally, he returned to our meeting and said, "In. But we take out the exterior troops as I say."

"Done!" cried Mark.

"Great and thank you," I said, leaning over and kissing his cheek. "God bless you, Colonel."

"It's a mission I believe in. I was horrified by the kidnapping years ago in Chicago when we went looking for your daughter. It has plagued me ever since, to be real honest. Just the thought of the little blond-headed girl in the clutches of those bastards--excuse me, Mrs. Sellars."

I smiled. "Just wait until you hear me talk about these sons-of-bitches when I get wound up, Colonel."

"Good, good. So. When do we leave?"

"We're going to assemble everyone in San Ysidro, California, just north of the border with Tijuana. From there we'll begin our intelligence gathering."

"What sort of air surveillance do you have?"

"Not much. Probably a light plane."

The Colonel waved Mark off. "That won't do. Let me make some calls. I'll put together a set of satellite views of Velasquez's compound. I know the Army and Border Patrol have computer hard drives filled with the stuff. But first we need to locate his *finca*. How does that happen?"

"We're going to need to go into Tijuana and ask the right people the right questions. I'll be posing as a drug dealer from Los Angeles. Melissa will accompany me, so we look like tourists."

"I've never heard of tourism in Tijuana. Isn't that an oxymoron?" the wizened old man said.

"It is. But actually, Tijuana is becoming more and more a bedroom community for San Diego. Property prices have soared in San Diego, yet there are hundreds of thousands of people working there who need good, affordable housing. Tijuana has seen a housing boom the last five years. In the mornings at the borders inbound to the U.S., the wait is three hours long. It's grown into a huge mess that no one on our side is doing anything about."

"That all makes sense," the Colonel replied. He turned to me. "What about you, Melissa? How do you feel about going undercover in Tijuana with your husband?"

Mark and I traded a look. "Actually we're no longer husband and wife."

"Oh. Sorry."

"No, I was reported KIA and Melissa remarried. Can't blame her one bit. It's lonely raising a kid by yourself, and the child misses out by not having a father, too. We're getting it worked out."

"Of course you'll be holed up in Tijuana in a hotel room for part of the time you're there. But you're adults. I'm sure you'll handle it, Chief. The Army always finds a way."

"Hoorah, sir," said Mark. "Hoorah."

We talked on then, late into the night, drawing up lists of weapons and military skills we were going to need. Through it all, I was nagged by the thought that Lisa might not even be there. After we'd spent a busload of money and risked a dozen lives, there was no guarantee that we would be any closer to Lisa than before. We finally settled on the alternative plan of grabbing anyone who looked gringo when we were leaving. Especially if they had indicated they wanted to come with us.

And there was another, even worse, path the op could take. The Colonel verbalized it, saying, "What if you go bursting in the front door, clear the house, and find your daughter dead of a gunshot wound. Would you go looking for Velasquez to take him out? Or would you just abandon the operation and exfiltrate?"

Mark took that one. "I, for one, will stay behind if necessary to find this rat bastard and kill him. I have a feeling I might do that in either case anyway, alive or dead."

"No," I said in a loud voice, "you won't be staying behind.

Lisa and I are going to both need you more than ever once we're repatriated. That's final and non-negotiable, Mark."

He slowly looked over at me. There was a glint of anger in his eyes, but he let go of that and began nodding. "You're right. Revenge isn't the mission, Lisa is. I can get carried away."

"So here' s where we are, Chief," said the Colonel. "I've printed out our arms and ordnance and HE."

"HE?"

"High explosives," the Colonel said to me. "Most of this stuff can be purchased right here in Arizona with the right contractors' card and ID. I'll tell you what. The HE is on me. I'm buying, and I'll transport it to San Ysidro myself. We in agreement, all?"

"Sure," I said. "As long as I don't have to touch it, it's great."

"Appreciate it, Colonel," Mark said. "Will you be making up satchel charges?"

"That's exactly what I'll be doing."

"Well, Colonel, I'm going to take my ex-wife and head back to our hotel."

"Well, good night, you two. Thanks for letting me in on the action."

"Our thanks to you."

We called a taxi and headed for our hotel. Tomorrow we'd be renting two four-by-fours and heading for San Ysidro by way of San Diego. We undressed--I showered--and we fell into our separate queen beds in the same room. That's the last thing I knew until morning when Mark was shaking my shoulder.

"Melissa," he said, his face grim, "wake up! We've got serious problems."

"What is it?"

"It's Tijuana, all over the news. They've just found a dozen gringo school children murdered outside Tijuana. NBC and CNN are reporting it was the Tijuana Cartel."

I sat straight up in bed.

"How soon before we leave?"

"I'm loading out suitcases right now. We're going to fly instead of drive."

"Agreed."

The terror had seized me again as I went back over Mark's words. Then my thoughts were interrupted by the CNN reporters on the scene. It sounded gruesome. It looked like the last place on earth anyone should be.

The school children were mostly girls.

And mostly teenagers.

Just like my daughter.

22

M ark and I were waiting for our flight to be called when my phone chimed. I fished it out of my shirt pocket and checked the ID. It was Isaac, my sister's son, the one who'd been living with us the night Lisa disappeared. I pressed TALK.

"Aunt Melissa, Isaac. It's all over the news. Mom called me and told me where you are and what you're doing. I'm leaving Chicago in thirty minutes, and I'll arrive in San Diego in about four hours. I'm going into Mexico to the scene, and I'm going to learn what I can about the victims. You guys can come with me, just remember I speak Spanish fluently."

My heart was bursting with thanksgiving. "Oh, Isaac," I said, "it is so wonderful to hear your voice. Yes, we could really use your help now. Please come, give me your flight info, and we'll meet you. Your Uncle Mark is going to be so relieved you've jumped in to help. Text me the details."

"Will do."

We hung up, and I turned to Mark.

"You're not going to like this, but this is the way it's going to go in TJ. Isaac is on his way to help. He speaks the language like a native. He and I are going to the scene of the murders. You will remain on the U.S. side because I do not want you showing your face in Mexico and later being remembered by someone not as a drug dealer but as a concerned father. That wouldn't work and would probably get you killed."

"What about you?"

"Wig and sunglasses. Give me fifteen minutes in a Target store, and I'm good to go."

"I don't think so. I want to be there and see this for myself."

"No. You're staying behind. I'm in charge of this operation, and this is the way it's going down. End of discussion."

"Wow. Who put you in charge?"

"I did. You're a warrant officer, and I'm a general. So I'm running things from here on."

He smiled through his distress. "All right. I can't fight you, I learned that way long ago."

I returned his smile. "Glad you remember."

He threw his arm around me in the airport waiting area chairs. I put my head back against him and closed my eyes. We were both dreading the next ten hours, and we knew it. The massacre could be any number of things, but one thing kept coming back to me: why would a group of American teenagers be in the Tijuana countryside at all? Could they maybe be other children kidnapped by the cartel? It was entirely possible and, in some sick, depraved way, could even make sense to an insane person.

Someone like Ignacio Velasquez.

We boarded a Southwest flight and touched down in San Diego after just enough time to down a Diet Pepsi and the mandatory bag of cashews.

We walked through the airport to the waiting area where Isaac was due to arrive. We found two seats side-by-side that faced the jetway. Mark pulled out his laptop and began working on his list of materiel and phone numbers for his soldiers. I sat back and shut my eyes.

It was all about to shift into high gear, and I needed to be rested and ready.

I realized that Mark's arm was still around my shoulder and that he was typing one-handed. I reached around, lifted his arm, and plunked it back down on his side of the imaginary line between us.

He looked at me and smiled. Then came a shrug.

I looked away.

23

"Señor Robles," said a Federal Policeman, "they haven't been disturbed. I was the first one here. I checked their pulses and made the call."

"Good man," said Robles of the Ministerial Police. "Please keep the press and the gawkers away from here. I don't want to wake up to a front page full of gory pictures."

"I have two men blocking the road where it crosses the train tracks. No one will be allowed beyond there."

"Okay, thank you."

Robles jumped down into the shallow grave. He counted the bodies as best he could. An even dozen. Seven males, five females. Robles put their ages as somewhere between twelve and seventeen. One boy had the beginnings of a very wispy mustache. Maybe sixteen years old, but no more. Eight bodies rested on their sides, their hands bound behind their backs with baling wire. Another four--their hands also bound--had remained upright on their knees, shot behind the ear each one of them. The Federal Police crime scene techs arrived and looked down at Robles. "I'm coming out. I'll retrace my footsteps. No harm to the scene."

The techs didn't respond. He had violated their crime scene, but he had done so on purpose. His own daughter had been kidnapped three months ago, payback for sending a ranking cartel member to hell in a shootout. He'd gone into the grave to look at faces. None belonged to Estrella, thank God. So there was still hope.

Just then, Julio Marzipan, the president's emissary, arrived with no fanfare and no special salute to him even though everyone recognized Marzipan. He came striding up to Robles.

"The President wants to speak with you. I can dial him up on my phone right now."

"All right."

A moment later, Marzipan passed Robles the phone Marzipan had called on.

"Mr. President?" said Robles. "Enrique Robles, sir. I'm the MP in charge."

"Robles," came the president's unmistakable voice with the Mexico City harsh accent, "You have twenty-four hours to locate the men who did this. We have a terrific chance to make good public relations out of this."

Robles' eyes rolled in disgust. "Yes, Mr. President."

"So I want you to take three of your best men and go into Tijuana. Hunt down the people who did this and execute them. I don't want a long, drawn-out trial in front of a terrified jury that will only let them go. Do you follow me?"

"I do, Mr. President."

"Are we on the same page?"

"Are you sure I'm the right man for this?" asked Robles. "The investigation is right here, not in town." Robles knew that if his name became known by the cartel as the officer of the law who'd executed the responsible cartel members, then his own daughter's lifespan would end. It would get his daughter killed in retribution, assuming she was still even alive.

"Oh, you're the right man, Señor Robles. Do you know why I say this? Because I know I can trust you. I know I can trust you to locate the men who did this and send them to hell with your guns. Am I right in this?"

"You are right, Mr. President. I can do that. But I still think--"

"Don't. Don't think, Robles. Just do what I've told you. My other phone is ringing. Call me when your mission in town is completed. Are we on the same page, Robles?"

"We are, sir."

Without a 'goodbye' the president ended the call. Robles returned the phone to Marzipan.

"I could hear every word," Marzipan told him. "You should gather your men and leave now. The president sounds anxious to move ahead."

"Yes, yes. All right. Who has the scene?"

"I do," Marzipan said with a sad look. "For what it's worth. I've never done this before. Any advice?"

"Keep everyone out of the hole except the techs. That's all

you need to do and if you do that they'll give you a useable workup in return. Everyone stays out, no exceptions."

"Thank you, Señor Robles."

"I'm going now."

With that, Robles began moving through his men, tapping them to join him. He then assembled them all inside his SUV and told them of the president's orders. Nobody blinked. It wasn't unusual for the president to mandate such a task after a horrible PR night like tonight would be. "Weapons, everyone. Each man must have an automatic weapon. Get them now."

SUV doors flew open, and the men dispersed to their own vehicles to retrieve their automatic weapons. In five minutes they had all returned.

"Good, then," said Robles, when the last door closed. "We're off."

24

Word of the slaughter reached Ignacio Velasquez just after noon that day. His first response was axiomatic: time to move his inventory because the Federal Police would soon swarm his *finca* in search of lost children. So he loaded his eleven girls into the Benz van and put Marcellus behind the wheel. Two armed guards were assigned, one to ride shotgun, one to ride swing, as they called it, meaning in the rear of the van.

Marcellus pulled the van onto Highway 2D, headed toward Tecate, where the cartel kept other emplacements. The girls would be hidden away underground in Tecate, safe from all prying eyes. Next to him in the passenger seat, Ramon fought to stay awake. He'd been up all night rounding up the inventory that refused orders and had been returned from their purchasers for the difficulties the children created by their refusals. The murder of such recalcitrants was routine; better to dispose of them than embarrass Velasquez a second time. He had his reputation to consider. The children were easily replaced, coming in daily from the United States and Canada.

A half hour later, the van came to a spot in the road where a green Ford SUV and a dead cow were blocking both lanes. It was evident what had happened as this was unfenced grazing land in Baja, southwest of Tecate, almost at the junction with Highway 2. Marcellus applied the brakes, which immediately caused Ramon to come fully awake and upright, cocking his automatic rifle reflexively.

"You're going to have to go see if they can move their vehicle," Marcellus told Ramon. Without a word, Ramon climbed out of the Benz and slung his weapon over his shoulder. He sauntered up to the green SUV and peered inside the driver's window. A red-headed young man and a somewhat older young woman were the only occupants. They appeared unarmed.

"Trouble?" asked Ramon.

25

Isaac had a good idea, which was that we would journey to the death scene from the east. So, we crossed the border at Tecate and came down on Highway 2. Just after we'd turned onto Highway 2D and were coming around a blind curve, a steer stepped into the road in front of our SUV. Isaac braked wildly, and we skidded sideways. But we collided, nevertheless. I was braced in the passenger seat, and the seat belt held me in place. Isaac, who is six-four in height, wasn't quite so lucky. Upon impact, his upper torso flew forward and his face smashed against the top of the steering wheel. Blood flew everywhere, and he pulled the waistband of his T-shirt up to staunch the flow. But I could see it was going to take more than that, so I was rummaging around in my backpack when a knock came on the driver's window.

I stopped my searching and slipped out of my sweatshirt and passed it to Isaac. I had a T-shirt on beneath. I bent forward to see around Isaac as he rolled down his window.

"Trouble?" said a Mexican man in a thick accent.

Isaac was swabbing his fractured nose with my sweatshirt but managed to nod to the man.

"We hit a cow," he told the inquirer.

The Mexican man looked at the dead cow between our vehicles then tossed his head back and laughed. "Really, you did? What was your first clue, Señor?"

"All right," said Isaac. "Let me back up, and then I think I can pull around and give you enough room to pass by."

"That would be good," the man said. "*Adios.*"

Isaac threw it in reverse and swung the tail end of our SUV around to where it was facing almost due east. He then pulled forward abreast of the Mercedes-Benz van and yanked the wheel to the left to get off the shoulder. As he did, his nose began spraying blood again, and Isaac hit the brakes.

From the passenger seat, I could look directly into the second of three windows on this side of the van. A girl was sitting there looking at us. I studied her face. A cold hand gripped my heart as I realized the hair color was right, the blue eyes were right, the slight pout, as she looked into my eyes, was right. Then her mouth moved. "Help me," she mouthed.

For a moment, I wasn't sure. Then it all became clear to me in the next instant.

I had stumbled across Lisa. There was no doubt in my mind it was her. We continued staring at each other while Isaac tended to his bloody nose. Then the driver of the van honked his horn for us to pass on by so he could edge around the dead cow. Holding my sweatshirt to his nose with his left hand, Isaac used his right hand to turn the wheel just enough for us to move on beyond the van. The girl's face slipped from my view as we moved along. Then I watched in my outside mirror as the van lunged to the left of the road, into the oncoming lane, to clear around the dead animal.

Then the van began receding down the road as it got back up to speed.

But I knew. I had found my baby--who wasn't such a baby now. For a minute I was speechless. Then I managed to say to Isaac, "Did you see her?"

He kept his eyes on the road ahead as he said to me, "See who?"

"It was Lisa in that van."

"What!"

"Yes. Turn around."

He was already slowing. We shot across the roadway onto the shoulder and Isaac threw our vehicle into reverse, backing, then down into drive, and we accelerated, skidding on the asphalt as we straightened out.

"Stay far back," I ordered. "We can't blow this by letting them see it's us and that we've turned around to follow."

"Of course, Aunt Mel," said Isaac. "Mama didn't raise no dummies."

"It's her, Isaac."

"I believe you. We need to get close enough to watch when they turn off."

"Yes, but please don't follow when they do. Unless there's a hill and they disappear. Then we can follow from a distance."

"I know, I know."

I looked down at my hands. They were shaking and toying with the glove compartment. I crossed my arms. "Oh, sweet Jesus," I said. "Thank you!"

Inside I was a jumble of feelings, mostly elation and relief laced with a terrible fear of losing her again. That wasn't going to happen, though. I wasn't going to allow that ever again. Not if I had to get a gun and kill every last one of these bastards, I was getting my Lisa back.

And I knew exactly how I was going to do it, too.

"Catch up a little bit," I said to Isaac. "I know how we're going to do this."

"How, Aunt Mel? There's only two of us, and we don't have guns and wouldn't know how to use them if we did."

"Get closer."

We raced along the road, 70 then 75 when they came into view again. The van's brake lights flared, which caused Isaac to immediately touch our brakes too, so we didn't overrun our prey. But then they kept going, thank goodness. Twenty minutes later we saw the roadside sign for Tecate and knew we had just entered the city limits. We followed the van slowly through the town, almost losing them when a traffic light let them through on a green then turned red for us. Isaac came up to the intersection, looked both ways, took a right, then a U-turn, then back up and another right.

"Good driving," I muttered. Hopefully, they hadn't turned off yet.

He floored it coming out of the intersection, and I thought I could just make out their silhouette just beyond the second light ahead. I began praying we'd not get stopped by the lights again. The first one let us on through. Then the second one turned red just as we got to the cross street, but Isaac didn't hesitate: he floored it, and we shot across the intersection and roared on down the road. Luckily John Law wasn't about and watching traffic. So we managed to gain some distance, and now there was just a block between us and the van.

Finally, it hung a right on an unmarked street and again started pulling away from us when we followed.

"Get way back," I told Isaac. "He's suspicious. I can feel it. In fact, turn down one of these streets and circle around the block. We'll catch back up to them."

Isaac did as I asked and we went all the way around, exiting the side street a block further on down the main road. The van was nowhere to be seen, so Isaac floored it, and we jumped ahead of other traffic. We shot past the city limit sign on the north end and quickly were back up to seventy miles an hour. Which was when we saw them, far off to our right, throwing up a rooster tail of dirt and dust as they sped due east on a dirt road.

"Should I?" Isaac asked, nodding toward them.

"Oh God," I said. "I don't know."

"Screw it. I'm going," he said and pulled a sharp right turn at the T-intersection off to our right.

We were flying along the dirt road for a good five minutes until we came to a huge home with red Mexican tiles off on our left. The entire place was surrounded by chain-link fencing with barbed wire along the top. Drawing up perpendicular allowed me a glance down the entrance road, back into a three-door vehicle barn. Sure enough, the Mercedes van had pulled in and was still unloading passengers, all girls it appeared as we shot on by.

"Good driving. Now let's disappear."

We had passed the house, and it didn't look like there was any person between our vehicle and the *finca* that might have been following us with their eyes. So far, so good.

"Now we know where your daughter is, Aunt Mel. How does that feel?"

Tears came to my eyes. "I don't know. Scared and excited, I guess. But I do know what we're going to do."

"What's that, Aunt Mel?"

"We're going to circle all the way around on this road and then head north for the border. When a left turn is available, I want you to take it. We're going back to *Los Estados*."

"What are we going to do there?"

"I'll make some calls, that's what. I'm getting my daughter back, Isaac. Today, make no mistake."

An hour later we had crossed the border and were headed due west by Otay Lakes and San Ysidro. At San Ysidro, we headed up the 5 toward San Diego.

I was going to need a bank. A bank with lots of cash.

26

On the way to San Diego, we stopped at a CVS and bought some medical supplies for Isaac's nose. I leaned over in the seat and got him cleaned up. Then I called Mark and brought him up to speed. I keep it purposely vague about my next steps—he would've screamed bloody murder to stop me.

California Bank and Trust in San Diego turned out to be the bank that could fill my withdrawal slip. I took the cash in a CPA briefcase. The whole thing took no more than an hour, and by two o'clock I had my million dollars in cash and an ashen-faced Isaac hurrying along the sidewalk to keep up with me.

He did everything he could to draw attention to us with his endless prattle and waving arms as he told me--repeatedly-- what a dumb idea it was to be walking down the sidewalk in a major American city with that much cash.

Finally I stopped and faced him. "What do you think, Isaac? They're going to take a check for her?"

"Yes--no--I mean I don't know, Aunt Mel. Let's just get in the car pronto."

So far his language skills had been about that useful: pronto.

This time we knew where we were going. Ten minutes later we were headed east on Otay Lake. Where it junctioned with 94, I asked Isaac if he would like me to drive. "You kidding?" he said. "I've seen your hands shaking with excitement all afternoon. I'll stay over here, and you just stay over there."

Hours later we turned south just this side of Canyon City. It was the same road we had taken out of Mexico--at least that was our hope. I was praying it was because I remembered the cattle feedlot on the corner where we needed to turn back west to locate Lisa's estate.

Sure enough, thirty minutes later the feedlot came up and Isaac looked over at me with a grin. "This is it. Get ready."

"I know."

We were less than twenty minutes from the *finca*. My pulse began pounding in my neck, and I broke out in a cold sweat.

As we sped west on the dirt road, I first saw a distant speck in the sky coming in our direction. Then, just as we arrived at the chain link fence, the helicopter swooped down on the house and settled onto the ground. We couldn't see that part with the estate blocking our view, but it had in fact disappeared back behind the mansion so we knew what had happened. We slowed and pulled along the fence. The gate was closed, but there was a guard station. So we pulled up and stopped.

"You stay here," Isaac told me. "Let me see if I can get us inside."

He stepped up to the guard station and rapped on the glass window. It slid open, and I saw at least two men inside. It wasn't small, more like a small living room in size so there could have been others, too. Isaac talked to the man through the opening for a good five minutes. Then I saw the man shrug and place a phone to his ear. His lips moved.

Minutes later, the front of the home opened and out through the patio and archway came a handsome man who looked to be fifty, his mouth hidden behind a Zapata mustache so I couldn't tell if he was smiling or scowling. Four Mexican men carrying guns with short barrels accompanied him. They all came up to the guard station, and he went inside.

Then he appeared in the window, and I could see him speaking to Isaac. Isaac stopped at one point and turned and indicated me with his hand. I had no idea what to do, so I lifted the CPA bag and showed it out the windshield.

Then the talking resumed.

Finally, the Zapata man came out of the guard house, and the gate rolled sideways until he could pass through. With two of his guards, he came up to my car and motioned that I should roll down the window.

"How much?" he asked. Nothing else, just "How much?"

I knew he meant how much money did I have.

"One million dollars USD. I want to buy a girl."

He leaned back and looked away.

"Who told you I have a girl?"

"I saw her in your van. I want to buy her."

"Saw her in my van? When was this?"

"This morning. Our car hit a cow, and your van was blocked. I could see the girl inside the window. She's the one I want."

"How do you know she is here with me?"

"We followed your van. We saw it turn in here."

"Very smart," he said, appraising me where I sat. His eyes roamed over my body.

"How would you like to be one of my girls?"

"I don't want to be a girl, sir. I want to purchase one."

"Which one would that be?"

"About sixteen, blond hair cut short, blue eyes looks right into your eyes when you look at her."

"Oh yes, Maria."

"Maria? Her real name is Lisa."

Suddenly he stood fully upright and scowled down at me. "How do you know what her name is?"

"I'm her mother, and I want to buy her from you. It will be a quick sale we can do right now, and you get the money, and I get the girl. Then I'm gone out of your life forever."

"How do you know I won't just take your money and bury you out in the desert? How you know that?"

"Because you're not stupid. Because you know the girl's father is very brave and very wealthy and that he will come down here and kill everyone he can find if something bad happens to me. I can promise you he will."

The man started laughing and laughed so hard he bent over at the waist. He spoke Spanish to his two guards, and they fell apart laughing as well. I looked over at Isaac, and he pursed his lips. Neither of us had any idea what was coming next. They might shoot us, they might bring Lisa out and take the money, they might tell us to leave and never come back--anything was possible.

Isaac returned to the car and climbed inside. The Mexican men ignored him.

They were all about the money. You never want to underestimate the persuasive powers of ten-thousand hundred-dollar bills.

"Do I need to count it?" Velasquez eventually asked, recovered from his coughing fit.

"No need," I said. "I know you'll come and kill me if it isn't all there. I wouldn't try to cheat you."

He looked at me, and his eyes narrowed. "No, I don't think you would. Because next time I will kill her. And you. And your husband and your other kids," he said, suddenly drawing a huge gun and pointing it at Isaac. Isaac cringed and slammed his head sharply against the window glass behind him. He came forward and shook his head violently.

"No!" Isaac cried.

"Get out of the car and come inside. I want to make sure you're serious about my inventory."

Isaac and I climbed out of the SUV, leaving it where it was, half-blocking the driveway into the garage. The CPA case was dragged out by me, and I held it by its handle. It weighed me down considerably. Ten-thousand of anything is heavy, I remember thinking.

Velasquez motioned that Isaac and I should lead the way, so we started up the driveway to the house. As we walked, Velasquez and his men were just behind us, chattering and laughing.

Isaac whispered. "They're saying they want to strip your clothes off and all of them--"

"Silence!" Velasquez shouted. Isaac's mouth closed and he looked away from me. But I'd gotten the gist of the conversation going on behind us. This could turn very ugly very quickly at any moment, and I steeled myself. My bottom line? I didn't want to leave there without Lisa. No matter what else they did or didn't do to us, I was leaving with my baby. The fear inside me squeezed hard against my chest, causing me to break out in chill bumps even in the soft desert air. Plus, it had been hours since I'd used a bathroom and just really needed to go. My mind wandered back over the movies I'd seen where the good guys got abducted by the bad guys. If nothing else, no one ever had to use the toilet. So much for all that: I did.

Over my shoulder, I tossed out, "*¿Adonde es el baño?*"

"Is inside. You can use it, and we don't even take pictures," said our new host. Again, more laughter.

I realized Isaac and I had become his toy, his plaything. My guess was that even he didn't know what he was going to do with us just then. He was just making up our lives as we all went along.

"Just go inside," we were ordered.

Isaac twisted the front doorknob and immediately an insane rush of dog barking erupted. Isaac hesitated. He looked around at our captors. "Jes go in," he was sharply told. So he took a deep breath and pushed the door full open and stepped inside. I followed right behind. The entryway was Spanish tile--what else?--with Clerestory windows over-head. Very civilized and very nice. I didn't know what else I was expecting, but it was a bit of a relief, and I immediately felt foolish and totally unsuited for what I was trying to do. And poor Isaac for agreeing to come along with his crazy aunt. There was a moment of regret that I hadn't made him stay behind in the U.S. when I returned this time.

Velasquez ordered us on into the large living area just ahead. We stepped down three steps and found ourselves in an expensively furnished family room--for want of a better word--where everything was rich, creamy leather and what looked to be solid mahogany, hand-carved furniture. Three Dobermans had followed us from the entry down into the living area. They sniffed me and sniffed Isaac and watched their master for instructions. It occurred to me that the dogs had been used to attack people before. Even now they were baring their teeth and lurking nearby.

Velasquez passed beyond us and then turned, extending his arms toward a long, low sofa covered in zebra hide. We sat where instructed, and I set the bag down between my feet, waiting.

"Anybody like some wine before we begin the game?" Velasquez said with a laugh.

"No thank you," I said. Isaac didn't answer.

Velasquez then walked over to a heavy coffee table and began unstrapping weapons from inside his sports coat and from around his ankle. He put down the small machine gun he was carrying. When he had finished, he picked the ankle gun up again. He pushed a small rod, and the gun opened up. He turned it butt-down, and all the bullets fell into his hand. Then he smiled at us very broadly and held up one shiny bullet for all to see, turning in the room so that even the guards knew there was one bullet in his hand and that that bullet was going back inside the gun. When it was reinserted, he snapped the chamber shut and spun the gun around an index finger. "Nice," he said, feeling the balance with the muzzle laid across the opposite wrist. Then he turned and pointed it directly at me. I flinched and turned my head to the side. If it had come to this, so be it. But at least I had tried to save my daughter.

I looked up, and he was spinning the chamber with the palm of his hand. Then he stepped over and handed me the gun, handle first.

"What do you want me to do?" I asked.

With his other hand, he made the sign of a pistol and pointed the finger barrel at his own head. He then mimed pulling the trigger with the muzzle pointed at his head.

"You want me to shoot myself in the head?"

"No. I want you not to shoot yourself in the head. Shooting yourself in the head means my zebra gets all messy. I don't like messy. So be sure when you pull the trigger that you avoid the chamber that has the bullet. Here. We get started with this now."

"And if I do it," I said, accepting the gun from him.

"You must do it six times. If you don't die, you get your daughter and keep your money. If you kill yourself, I get the money and the daughter. And the man you have here? He gets to walk outback across the field where we have our landmines. He will probably shake your hand in heaven just fifteen minutes after you. What is your name?"

"Melissa."

"Melissa. We are going to bring your girl out. Javier," he said to one of his stooges, "bring me Consuela."

Javier disappeared, and Velasquez made himself a drink with ice and rum while we waited. One big swallow later and the man Javier returned with--with...my daughter.

It was Lisa--at least I wanted it to be. It was the girl I imagined her to be over all these years gone by. Her eyes and skin were clear, and she looked to be in good health. She didn't make eye contact with me this time, keeping her gaze fixed on the floor before her.

"Can you look at me?" I asked her.

She didn't lift her eyes.

"Consuela, this woman says she is your mother. Look at her and tell me what you see."

She looked up then, and I was positive--the bone structure, the restless eyes--that it was my girl. She smiled and nodded at me. Then her eyes dropped away again. A warmth spread through my body like that first drink of alcohol, soothing, and all the usual, balled-up, coiled loss I had carried around for ten years suddenly seeped out of my soul and disappeared out the windows that looked out on the giant, landmined pasture in this horrible/beautiful place. I could have died at last, peaceful and filled with the knowledge that she was alive and looking like she had come through whatever hell had been struck for her. We were together at last, and it was over.

Until Velasquez stepped between us. He peered down into my eyes and again made the finger-pistol to the head pantomime. I knew it was time.

Almost without fear, I placed the muzzle against the side of my head and fixed my daughter with my eyes and pulled the trigger. It was over in an instant, and I still was looking at my child.

He nodded at me and held up one finger.

Without hesitation, I snapped the trigger again, this time with my eyes tightly shut. I looked back at him.

Two fingers.

"Spin the chamber," he said and came and took the gun from me and spun the chamber with the palm of his head. "This way you're not moving closer to the bullet by statistics. Do you like statistics, Consuela's mom?"

"I don't know. I don't have math in me."

He handed the gun back to me. I looked to my left on the sofa and saw Isaac sitting there, all but paralyzed waist-up, his legs jittering up and down and tears streaming down his face. His eyes were closed, and his lips moved silently. He was always the sensitive one in my sister's family, the one who went to church camp at a young age, the one who even today proclaimed that when he married, it would be in a church, "Of some kind or other."

When I received back the gun, I spun it again for luck I told myself, using the palm of my right hand.

Then I placed the barrel against my head and started to pull the trigger. But this time I paused. Suddenly I knew. The bullet was right there, waiting to click over and fall beneath the hammer of the gun as it slammed forward its firing pin.

I stopped and withdrew the gun from my head. With a great smile, I looked around at my captors and spun the cylinder again. "It was right there about to kill me," I explained. Nobody said anything. They just looked at me.

Then I raised it up and in one fluid motion pulled the trigger again and was awarded the loud "Click!" of the hammer falling home. I rolled my eyes and smiled at Velasquez. "What can I say? I'm still here, Mr. Velasquez."

"You are, and you are very brave. I am hoping you win against the gun."

"Oh, this isn't against just the gun, Mr. Velasquez. This game is against life and all its hell. This game is for my daughter, for her father, for all the childless mothers of lost children you have stolen and sold and murdered. You will see, Mr. Velasquez that at the end good will win. Just like this afternoon, here in the middle of nowhere. Now watch. Go ahead, raise four fingers and watch my eyes as I pull again."

Without another word, I brought the gun to my temple. A quick snap and again a loud silence.

"Four fingers, indeed," I told him. "Thank you."

"Yes."

"And while we're at it, how about five and six?"

I placed the gun to my temple and pulled the trigger twice in rapid succession, expecting to die and ready for the darkness that would surely follow someone with my luck.

Snap! Snap! Said the pistol.

Then I was laughing and crying at once, rocking back on the couch and, because I hadn't found the bathroom, wetting myself. But I didn't care, and I thought, Fuck his zebra. Followed by the crazier thought, He should be ashamed, skinning Zebras for his stinking ass.

Like I said, my thoughts from then on that day made no sense. I had never been so frightened and so determined. I had been prepared to die for my child. Any mother would do the same thing.

Which was something Mr. Velasquez hadn't counted on in making such a cheap bargain for my daughter:

Motherhood.

27

Velasquez's men escorted us back to the SUV. The kidnapper-in-chief, the sex-trafficker in chief, Ignacio Velasquez, was suddenly "called away" and left the room. This was just after I didn't kill myself. "Release them all," he said to Javier, and doors began opening.

Isaac got behind the wheel, and I put Lisa in the front passenger seat. Into the backseat behind her I climbed, along with my briefcase containing one million in cash. Isaac peeled backward out of the gate in the fence, rolled back against the far shoulder, and shot the car forward toward Tecate and the road to San Ysidro and our hotel. Within minutes my daughter turned to look at me. "Are you really my mother?" she asked.

"Yes, I am." It was all I could do to restrain myself from grabbing her and hugging her for the next hour. But it had occurred to me that I didn't know her; I didn't know how she would react. So I stayed relatively level.

"Thank you for coming to get me. It was hard."

"I know it must have been. We'll talk about all that. The first thing is, I want to get you to an ER and get you examined all over. It won't take long, just a few hours, but I want a team of American doctors and nurses and lab people to check your health. I think we'll go to UCSD Hospital in San Diego for that, Isaac. So why don't you put that in your GPS and make that stop one? As soon as I can get cell out here, I'll call Lisa's father and tell him where to meet us. Then I can bring him up to speed on everything. Your father is going to be very excited to see you."

"Is he the one with the red hair?"

"Red hair, your father? No, you've never seen your father. Uh, who do you think might have had red hair?"

"Oh, my father has red hair."

"How old were you when you last saw him?"

"I don't know. I was young."

"Of course. I don't doubt someone else came along in your life with red hair. We'll figure out who that was. We're going to need a long time to learn about you. And you about us. But don't worry, we have that, lots of time."

She turned back around and faced the windshield. Her head was canted slightly to her right so I could tell she was looking out to her right as we made our way. Again, I had been struggling with the urge to touch her. I don't know what I wanted to do with her, but it was about physical contact. Maybe a hug? That would have been good. But there was no time for it back at the *finca*. What would she do if I just reached forward and began massaging her shoulders? Or ran my fingers through her blond hair. Would that be something a mother would do with a sixteen-year-old after years apart? I honestly didn't know, so I decided I would stop trying to think my way through some of these things and instead just watch carefully and see what I learned about her.

"Isaac, I'm wondering if Lisa might be more comfortable in the back here with me?"

Lisa said, "No, no, not necessary. I'm fine up here. What do you want me to call you?"

"Mom? Are you comfortable with Mom?"

"I don't know. What's your name?"

"Melissa."

"Can I call you that at first?"

"Yes, of course."

"And what about my father?"

"You can call him Mark if you wish. Melissa and Mark."

"Do you have Mexican soap operas? ¿Uno Familia Con Suerte? But my favorite when I was little was Wild Heart."

"I think all the providers have at least a hundred Spanish language shows now," Isaac volunteered. "I watch some of them for language practice."

"Can I watch them?" Lisa asked.

"Of course you can, sweetheart," I answered. "We'll also need to look into school for you. What grade are you in?"

"What grade?"

"Yes, how far have you gone in school?"

"Gone to school? I didn't go to school. We had nothing like school. No, we learned to cook, to clean, to care for babies, to please some mens."

"Please some mens? What's that mean?"

"You know, how to do good sex to them. If we don't do good Iggy don't get paid."

"She means Ignacio, I think," Isaac told me. "Iggy-Ignacio."

"Si. Iggy es Ignacio."

I was trying not to break into tears. I had known there was the possibility of anything happening to her. I just hadn't expected she would be so blasé, so open about the sex teachings. More than ever, then, I wanted medical professionals to test her for everything. Only God knew for sure at that point what might be found.

"Isaac, aren't we going quite slow?"

"I'm doing seventy, Aunt Mel. This one-lane road shouldn't be driven much faster. Do you want me to speed up?"

"Not if you think you're at what the road can handle. So, have you found UCSD Hospital yet?"

"Yes, it's in the GPS."

Then I turned back to Lisa. I didn't mean to interrogate her, only to try and understand her. She was my daughter, after all. "Do you read and write English?"

"No. I hear English because most of our mens talked it. How much? How much for? Would you do this to me? Can I do this to you? Would you like to have my baby? What about doing this?"

"Commercial phrases, Aunt Mel. Don't worry. She knows more than that."

I wasn't worried like Isaac thought I might be worried. I was way down the road on that. I was worried by now that she still might decide to just up and go live with some man. Evidently, there had been absolutely no grounding in the importance of family and parents, and now she was sitting like a ripe plum on the branch, waiting to be pecked.

"You are going to live with me, Lisa," I said solemnly as if making a vow.

"I am? What would I do there?'

"Well, we'll see about school, first. There is much for you to learn."

"Then I don't live with you. I want to be in my room with my TV, so I can watch MTV and Telemundo and do my nails and text to my friends in TJ. School is boring."

"How do you know school is boring?"

"Iggy said that."

"Velasquez told you school was boring?"

"Yes."

"Do you believe everything Mr. Velasquez told you?"

"Yes, I do. Iggy is a very smart man. He's not my father, he's better than my father. He's my uncle."

"Iggy isn't your uncle. Iggy is a man who kidnapped you."

"No one kidnapped me. I wanted to go with Iggy to Mexico."

"Really? Where were you living when Iggy took you away?"

"Santa Barbara."

"What?"

"Santa Barbara."

"How do you know this?"

"My Girl Scout card said Santa Barbara."

"You were old enough to be in Girl Scouts when you were taken away by Iggy?"

"Uh-huh."

"Do you know your name?"

"Yes. Do you want my American name or my Mexican name?"

"Let's start with American."

"Susannah Upchurch."

"How do you know that?"

"Because that's what everyone always called me. My dad is Franklin Upchurch, and my mother is Madeline."

"What? Are you sure of this?"

"Yes, I am sure. I was with them when I was little."

I could hardly believe my ears. If what she was saying was true, I had the wrong girl. My mind jumped ahead three spaces. They brought the wrong girl when Ignacio sent Javier to fetch her. They brought some other blond girl.

"Susannah, were there other girls with you who had blond hair?"

"Everyone has blond hair."

That wasn't going to work. Blond/blue was the paradigm, I told myself. Try something else.

"Were any of the girls unusual in any way? Anything stands out in your mind?"

"Well, I lived all over. My favorite girl was *Pollo Loco*. She lived down south, and she lived in the chicken house after she didn't get the job in Arabia."

"Tell me about this girl, please."

"I was older. She was very sick when she arrived. The nurse gave her medicines and kept her in bed. Then one day she got up and came outside to play with us. She loved the chickens at that place. After I was gone, she let the chickens loose. I only heard about this. Then they took her to Saudi Arabia, but he couldn't sell her. So they came home, and he put her in the chicken pen to live. That's all I know."

My heart was racing. "How long ago was this?"

"Last summer."

"Where was this?"

"At the ranch. Ignacio collects his babies, his chickens. The young girl turned them loose, so she has to live in their fence."

"My God!"

"But it's very good there. It doesn't get cold like nights in TJ."

"Susannah, if I asked you to, would you guide us down to the chicken ranch?"

"I don't know. I guess I would. Would Iggy get me back?"

"No, I promise."

"No, that's not what I mean. I mean I want Iggy to have me. I love him. He took me away from a very bad man in Santa Barbara."

"Your own father?"

"That's the one. Bastard!"

"Do you know the roads to take to get back there?"

"Of course. We drive there many times. Sometimes we live there."

"All right, here's what we're going to do. Isaac, let's head back to San Ysidro after all."

"What about the doctors?"

He was right. Would I offer Susannah less medical care than my own daughter? It was a terrible thought because it would slow us up. But I knew I had to do what was right for her.

"All right, keep on to UCSD. We'll get her checked out then we'll go back to Mexico and let her direct us."

"We taking Mark and the Colonel this time?"

"Yes. We're going to need them."

I was totally deflated. After all the hell I'd been put through I still didn't have my daughter. Don't get me wrong, I was happy we'd managed to tear Susannah away from that horror chamber, but Susannah wasn't my Lisa. I wanted to cry but held back, knowing that Susannah would catch on to how anguished I was that it was her with me and not Lisa. Instead, I began chewing the inside of my cheek until blood could be tasted. Then I swiped the back of my hand across my eyes and said something about how hot it was. Unspeakable images raced through my mind, taunting me with what Lisa was going through because I'd been there. Then the tears couldn't be held back, but I made sure no one noticed. Alone in my pain, again, but a feeling of determination rising up through it all now. In the end, I was more determined than ever to get to Lisa and save her. I vowed this incredible mixup wouldn't hold me down any longer.

Two hours after, we were in San Diego, where we found the hospital and took Susannah into the ER. There was no insurance; I put it on my American Express. It came to right at five thousand dollars when they finished with her four hours later. They had performed a complete physical exam, psychological assessment, blood work, chest x-ray, and body scans. I was surprised it didn't cost more, but that was it. Susannah was crying when she came back out to us.

"I'm never doing that again."

"We know, sweetheart. But it was important to get you checked over."

Then we headed to San Ysidro and Mark and the Colonel. I had spoken to Mark twice by phone and James once by phone while I was waiting in the hospital. I also got to tell Gladys goodnight and give her a long-distance phone kiss.

Mark was adamant: I was not going with him to get Lisa out of the chicken farm. I was going to stay at the hotel with

Susannah and keep an eye on her while Children and Family Services assessed her Santa Barbara home. I got the ball rolling on that with a phone call; Susannah's future whereabouts were in the works, but CFS made a temporary placement to me.

It was just for forty-eight hours, but it was something I gladly ran with.

28

We arrived at the San Ysidro Restoration Hotel sometime after dark--I say "sometime" because I was too tired even to lift my wrist and check the time. Mark and I—twin beds—took the adjoining room and put Susannah in there. She had no toiletries and no clothes, so Isaac made an emergency run with her to Target. They came back after nine with four brimming shopping bags. Now Susannah had enough to sustain her for a few days while we went after Lisa.

The next morning, Mark, the Colonel, and I met around our suite's dining table and laid our plans. Susannah would go with them--contrary to what Mark had earlier said--because only Susannah knew where we were going. Which meant I would be left behind all alone. There was no justification for that, so Mark finally relented and agreed I could go. Truth be told, it wasn't his choice to make. I was going to take Susannah with me and go without them if I had to--but I was going one way or the other.

Susanna joined us at the table. She explained that there

were many men at the chicken farm. All of them carried guns on their shoulder and guns in their holsters. There were also places where the children were never allowed to go--mine fields, she'd been told during her earlier years. "You just don't go over there," she said. So we had her draw us a map, and she was able to locate six guard towers in addition to the mine fields. When she finished, the Colonel and Mark exchanged words. In their opinion, they were outgunned and would be even with the soldiers-of-fortune they had recruited. Evidently much had happened while I was gone, including the arrival of these men and the arrival of the guns and ammo and armaments needed.

Susannah drew more maps, and the two soldiers put their heads together. Then they sent for a retired sergeant newly arrived to help. He had been an airborne assault officer and served in two wars. Billy Prekam was his name, a stout, bowlegged man who came bounding into our room wearing cargo shorts, a T-shirt that said *Sea Shepherd* and carrying a baseball bat. "Let's fuck someone up!" he said to Mark and the Colonel, as Susannah and I were at the other end of the table, and he couldn't see us when he first came in. "Ooops! Sorry, ladies. My bad."

"I've heard worse," I told him. Susannah rolled her eyes.

He was invited to sit down. Mark and the Colonel went over the hand-drawn maps with him. They then went over the satellite photos provided by the Colonel. I was listening intently during all of this, making damn sure that my daughter wouldn't be jeopardized by the ultimate go-to plan the soldiers decided upon. But in the end, there were no guarantees—not just for Lisa but all the captives at the *finca*. I interposed my thoughts, which the men seemed to consider the comments from someone who worries too much. Then I got up next to them and explained why the plan they were proposing was going to get people killed. It couldn't help but get people killed. The children, in my opinion, would be used as human shields and some of them would probably die.

I looked to Mark for help and gave him a look that said he didn't have my buy-in. There were enormous implications to this, and he knew it: for one, if something tragic happened to Lisa it would be on him and him alone because I wasn't in the boat with him. I opted out. We took a break and Mark and I stepped out into the hallway where we could be ourselves and say what we needed to say to each other.

"This isn't what I signed on for," I told him.

"Seriously? What did you think was going to happen? You were with me at the Colonel's. You heard about the soldiers and guns and explosives. Where were you then, Mel? This is all a surprise to me and it—it—"

"It makes you look foolish?"

"That's exactly it!"

"Now think about that for a minute. Do you go home with your daughter or your pride intact? Because this plan isn't going to give you both."

"All right. Assuming for the sake of argument I agree with you. What is the alternate proposal you would make?"

"Take the money and buy her. She's a commodity, she's inventory to this bastard. So pay the going-price for a beautiful sixteen-year-old American girl. Give them what they want."

"There's a thought."

"No, it's out plan now. I'm the general, remember?"

He slumped against the wall. "Let me run it by the others."

I put my hand squarely in the center of his chest. "No, there is no running it by. This is how it's going to be."

"Wait, Mel. How do we get from a small military action clear over to giving them what they want?"

"One thing. It ain't your million dollars. And it's not the Colonel's. And it's not the Devil Dog's, or whatever you call the new guy in there. You know whose money it is? Mine. I earned it and I get to spend it like I want. If it will guarantee my daughter's safety and guarantee that I'm not jeopardizing other children, there is no alternative. Now you get back in there and tell these guys this is what we're going to do. Agree?"

He backed away, drawing my hand into his and holding it. Ever so slowly he began shaking his head side-to-side. "Now you know why I'm going to hate losing you, Mel. You're the real deal."

I could feel my face reddening. Slowly, I withdrew my hand.

"Just bring my daughter home."

We went back inside. I watched Mark as he sat down with his soldiers.

Mark looked grim. "This isn't a place where we can successfully launch an assault. Too many will be killed, and we cannot afford that. Plus, there is the safety of the children kept there. We don't know where they are, we don't know how many, and we don't know what our own daughter looks like to carry her out of there. I don't like this, Colonel."

The Colonel's face turned red, and he said, "I was attached to the Corps of Engineers. I know next-to-nothing about assaulting enemy prisons. Zero, *nada*."

Clearly, it was up to Mark to make the next call. We waited while he rolled it around in his head.

"You know what we're going to do?" he said at long last. "We're going to bribe someone."

"Who might that be?" the Colonel asked.

"The Federal Police commander for Baja. We are going to give him the suitcase full of money and let him come out with Lisa. Half up front, half on return with our daughter."

I immediately liked the idea. The idea of bribing the Federal Police resonated with me.

So we put it in play.

Mark and the Colonel drove across the border at San Ysidro and found the offices of the Federal Police in Tijuana. He later called me to report that the commandant had accepted the five-hundred-thousand and immediately left for the chicken farm. He didn't even have to take Susannah. He knew exactly where it was. All of which made me wonder just how closely aligned the Tijuana Cartel was with the Federal Police, but I knew better than to ask. This operation was way above my pay grade, and all I could do was wait around the Restoration Hotel with Susannah and watch TV. She wanted to go shopping after a couple of hours of this, so I took her up to Seaport Village and bought her some shirts and jewelry. Her tastes were very adolescent, but she was happy with what we found for her, and that was all that mattered. When we arrived back at the hotel, Family Services was waiting in the lobby. The caseworker reported that a preliminary study was done at Susannah's home and the report was inconclusive. So they were making a temporary two-week placement of Susannah with a foster family in Santa Barbara while the home study continued. We said goodbye right there in the lobby after I called up and had Isaac grab her things and bring them down in my small suitcase. That left me with my "Captain's Club" bag for my things. Isaac and I sent her off like that, outfitted and dressed, to face God only knew what in her life. It was going to be so hard for that child that it made me cry after she was gone.

Now I could only wait to see if there would be another girl to take that one's place.

It was getting later, and by dusk, I was totally climbing the walls. Isaac went down to the pool to wait there while I ordered dinner and ate alone in my room. *Rachel Maddow* kept me company over chicken and creamed peas and homemade rolls.

Finally, my phone chimed.

It was Mark. "Set three places at the table tonight, Mama."

"Tell me!"

"We have Lisa! We're coming home."

The phone slipped from my hands while I broke into the most violent sobbing and wrenching crying I'd ever experienced. Tears fell from my eyes as I stumbled around the room, foolishly trying to make the place presentable for my daughter. Nothing helped, of course, but it kept me occupied for the next little while.

Just after eight o'clock I heard the door open and went to investigate.

There she stood. Looking exactly like I thought Lisa would look at sixteen.

We stood fifteen feet apart and just stared. Her chin trembled. Mark cleared his throat behind her. The Colonel had gone on to his room.

Ever so slowly so as not to alarm her I began moving toward her. Astonishingly, she at the same moment started walking toward me. She held her arms outstretched, and I felt her wrap around me as I passed my arms around her and laid my face against the top of her head. Crying broke out among the three of us. No words could express our feelings.

Then I held her at arm's length. "Let me memorize you," I said.

She instinctively seemed to know what I meant.

"You're home, I'm your mother, and this is your father. What's your name?"

"They call me *Pollo Loco*. It means crazy chicken."

"No, what's your real name."

"Lisa. My name is Lisa, and I'm hungry."

WE FED her then we drove her back to the hospital ER and repeated the earlier set of tests and examinations. It was quieter in the ER this time and altogether took about two hours. While we waited, Mark made arrangements. He used his own money to pay the soldiers who had come into town to help us. He had his back pay and insisted on handling that himself. He told me he had paid them as if they had undertaken and completed the actual mission. We both thought that was fairer than fair; the Colonel agreed.

The Colonel caught a Southwest flight into Phoenix that night, and Isaac tagged along to check out ASU. He wanted to learn about teaching assistantships while working on a Ph.D. in Arabic. Working for the CIA was his goal, and he evidently knew what it would take to get there.

Then the ER doctor came out and brought us up to speed. Blood tests looked normal; major organ functions were within acceptable limits; the physical exam revealed a slightly undernourished, slightly underweight sixteen-year-old girl who bordered on anemia. We were told to take her to our family doctor when we returned to Glencoe and repeat everything. They didn't need to tell me that; I was already lining up doctors and dentists in my head while I was waiting in the ER. Funny aside: Mark wouldn't let her out of his sight when she went off with the ER doctor and nurse. He went right along with her and waited outside her curtained exam room. No way was he ever going to be without her again, he swore. He was stunned, as well: she looked just like him, and Rebecca, his mom. She had Mark's eyes and his mom's facial structure. Her blond hair was considerably darker than I remembered.

Just before leaving the hospital I asked Lisa if she would show me her lower left side. Without hesitation, she pulled her T-shirt away from her body and pulled her jeans lower.

The sailboat was still sailing the downy seas of my precious Lisa's low back. Now I had no doubts.

My baby was back with me. I remember thinking, *It would scare you to hear how much I love you. It would probably scare me to say it out loud. I would've killed for you. I would've moved mountains. I cannot tell you these things yet, but I will at some point.*

My phone wasn't in my pocket. I had to run back inside the hospital and grab my phone, which I'd left charging in the waiting room. The ER doctor came strolling through and stopped beside me.

"She's very young," he said, "but that's no reason she can't be an excellent mother just like you."

I looked at him, astonished. "What's that mean?"

"You know, your granddaughter. Lisa's baby."

I was stunned. I couldn't speak. He walked on past and disappeared through a door on the opposite wall.

Just like that. I was a grandmother. My heart raced; my eyes clouded over. Then I fainted.

Twenty minutes later I was lying in an ER room, shoes removed and a damp cloth on my forehead.

A pretty young nurse was sitting in the chair beside me. "How long since you've eaten anything, Mrs. Sellars?"

My mind worked back over the past few days. "Probably just hours."

"We're giving you an IV. When you feel ready, you can stand up. Shall I call your husband?"

"Yes."

Mark came inside the curtained room, followed by Lisa. Tears rushed into my eyes when I saw her. It was the last thing I could have expected.

"Where's your daughter?" I asked her.

Mark looked at me, incredulous. "Wait, what?"

"She's dead."

Which is when I lapsed into unconsciousness again.

IT WAS JUST TOO MUCH after all I'd been through. I was a grandmother, Lisa had given birth, and Mark was a grandfather.

The next morning, I came awake in my hospital room. In a panic, I realized Lisa wasn't in the room, though I don't know why I thought she would be. I plunged the CALL button, and a nurse came. "You're awake!" she said in a bouncy voice. "Let's get you into the bathroom."

We did that. Then she sent for breakfast. It arrived thirty minutes later, heavy on the protein: eggs and bacon. Plus orange juice and toast. They even brought a cup of decaf.

Mark and Lisa arrived and arranged themselves around my bed.

"How did she die?" was the first thing I asked.

"She got sick and we had no medicine. It was quick."

"How old was she?"

"Three years old. She looked liked me."

She started crying then, and took the chair beside my bed. She drew her legs up under her and turned her head to the side. I reached out and touched her ankle. "Hey, we can talk about it some other time. I'm sorry."

"I'm sorry, too."

"I'm being discharged," I said. "We can go home in about an hour."

Mark said, "I have us booked for O'Hare on a three o'clock flight. Can we make it?"

"Easy," I said.

Lisa stood and leaned over. She reached and took my hand in hers.

I could have died right then and there and been totally at peace.

"I'm glad you're okay," she said. She then bent and kissed my forehead.

"Thank you, beautiful Lisa."

Then we flew home to Chicago.

29

L isa chose the bedroom at the end of our upstairs hall. It had previously done service as a second guest room and was very Country French in furniture and wall hangings. I could see why she liked it there; the place had a strong, substantial feel. So we moved her in there and began shopping for clothes. And books. And videos. Add to that computer lessons from Geek Fleet.

Her third week back with us, I came home early with a headache. James was in trial and Gladys was still in school as it was just after midday. Upstairs I plodded to my bedroom, where I slipped into sweatpants and a T-shirt. Usually, I'll go downstairs to the workout room when I'm headachy and sweat it out. Just as I was leaving my room, I heard a small cry from Lisa's room.

I wasn't snooping--I walked toward her room in my bare feet, and I suppose my footsteps were muted.

Outside her bedroom, I stopped, as she was obviously on her new phone.

But with who? It must be Mark, I finally decided. Mark was living in Glencoe with his parents and saw Lisa nearly every day. I didn't want to interrupt. As it turned out, I heard her end of the conversation.

"Just tell me she's okay." Lisa sounded like she was pleading. "Don't make jokes."

Long pause.

Then she said, "I don't know what they have. Nobody has told me."

Another pause.

"Now that would be stupid. They'd be all over me."

At that point, I rustled my feet on the carpet and knocked on her door frame.

"Lisa?" I called. "Can I come in?"

"Just a minute!" Then, "Okay."

The phone was nowhere to be seen. She was sitting at her small desk, casually leafing through *Seventeen*. I had asked her to snip out pages with cute outfits she'd like. She had; there were a few off to the side.

"Friends?" I asked.

"I don't have any. I've only been here three weeks."

"Oh, I just thought I heard you on the phone."

"You did? What was I saying?"

"You seemed to be asking how one of your girlfriends was doing. Who was it? No, I'm not going to pry. Yes, I am. You've only been here three weeks. I'm asking myself, who could she possibly know? Would you set your old mom's mind at ease and tell me if you've found some buddies to pal around with? That would make me very happy." There it was; I was prying and couldn't help myself. Screw it.

"No, it wasn't that. I was talking to someone in Mexico."

"Mexico isn't on your cell phone plan."

"I added it," she said. "I had to call someone."

"Now that worries me. What would you be calling someone about?"

"This and that. Just asking how my friends are doing. Nothing else."

"Everyone okay?"

"Yes, everyone's okay."

I sat down on her bed and put my arms behind to support me. It felt fantastic to be in my daughter's room with my daughter there actually talking to me. Instead of the dreams and fantasies, I'd harbored all those years about having times like this with my daughter, it was real. No fantasy, no dream.

"Lisa, please tell me about your baby. How long was delivery?"

"Three days."

"Wow. Who was the father?"

"Javier Menendez. He's the one who was always with me."

Javier, Javier, Javier. I was running it through my mind. It was a man named Javier that Velasquez had sent to bring me, Lisa. He had returned with Susannah instead. Of course; he didn't want to give up Lisa, who he was having sex with. It was beginning to come together in my mind.

"Was that Javier on the phone?"

Her face fell. "Yes."

"Did you call him?"

"He called me. He's lonesome and misses me."

"Do you miss him?"

"Good God, no way!"

"Good. Are you done with him?"

"I hope the ground opens up and he falls in. I hate that man!"

I brought my hands around and leaned forward, forearms on my knees. She was still bent over her desk, casually turning magazine pages without really looking. There was more here than I knew. But I decided not to push it. The last thing I wanted on God's earth was to alienate my daughter. The very last thing. So I changed the subject.

"We're going out of town next weekend. To Chicago, actually, where we're going to stay overnight and see a play. The Curtises are going with us. Would you like to stay with your dad and grandparents while we're gone?"

"I'd like that, yes."

"Good. I'll tell your dad, and he can work it out with you. I hate the idea of being away from you, but we both need to learn to be apart without being overly anxious, you and I. At least I do."

"Oh. Okay."

"What, you don't want me to go?"

"No, it's okay. I'm just going to miss you guys is all."

"We'll miss you, sweetie. But we'll be back bright and early Sunday morning. We can all get brunch or something."

"Okay."

She was still absently turning pages. Her back was to me, and her T-shirt hung away from her jeans, so I had a view of the lower left kidney.

I could see her sailboat. It had come home to port.

My God, I was getting maudlin. I guess that's what a kidnapping does to a mother.

30

Ignacio Velasquez hated getting undressed for bed. So he let others do that for him--the twelve-year-olds, the fifteens, the seventeens. They would then spend the night with him. When he was done with each one, he would pass her along to his lieutenants. Which is how Lisa Sellars fell into the hands of Javier Menendez, the next-in-line who was given the young girl when Velasquez had had his fill of her youth and innocence and beauty.

Javier didn't wait long. She was pregnant two months after falling into his clutches when she was thirteen-years-old. She gave birth to a daughter, a beautiful brown baby named Elena Sellars by her mother. Javier surprisingly allowed the girl to keep her baby. Ordinarily, the *putas'* fetuses were aborted; Lisa was allowed to carry to term. The mother and her baby were kept close by Javier and, when the baby was three, the mother celebrated her sixteenth birthday. Two months later, Lisa was bought and paid for with a bribe from her mother Melissa, delivered to Ignacio Velasquez by the chief of the Federal Police in Tijuana.

Velasquez got the million. But Javier wanted more than the ten thousand dollars he received out of the bribe. He was hungry, and the easy money--especially the ten-thousand that was all but tossed at him--only whetted his appetite. So he made a plan, a plan that he took first to Velasquez himself.

"You gave my wife away for ten thousand dollars," Javier began. He wasn't at all afraid of Velasquez; they were cousins and had played cowboys and Indians together since they were just into long pants.

"But I got much more than that for the *puta*," Velasquez smirked. "She almost earned what she cheated me out of in Riyadh."

"I want more for her. I want those people to pay me one million dollars for my *puta*."

"So what will you do?" Velasquez asked. He knew Javier had a good mind and that he--Velasquez--would take the larger portion of any other money Javier managed to drag home.

"I have her baby, Elena. She lives with me, and she is a good baby. But I would snap her neck in an instant and throw her to the pigs if someone doesn't pay me."

"Of course."

"I have spoken to Lisa in Chicago. She told me the people who purchased her are quite wealthy. She can get their money to buy her baby."

"Do Lisa's parents know about the baby?"

"Lisa told them the baby was dead."

"Why do that?"

"So they wouldn't try to steal her back. That would get her baby killed. She is looking for assets of her parents to buy the baby from me."

"And from me. Don't forget my first bite."

The men laughed, Velasquez more raucously than Menendez.

"So what do you want from me?" Velasquez asked.

"I need some person to go to Chicago."

"For what?"

"To kill Melissa Sellars. She is Lisa's mother."

"Why her?"

"Because then Lisa's father will pay up."

"To protect his grandchild."

"Exactly."

"Who do you want?"

"I remember the man who killed the Tijuana police. He cut off their heads and rolled them in the door at the police station. That man knows what I need."

"You have talked to him?"

"I have. His name is Ishmael Montague. He is from Argentina."

Velasquez smiled and held up one hand. "Who do you believe hired him for Tijuana?"

"Hired him to kill those policemen? You?"

"Aiiiee, Javier. You forget so fast. Of course me! I will give him to you for Chicago. He will find your wife's mother."

"She is not my wife. She is my whore."

"Whatever," Velasquez sighed heavily. "The whore who had your baby. That's a wife, Javier."

"She is not my wife."

"All right, Javier. We are done here. I will make some calls, and you will meet this Montague in Tijuana at our cantina."

"All right. Thank you, Iggy."

Velasquez brushed Javier's words away with a wave of his hand. "Forget about it. You my cousin. You get the best I have. You always did."

One week later, Javier met the man in the dark hat in the Tijuana cantina. The man was waiting at the last table. He was alone, smoking cigarettes from a red box, and where his jacket slumped open, Javier could plainly see the man's huge gun. It looked like a Smith and Wesson .44 Magnum, the gun of *Dirty Harry*. So pretentious, Javier thought to himself, but so powerful. The man was evil incarnate-- exactly what Javier needed.

Before Javier could join his man and sit at the table, Montague raised a hand and stopped him. "Wait. Before you sit down, do you have my money?"

Javier reached inside his jacket and pulled out a fat enve- lope. "A hundred now, a hundred after."

Montague counted the money, arranging it in stacks of ten thousand dollars each. When he had assembled ten such stacks, he swept the bills together and stuffed them back into the envelope. That was worked inside his coat pocket, all the while Montague keeping eye contact with Javier.

"Just give me her name and address. You promised a picture as well."

Menendez snaked his phone loose from his pocket and held the screen up to Montague's face.

"This is the woman. I received this picture last night. My *puta* took it of her mother over dinner."

"Not bad. How dead do you want her?"

"Dead enough to frighten her ex-husband into paying."

"What about your *puta*? What do you want with her?"

"Leave her alone. Unless she gets in the way."

"What about anybody else?"

"Kill anybody who gets in your way. But don't miss the mother."

Montague took a swallow of his beer. "What of the mother's husband? Will he be a problem?"

"This *pinche* is an *abogado*. He's useless and he's weak. Just avoid him."

"When do I do this?"

"Immediately. Iggy wants his money."

"Done. Leave me now."

"Thank you, Montague."

Javier disappeared back outside in the bright sunlight, climbed into his pickup truck, and headed back to the *finca*.

The mother was already dead.

She only needed to hear about it now.

31

The killer had been to Chicago before, and he had killed people there. As his Los Angeles-Chicago flight circled O'Hare airspace, he looked down at the vast spread of city lights. "Somewhere you are waiting," he muttered. "We have a meeting, you and me."

The 757 landed and taxied up to the jetway. During the offloading of passengers, Montague remained in his seat with his face averted. He was wearing his dark hat and fake sideburns and mustache. Anyone who did pay any attention to him would give the police the wrong description if it ever came to that--which was highly doubtful.

He had decided to choke her with piano wire. That was the easiest and most efficient way without the necessity of purchasing a gun, which might be traced. The plan was to take her in her parking garage at work.

With his false driver's license and prepaid Visa, he rented a black Accord and headed downtown. It was almost seven o'clock; still, he wished to stake out her house that night. He wanted to do this because he meant to kill her the next day. He'd already purchased his return flight ticket and didn't want a delay.

From Chicago, he drove north past Evanston, past Winnetka, and into Glencoe. There was no GPS being used. GPS could later be traced by the police, and rental cars that had followed a GPS signal were a common search item for homicide dicks. Montague knew this and left the in-dash unit switched off.

Montague had done his research. He knew the town was one of the wealthiest in America. Driving past the lakefront houses toward Melissa Sellars's home, Montague whistled and shook his head. Such blatant displays of wealth by the town's inhabitants. People like Montague would never display their wealth--and he was very wealthy. It attracted missions such as the one he was on that night. Wealth brought out not just the curious but also the evil ones. No, Montague lived in the shadows, far from the pretty homes and lakeside neighborhoods in Buenos Aires. It was nothing like what he saw as he drove down street after street.

Three miles inside the city limits he located her address several streets inland from Glencoe Beach. He drove on down to the end of her street and drove past her home a second time.

There was no doubt. He had found her.

32

L isa called Mark the night before Montague came to Chicago. She had something important to tell him. So, Mark drove over to his ex-wife's house and rang the bell. Lisa answered and asked if they could go somewhere to talk.

They climbed into Mark's pickup and headed to the Leather Cheshire, a restaurant-club downtown. Inside, Mark told the hostess they needed someplace quiet, and she led them to a table all alone in a dark alcove. She plopped down menus and said she'd be back. Mark said no, they were ready to order, and he ordered two coffees just to get the waitress to leave them alone for awhile. He told the frowning woman they'd probably want dinner in about twenty minutes, to check back.

"So," he said, leaning back on his side of the booth. "What brings my daughter out to talk to me tonight?"

Lisa was fighting back the tears. She wiped at her eyes with both hands and then broke down. "I talked to Javier."

"Okay, which one is Javier?"

"He's the one who got me pregnant."

"The father of the baby that died?"

"Dad, I don't know you at all, and I don't know how you're going to take this. The baby didn't die. I lied to you guys about that because I was afraid you'd go back with a gun. Especially you, with the Army stuff and all. It would have got you killed. Maybe her, too."

"Damn, Lisa, always tell me the truth, daughter. I'm not like that at all. I do smart, not stupid. Okay?"

"Okay."

"A baby?"

"A little girl."

"So what did you and this Javier discuss?"

"He has my baby. Her name is Elena, and she's three."

He did the math. "You gave birth when you were thirteen?"

"Uh-huh. Yes. They do that down there. He has Elena now, and I told him I want her. He said I could have her, but he wants more money from you."

"How much more?"

"One million dollars. Just like before except this time you deliver the money to him. He's going to break off from Iggy and take the baby to Ensenada and wait there for you to come with the money."

"We'll do it. Your grandparents will supply the money in a heartbeat. So what's the first step?"

Lisa was again crying, this time loud enough that the waitress returned. "You okay, sugar?"

"I'm okay."

"She's okay. It's just a hard story. Thank you."

The waitress left.

Again, "What's the first step?"

"That's not everything. Javier is sending someone after mom. He's going to have her killed, so you know he's serious. He's going to have her killed, and my baby dies forty-eight hours later if he doesn't get the money in Ensenada by then."

"Jesus! Well, how long have you known this?"

"Since yesterday. I didn't know what to do. These are horrible people, and I don't want my mom or dad getting hurt by them. Then I knew I had to tell you."

"Tell me what else he said. Everything, Lisa."

"The man is coming tomorrow. I am to remain in my room and not interfere. If I interfere or tell anyone--"

"They kill Elena."

"Worse. He said he would hurt her first!"

The crying turned to sobbing and Mark went around the table and sat down beside his daughter. He put his arm up around her shoulders and pulled her close. With his free hand, he took her hand in his and held her while she got it all out. After several minutes, it subsided and she was reaching for a napkin to clean up. Mark moved slightly away and withdrew his arm.

"We're not going to let Javier hurt your baby. I'm going to get her back."

"What will you do? I know if the man doesn't call Javier to say Mom's dead he will kill Elena. So you can't just have him arrested, Dad."

"No one said anything about arresting anyone, sweetheart. That's not what we're going to do at all."

"What will you do?"

"Pass me your phone."

She passed him her new phone.

"Which one of these is Javier's number?"

"It starts with a six-one."

"Okay." Mark dialed the number and waited.

"Dad, what are you doing?"

"I'm going to tell him I'm on the way with the money. I'm telling him that if he hurts Mom, there will be no money."

"Dad! He'll hurt my baby!"

"No, he won't. Just wait."

Lisa could hear the phone ringing. Finally, a recording answered and invited the caller to leave a message.

Mark ended the call. "I won't leave a message. I need to talk to him myself. We need to wait a few minutes and I'll call again. How about dessert?"

They ordered two desserts and chatted while they slowly ate and had seconds of coffee.

Then it was time to call again.

Mark dialed the number for Javier.

Again, the phone rang and rang. Then a voice came on and said the number was no longer working.

"Damn!" Mark exclaimed. "Is there any other number for him?"

"No. That's the only one I have. I don't know what's wrong."

"All right. First of all, I have to move your mom. Someplace the killer won't look. Then I have to set a trap."

"Oh, Dad, you know how to do this? Are you sure Elena won't be hurt?"

"Honey, there are no guarantees about anything. Call Mom on your phone. Tell her to stay inside and lock the doors. Tell her I'm on the way and don't call the police. If they get involved your baby's life expectancy is very short."

"I'm dialing her now."

"Hang on."

33

M ark and Lisa got to my house less than ten minutes after Lisa called me and scared me to death. "Mom," she said through her tears, "stay in the house and lock the doors. Dad's driving me. We'll explain." I went around and locked the doors. James wasn't home yet, but he soon would be. Gladys was with me in the family room watching videos while I read. It was one of those nights where we just liked to hang out, make popcorn and hot apple cider, and get sleepy.

The garage door went up--Lisa's phone was programmed to open it--as I leaned out the door leading down into the garage.

"What is it?" I called. They came bounding out of the car and up the steps.

"Does James keep a gun here?"

"I don't know. Yes, in the attic I think there's one his father had."

Mark pushed past Lisa and she came up the stairs behind him.

"Will someone please tell me what's going on? Do I need to hide Gladys?"

Mark cried out, "Where's the attic? Where would the gun be kept? What would it be in?"

"His dad's foot locker. Hallway closet, a ladder pulls down."

Mark was off. Lisa locked the door at the top of the stairs and turned to me. "It's all my fault. I am so sorry to bring this here."

Whatever trouble we were in, I wasn't going to let Lisa frame it as if she brought it here.

"You didn't bring something here. We have our daughter back, and her life is what it is. We love you, and we'll take care of whatever--"

"Found it!" Mark cried down through the attic opening. We had moved into the hallway and were waiting when he yelled. "It's a .45 ACP 1911. Great gun, full magazine. Shells might not even fire, but he won't know that."

Mark started climbing back down the stairs, the gun stuck inside the back pocket of his jeans. Then he turned to me.

"Lisa's baby didn't die."

Shocked, surely I didn't hear things correctly. There was a baby alive?

"Whose--"

"I lied, Mom. Elena didn't die. She's three years old."

"We have a granddaughter? Where is she?"

"Javier has her."

"I remember that bastard," I said, his face coming back to my mind. "He's the man who brought me Susannah instead of you. He's a son-of-a-bitch."

I don't usually swear like that, but Javier was at the top of my shit list. And now he had my granddaughter?

"That bastard has sent someone to kill you, Mel," Mark said. "He could even be in town already."

"My God, James!"

"I think James will be okay. It's you he's after."

"But why?"

"Long story short, to get more money out of us."

"He's selling us Elena."

Mark added, "But he's killing you first. Or trying to. Luckily, Lisa called me, and I'm all over it. Let's all go into the kitchen and have a seat."

I knew what he was doing. The family room opened on the street side of the house. The kitchen was on the back side, behind an electronic security fence. The whole place was rigged with cameras and sensors by ADT. I grabbed Gladys and steered her by the shoulders into the kitchen even while she was trying to get away and return to her video. I spoke sharply to her, and she gave it up, shoving my hand away and walking on her own.

What age does it start? I remember thinking. What age is it where they no longer need you--they think. Then what age is it when you've held on too long, and they don't need you anymore? Lisa was at one end of that age spectrum, Gladys was at the other. Except I wasn't letting anybody go. Hell, that night I wasn't even letting Mark go. "Stay here in the kitchen with us," I told him when he said he'd be right back, that he was going to check the cameras. He smiled and went ahead, regardless of my worry.

I needed to be kept busy. I poured more cold apple cider into a saucepan and began heating it. I stood over and watched the bubbles start, thinking. So, I had a granddaughter. "How old is she?" I said over my shoulder to Lisa.

"Three. She looks just like me. With dark skin, of course."

"Oh, the father is who?"

"Javier. I think."

"Oh, my God."

"It's all right, Mom. I'm all right. I survived, and now I'm home."

I couldn't help it; my eyes filled up with tears at the thoughts and pictures in my mind of a younger Lisa being abused by those animals. But then something else happened. It was like when I was shooting myself in the head but didn't. That was the first time I felt that overarching anger in my soul, the kind that's willing to die for the right outcome. That's what I felt as the bubbles increased and the apple cider smell filled the kitchen. In fact, I was mad as hell. The thought of those devils blithely sending someone to kill me, to end my life, all for money. I knew then that if I died, it was going to be for some greater cause than money. It was going to be for my kids and grandkid. Nothing less would take my life.

Mark returned from checking the cameras. "I texted my dad. He's bringing over my guns."

"Is that safe?"

"James isn't home yet. He can pull into the garage in his spot, and we'll close the door behind him. I can get my guns and send Dad on his way. No need to worry, it was Dad who taught me to shoot long before I joined the Army. He's strapped and ready for anything."

"All right."

"It'll just be a few."

It was then that I handed out mugs of hot apple cider. Soon we were gathered around the table, my husband's pistol on the table next to Mark, waiting for his father to call and tells us to let him into the garage. We had a long moment then of just being together. It felt right, Mark, me, Lisa and Gladys. It felt like a whole family. Not a happy family, but it felt complete just like we were. Then Marks' father, Charlie, called. He was coming up our street. Mark grabbed the gun and went into the garage. We heard the garage door rattling up and heard a car come roaring inside then the motor shutting off. It was silent, but then a door slammed, and the engine started up again and then shortly after the garage door closed again.

Mark returned carrying two guns that looked like the ones you see on the SWAT team shows.

"He went back home. Okay, Mel, let me show you how to operate this weapon."

He showed me the charging handle, how to set the safety off, point, and squeeze the trigger. Don't pull, squeeze. I was determined and memorized every piece of it. If the man came inside my house, I was fully prepared to shoot him dead.

Mark said he had called James and told him what was up. He's made him promise not to call the police. James was driving home as fast as possible.

"I'm going to sit with the video screens," Mark said. If you hear shooting stay in here, point your gun at the door, and shoot anyone you don't recognize."

"Really? Anyone?"

"Yes, really. If they make it this far, that will mean they got past me. Then it's up to you, Mel. You must shoot him to save these kids."

"I will," I said. "And I won't hesitate and ask questions. I'll shoot first."

"I'm down with that. All right, here I go."

Mark went into the other room, and the girls and I huddled closer to the kitchen table.

An hour later, James' Volvo could be heard pulling into the garage. I breathed a huge sigh of relief. Now there were two men against one.

"Hold your fire, Mel! James is coming in. Point your gun at the floor."

I did as I was told and James came charging in. He immediately took the gun from me and checked the safety. He released the magazine, checked it, and slammed it back into the gun and pulled the charging handle.

"Locked and loaded!" he exclaimed.

Mark watched all this. "You've done this before."

James smiled grimly. "ROTC. University of Illinois. We had summer camp and learned to shoot."

So, we were set. Two men who loved me, each of them armed, and me safe with my daughters.

But suddenly I felt a stab of pain for the one who wasn't there. For the empty place at the table.

Elena. There was one more chair, and it was hers.

THE NEXT MORNING, I was needed at the studio. I got up and looked downstairs. Both Mark and James were still awake, manning their places at the video screen and the back of the house.

"I've been roaming the house all night," James told me and kissed me good morning.

"You must be exhausted."

"I called the office and told Sylvia to cancel my day. Mark and I are going to trade off today so we can get some sleep."

Mark came into the kitchen then, where James and I had drifted. I wasn't surprised to see the two girls already there, sharing a Raisin Bran box between them. They were chattering and really getting to know each other, and that gladdened me.

"I need to go to Chicago," I announced. "How do you guys want to do this?"

"No Chicago. Not today," Mark barked. "We can't guard you there."

"Sorry, but I can't miss it. Should I call the police to come?"

"No."

I knew why. The man had to be killed. It would never stop otherwise.

"So what do I do?"

"I'll ride shotgun with you," Mark said. "The guy is after you. I should be with you. James will stay with the girls."

"I have school," Gladys announced.

"Not today, honey," her dad said. "You and Lisa are staying with me today. Don't worry, we'll make it fun. Like pizza for lunch kind of fun."

"Mommy, what's wrong?" Gladys wanted to know. "How come everyone's here?"

"We're having a family meeting," I told her. "Mommy and Mark are going to Mommy's studio while Daddy stays with you and Lisa. Is that okay?"

"Works for me, Mommy," said Gladys.

I couldn't help but laugh. I wondered where they got that stuff. TV, that's all it could be.

At 7:30 a.m. Mark and I went into the garage and climbed into his pickup. He was openly carrying his rifle and had the handgun stuck inside the waistband of his jeans. He had scanned the video screens for anyone nearby and saw nothing unusual. So we raised the garage door and started backing out.

At just that moment, Lisa came bursting out the front door, running for my truck window.

I rolled down the glass.

"He's a Mexican, and his name is Ishmael. He cut off the heads of some police officers. I heard him bragging about it to Iggy."

"Thank you, Lisa, but why are you out here? You could have told me inside."

"I--I--just love you and want you to be safe."

At which moment, Mark gunned the engine and waved Lisa back. We watched her turn and go back inside the house. While we were having our moment, Lisa and me, Mark was scanning the streets and shadows around us, looking for whatever might be lurking.

Then we were backed out, pulled forward, and moving down the street. When we made a left turn at the far end, I noticed a car come from our right and slow down to let us go first at the stop sign. Mark watched the car in his rearview mirror. Then he turned randomly off on a side street.

The car followed us. I turned to look.

"It's a black car. Something Japanese, I'm thinking."

"Honda Accord," Mark said, and I was surprised at how fast he'd gotten to know all the cars since returning from

Afghanistan. But that was Mark: he lived and breathed guns and cars. It was just who he was.

We turned right at the first corner then right again until we were heading back toward the main road. The Accord followed us exactly, making no effort to disguise that it was following.

"I'm going to stop and go back and question this guy," Mark said. He slammed on the brakes and jumped out of his side. Back behind him the Accord slowed then suddenly began backing away at high speed. Something was definitely up. Mark ran back to the truck, jumped in, and turned around to chase after the car.

By the time we got back to the corner, the black car was gone. We had no idea which way to turn, so Mark backed up again, and we headed back to the main road.

"I can only assume that was him," Mark said.

"Them," I corrected him. "I definitely saw two heads in the Accord."

Mark looked over at me. "Sure?"

"Positive."

"All right, then."

We hurried up to the stoplight and made a left then a right onto the main road to Chicago. Our speed picked up and almost instantly we were hemmed in on all sides and behind by aggressive, in-bound Chicago traffic.

"Watch the mirrors," Mark said. "I'll take the windshield."

Twenty minutes later we bypassed Winnetka and continued

south. I had been watching the mirrors, making sure the black car wasn't around.

"You know what could have happened?" Mark asked. "There could be more than one car. A second car could be following us on our bumper right now, and we'd never know it. In fact, it wouldn't surprise me at all."

"You think he brought more than just himself?"

"I don't know that he brought them. These cartel people are connected everywhere. Lining up a few more warm bodies to help him track and kill you would be easy for him. Luckily for us, these aren't the most sophisticated killers in the world. But the flip side is, they have no fear. They'll gladly take a bullet to impress the cartel chiefs. That's what we're dealing with today."

I couldn't think of anything to say in reply. The whole insane thing was more than I could comprehend. I'm a quiet woman, haven't known any violence in my life, and the idea that someone was out to kill me was just a little absurd. Why? Because I hadn't done anything. I had paid them for Lisa. And I was willing to pay them now for Elena. So where did this killing me come from? It made no sense, and I was having a hard time accepting that that's really what they wanted.

Until we hit the Chicago city limits.

Then everything changed.

34

We were stopped at a red light, and I know, for me at least, I was feeling a little better being back in the city where there were lots of people around.

Wrong.

A car across the intersection in the left turn lane with its blinker flashing came out and began a long, looping turn until it was directly across from us. Suddenly it straightened out and came right for us, ramming us in the front end. At the exact same moment, a car behind--a white SUV--rammed into us from the rear. I saw this one coming, and I remember thinking to myself, this can't actually be happening.

But it was.

The next thing I knew, there was a man at each of our windows, and they were firing their pistols at us. Mark shot back at the man on my side. Then I saw Mark's head explode toward me as a bullet came through his window and passed through his head and struck me in the temple. I slumped forward and at that exact moment felt a searing pain in my chest. The men must have panicked just then because the shooting stopped as abruptly as it had begun. I heard a man cry out, "Get the bitch's picture, pendejo. We need the proof!" Suddenly, the sirens were coming, and there were no more voices.

Then it was dark, and I was falling into a warm black pool and disappearing into its folds like velvet.

A THOUGHT. Where am I? An eye opening. Lots of tiny blinking lights, hushed voices.

Then out again.

Both eyes open. I try focusing but cannot. It is all double images. Then I see a face and try to make it out.

Detective McMann. From when Lisa was abducted. What was she doing here? Then it was black again.

The next time my eyes opened I knew it was dark outside. A nurse stood beside my bed. She was holding an instrument in my ear.

"Hello, Melissa," she said solemnly. "Are you feeling like you want to wake up a little bit?"

"Where am I?"

"Hospital. You were shot."

Parts of it came back to me. "Who shot me?"

"You'll have to talk to the detective about that. She's down in the cafeteria."

Then another flash of memory. "Where's Mark?"

I heard a voice off to my left and recognized it as my husband. James had been waiting.

"Mark died," he said. "I'm sorry, Mel. But he shot one of them. Put a hole dead center between his eyes. Detective McMann and the others are running ID on him now."

"How long have I been out?"

"One day. You've been in and out but these are your first words."

"Where are the girls?"

"Home. I hired a security team to stay with them. They're well-protected, believe me."

"Home? Are we going home?"

Then I was out again. The next time my eyes opened, it was morning, and several men in white coats were standing at the side of my bed. In front of them was a stout woman with gray hair parted down the middle and a button on her frock that said something like, "Ask me. If I don't know, I'll ask another woman."

She reached out and touched my arm.

"Damage report, Melissa. Do you want to hear?"

"Yes."

"We removed bullet fragments from the left side of your face. You'll need some minor plastic surgery at that site. You were shot in the right chest. Pneumothorax which we repaired. A defensive wound through your right hand where you raised a hand to defend yourself. Don't try to lift that arm; you can't. You were also struck in the low back when you flew forward after the chest shot. This bullet missed your kidney by less than an inch and traveled straight down. It exited out of your thigh after nicking the thigh bone. You were very lucky. These are students standing behind me. I'm Doctor Lewinsky, and I'm your treating. I expect you'll be able to leave here by tomorrow morning, barring any unforeseen developments."

"What about Mark? How did he die?"

"Gunshot wound to the head. Fragments of that bullet pierced the side of your head and face."

Detective McMann appeared later that morning.

Her first words were, "Mark died protecting you. He shot the man outside your window. Right between the eyes. Then Mark died when he was shot in the head by the man on his side. He could have saved himself by shooting the man on his side, but he didn't. He chose to save you instead."

Hot tears for Mark filled my eyes, but I was too doped-up to feel much more. I said a silent prayer and thanked Mark for saving me. He had always been there for me, I told him. I would never forget him. Then I was out again.

THEN I WAS HOME. For the most part, I was ambulatory. It was slow-going, but at least I was up and around mostly with the help of a cane. This was thanks to my nicked thigh bone and the wound to the leg which had required cleaning and sewing. The leg was extremely sore and throbbed at night after the Oxy wore off. I quit the pain pills the next day. It was my decision because of how terribly addictive they are. I just didn't want to add that to my list of woes.

Lisa came to me the first afternoon I was back. She sat beside me on the couch then leaned forward, her head slumped down on her chest.

"We haven't got to talk yet," I said. "Except I think you told me in the hospital you hadn't heard anything?"

"He hasn't called me."

"He has your number?"

"I'm positive he does."

"You've tried his number again?"

"Way more than I should have. It's out of service. They go through phones like we go through coffee cups. That's why they're so hard for the DEA to track down and kill. We were always moving on a moment's notice. Kids running and crying, women throwing clothes and belongings into pillow-cases, running for the trucks, tearing out. It never stopped."

"What do we do about Elena?"

She turned to me with her eyes brimming over. "Honestly? I don't know. I mean--I mean--"

"Come here."

She leaned against my left side--my good side--, and I grasped her shoulders with my arm. Together we both just sat there several minutes. We were beaten down, and we had no ideas left, no plans, no sense of where to even start.

Elena was lost to us, and Javier wasn't calling.

WE BURIED Mark in a grave dug through snow and dirt. Lisa tossed the first handful on his casket when all was said and done. I tossed the second. We stood shoulder-to-shoulder, crying with our heads together as a strong wind threatened to peel away our topcoats and hats and pierced our gloves.

James drove us home in total silence. Lisa was up front with him; I was riding in back with Gladys. Armed security officers followed us in a van.

It weighed heavily on my mind that Mark was Lisa's biological father while I wasn't her biological mother. I realized I'd always felt like that fact gave him a little more right to have her in his life than I did. Compared to him, I was a mommy-come-lately. Now that he was gone I wasn't sure I'd be enough for her, just me without him. Would she need to go find her biological mother? I didn't know. It didn't frighten me, either way. It just made me feel that much more sorrow for my baby, my girl, my Lisa. When was life going to stop hammering this kid? I wondered. Hadn't she suffered enough?

James took the last turn on Oak Drive and came up our street, pulling into our driveway. It was then I saw her standing beside our front door, her back to the wall, smoking and smiling as we pulled in.

Susannah. My original Lisa had come home too.

There had been no forewarning, no calls from her; I had no idea she even knew what state I lived in, but then I remembered Isaac talking to her on the way to the hospital after we rescued her. She'd been asking him all kinds of questions about Chicago and fun things to do, and I vaguely remember Isaac telling her that the town where I lived-- Glencoe--was very ritzy and she would hate it there.

That remained to be seen. Hopefully not so.

35

"He could leave at any time," Susannah was telling us after supper. We were all gathered around the kitchen table and had just wolfed down pimento-cheese sandwiches and tomato soup. Now we were nibbling Fritos, and Lisa was brewing coffee a cup at a time in the Keurig and passing them around.

"Where is he again?" I asked her. "Rosarito Beach? Is that California?"

"It's Baja California. South of San Ysidro about thirty or forty miles. It's a cool place with lots of beach, cheap housing and tons of great food. We stayed in this house before. I think it belongs to Iggy, but anyone can go there anytime."

"And you're sure Elena's with him?"

"She was when I talked to him this morning. She and the twins he had with Marisa. Marisa is there too and Juanita, who's Javier's older sister. She's always with him."

"Why did you call him?" I asked.

"Iggy won't take me back. He said I should call Javier and he gave me his phone number. So I called him. He asked me about the time I was with you, Melissa. He asked me if I'd seen you again. I said no. He said good. He said some other choice things about you, too, but I won't repeat those."

"My God," Lisa said from behind me, "Tell me everything he said about Elena."

"Nothing, really. She was just another name to him when he was telling me who all was there. He wanted to know did I want to come to help Juanita with the kids and I asked him which kids. That was when he said it."

"How did you leave it with him?" I asked.

"I said I was coming down."

"When?"

"He told me to bring money. First, he said I should try to steal money from my parents. We're not talking again, them and me, but that's a whole other story. He mentioned Lisa's name and told me he had scored huge with her parents."

"That's a joke! Just the money my Mom gave Iggy for me. Nothing since."

"That's cool," Susannah said. "I'm not saying give him anything."

I had been thinking several moments now. Then I jumped in.

"Susannah, could you take me to his house?"

"Sure. I've been there lots."

"Would you take me and not tell him?"

"I don't know. What are you going to do to him?"

"I haven't decided."

"Will I be staying with him?"

I surprised even myself just then. "No," I said, "you'll be coming back here with this family. You'll live with us while we figure out your life."

"Figure out my life. That' s a funny way to put it," Susannah laughed. "I need to write that down."

"So will you take me there?"

"Will I have to go in?"

"No, I'll be the only one going in."

"What will you do to him? Are you going to kill him and take Elena?"

"Yes. That's exactly what I think I'm going to do."

"Mom!" cried Lisa.

"Mel, honey," James began, but I raised my hand. "Everyone just hold it. This man just killed a man I loved very much. Then he stole my daughter and raped her. Now he has my grandchild. My answer for his life is much easier. He has to go."

"Wow," said Susannah. "You're serious. And you really mean it about me coming here with you?"

"I do. You won't be staying here forever. Neither will Lisa. But we need to help you two get a start in life. At first, you will be living here with us."

Susannah rolled her eyes at the ceiling and dabbed at her eyes with her napkin. "Wow," she said. "Just wow."

James leaned toward me. "You know I can't allow this Mexico thing, Melissa," he said under his breath.

I looked hard at him.

"I don't remember asking you. Nor do I remember turning over my life to you. I married you, and, if you'll remember, no one gave me away. I kept me, and you kept you. Now you do whatever you need, but I'm going after my grand baby, and that's final. From here on you're either with me or you're not. And I won't accept not."

He looked shocked, then amazed. But then his eyes opened wide, and a smile crept across his face.

"How can I help?"

That was the last he had to say about it.

36

I stood right there and heard Susannah talk to Javier with her phone on speaker.

"My dad gave me fifty-thousand-dollars. I'm on my way down to you."

"My beautiful girl! When will you be here?"

"Tomorrow. I'm bringing my mom to meet you. She wants us to get married."

Long silence. The wheels were definitely turning.

"Your mom? Here? I don't think that would be--"

"It's the only way, Javier. Otherwise, I don't get to come."

"Well, then bring her. But she can't stay or nothing."

"She just wants to see where I'll be staying. Plus she wants to meet you before she hands over the money."

"She's welcome to come and do all that. We'll have it all cleaned up and sparkling, so there is no problem."

"Excellent. Now you're at the place two kilometers south of Rosario Beach?"

"Yes. We have been here before with Iggy."

They hung up, and Susannah looked at me.

"How'd I do?"

"You were perfect. We'll be driving out. You have a license?"

"No."

"Can you drive?"

"Absolutely. My California license just got lost."

"So you still have a valid license you just don't have the license card itself?"

"That's it."

"You can help me drive then."

Two hours later we were packed and loaded. Susannah borrowed some of Lisa's jeans and a sweatshirt. I told Lisa we'd get her more.

Why the car?

Before we piled in, I rummaged through the tool chest in the garage. I found an old roll-up cloth that had pockets on the inside for a screwdriver set. I dumped the screwdrivers on the work bench. Then I smuggled out James' father's handgun. It fit inside the sleeve, which I could then roll up. It had two shoelaces sewn to it to wrap around and keep it closed. Except, instead of wrapping and tying off, I rolled it up with the gun inside and the package up under the dash. There was a flange there with a hole on one end that I could thread the shoelace through. Then once around the bag and a slip-knot. I tested it from the driver's seat several times: bad guy coming, reach up under the dash, pull the loose string and the gun rolled down into my hand. Very slick. The inbound Mexican border never stopped and searched, but just on the off-chance they did, I was ready.

We drove straight through. Each of us took a four-hour driving shift followed by a four-hour free time, which I usually used for catnapping. When we arrived at the Mexican border at San Ysidro, I was driving, and I was exhausted. I was so tired I was hearing voices and seeing things--not quite, but almost. The border crossing went without a hitch--no search. Susannah told me it was a felony and automatic prison to get caught with a gun in Mexico. I thought sure, that's why all the cartels and gangs have guns because they're afraid of prison. Right.

We drove straight south from the border, about thirty kilometers to Rosarito Beach. Once we arrived there, we stopped at the Rosarito Beach Hotel and used the restroom inside the lobby. Susannah would drive the final two miles to the hacienda because she knew the way.

We headed out of Rosarito at two o'clock in the afternoon. There was leftover fog that hadn't burned off yet as we were driving along not a half mile from the ocean. Then we came to a turn-out, which Susannah took. Down a short hill we went, bouncing along in the gravel road ruts until we reached the bottom of a hill that overlooked the Pacific. It was beautiful there, but beauty was the last thing on my mind. My heart was pounding as we pulled up in front of Javier's house and Susannah turned to me. "How do you want to do this?"

"We'll go up to the door and knock. If he answers, you yell 'Yes!' and I'll take over. If it's not him yell 'No!'"

"Yes or no. Got it. Should I go in first and make sure Elena's there?"

"No, we lose the element of surprise by doing that. I want a quick, clean shot, a run inside to scoop up my granddaughter, and a dash for the car. This is isolated down here so nobody should hear the shooting."

"Don't worry about that. There are so many guns down here that there's shooting all the time. The whole felony law thing is a joke."

"All right. Well, that's good to know. Are you ready?"

"I am."

"Lean back."

I reached across her legs and pulled the shoelace. The gun dropped into my hand, and I freed it from my makeshift case. Then I pulled the slide back like I'd seen James do that night. I moved the safety and--here was my uncertain piece--I assumed I had moved it off since James had most likely left the safety on. If the gun didn't fire the first time, I would have to have the presence of mind to switch the safety the other way and try again.

I saw a face in the front window. It appeared to be a child standing on a piece of furniture and peering out. I would need to be very careful about where I was shooting. We opened our doors and climbed out. Susannah put the car keys in her pocket, and I thought nothing about it.

Up to the front door we walked. It was made of vertical

planks of wood stained reddish-brown and had a wrought iron handle and knocker. At that moment, I was holding the gun just behind my back. I had my finger on the trigger. I took a deep breath. I double-checked with my insides: I had zero compunction about shooting the man who'd raped my daughter and was now raising my granddaughter to be sold like livestock into the hell he had awaiting her. With my left hand, I reached up and rapped the knocker three times. Footsteps could be heard inside along with children squealing. "Someone's here!" a small voice shouted.

Then the door opened.

"Yes!" cried Susannah.

The man looked right into my eyes. "You Susannah's mother?"

"I'm Lisa's mother, you rotten bastard!"

With that, I swung the gun up, centered it on his forehead and pulled the trigger.

The gun went "Click!"

I pulled the trigger again. This time nothing happened.

The look of horror on Javier's face suddenly shifted to rage. He threw the door open, knocking me backward onto the seat of my pants. Then he came for me.

I worked the slide on the gun again and pulled the trigger again with the barrel trained on his midsection.

"Click!"

In one motion I pulled my legs up under me, stood, and ran for the car.

Which was when it occurred to me we didn't have Elena, and I didn't have the keys.

There had been no plan B, I realized in horror. There wasn't a backup plan in the event the gun misfired.

But it had, and now I was dashing around the car with Javier in hot pursuit. I ran across the gravel up onto the stunted grass and sandy soil and kept going beyond the house. Down the hill I ran about two hundred yards. Then I was running on the beach, heading south of the house.

My ears didn't lie to me: he was right on my tail, just about to grab me, where I zagged left. At that exact moment, he made a dive for me and narrowly missed. I jumped over him on the ground and headed back the way I had come. But then I slipped in the sand and went down. My hand went beneath the sand. I came up holding a sea shell. Or half of one. I almost dropped it and ran again except he was hovering over me and then falling onto me and pinning me down on my back. His hands encircled my throat, and the choking began like I had known all along it would. I had known he would eventually catch me and kill me.

Wildly I struck out at his face. My right hand without guidance from me flew instinctively up and swiped at his face. But I was still holding the shell. When I swiped at him, the shell zipped across his throat. Suddenly his hands released their grip on me, and he reached both hands up to his throat and held them tightly.

"Get help, please."

"You were going to kill me," I said.

It then looked like a red blooming flower an instant later as the blood came oozing over his hands and ran down his forearms. He moved his hand on his throat, attempting to staunch the flow.

But it was no use. The blood was pumping out of the side of his neck, long spurting streams as his hands fell into his lap and he slumped sideways off of me. I edged out from under and saw that I was covered in his blood. I began running back the way I had come.

The front door was still open. I dashed inside.

"Susannah!" I cried.

An older, tired-looking Mexican woman appeared out of a hallway. She was carrying a child about four years of age with very pale skin. The child turned in her arms and showed me her face.

Lisa. Twelve years ago.

There was no doubt whose toddler this was. The woman held her out to me and I took her in my arms. Her head lolled to the side without a qualm. She'd been held and passed around by many different people; she didn't at all complain about my taking her up.

Just then, Susanna came out of the hallway.

"The rest of them are Maria's kids. Half of those are Iggy's, and half are Javier's and another guy. Juanita takes great care of all of them just like they are her own. No problems, Melissa."

I began backing toward the door, almost daring the woman to follow after me and try to stop me.

But she had no intention of doing that. Instead, she held up a hand and motioned for me to pause. Instinctively I knew it was okay to do so. Then she came to my granddaughter, bent low, and kissed her on the forehead. "*Vaya con Dios*," she said, her face crestfallen. "I love this baby," she told me.

"Thank you for caring for her," I said. Susannah passed by me and turned me to head for the car.

Following Susannah, I was sure that at any instant Javier was going to come back to life and come running after me and kill us all.

But he didn't.

We stopped at the hotel again. I lurked in the arches in the shadows while Susannah bought a shirt that said *Life's a Beach*. Then I crept into the restroom and discarded the bloody shirt. I proceeded to wash away every last speck of Javier's blood, even wetting my hair and finger-combing it then drying what I could with paper towels. The shirt fit a little large, but hey, who was complaining?

Susannah was still driving, and I had Elena on my knee. I was strapped in; she wasn't. So in San Ysidro, after an hour wait at the border crossing, I went into a Walmart and picked out an approved child's car seat. We strapped it in and headed for a McDonald's where we could get a kid's meal and two burgers with fries and three boxes of milk. We sat in the car and munched without talking.

Then, out of nowhere, Elena poked a fat finger at the McDonald's and said, "Mickey D's!"

Susannah burst out laughing.

"She got that from Lisa. That's what Lisa calls McDonald's."

"Then you are the right one, aren't you?" I said to my new granddaughter.

She gave a little sideways smile and put her head back in her seat.

"Mommy?" she said.

"We're going to get Mommy in about one day."

WE PULLED into my driveway in Glencoe late the next day. The baby was asleep, and I was driving. Susannah was in the passenger's seat, her bare feet on the dashboard. She was flipping through a magazine.

When the garage door started rolling upward, here came Lisa through the door from the kitchen. She flew down the steps and threw open the back door.

Mother and child, reunited.

Grandmother, child, and grandchild...starting from scratch.

I couldn't wait to get started.

37

I t was a flophouse in Little Italy just west on Harrison. The front desk was one clerk inside a bullet-proof glass cage and four huge Philodendron plants sadly nodding in the intermittent airstream rushing in through the front doors. The floor was tiny white tiles, and the walls wore coat number 79 of interior paints.

Ishmael Montague, wearing khakis pants and a golf shirt, sunglasses, and a baseball cap, came breezing through the front door and jogged for the single elevator car. He stood at the buttons, madly hammering the up arrow and anxiously shuffling his alligator-shod feet. Across his left arm was draped a nicely folded London Fog, in the folds of which was concealed a Glock 26 with the small clip for easy concealment.

No one in the lobby paid him a bit of attention, though at one point the desk clerk, fed up with Montague's hammering of the up button, turned away from a registrant and shouted, "Hey!" toward the elevator. He didn't pay any more attention than that, however, and turned back to his newest guest. Montague saw that he had drawn attention to himself and recoiled. Attention was the last thing he wanted. Which was why he was casually dressed like so many other men in downtown Chicago on that warm spring day.

Finally, he was aboard the elevator alone, the rickety machine bumping and clacking him aloft, as it were. He got off on four, dug in his pocket for the key--an actual, metal key, not an electronic one--and let himself into his room. Maps were strewn around, and there were a dozen or more telephoto shots of his prey pinned above the small desk. Montague dropped his pants, kicked off the alligators, shrugged out of his shirt, and trod barefoot and fully nude into the bathroom where he spun the hot and cold handles of the bathtub. Minutes later he was in the tub, holding a yellow street map above the steaming water. With his eyes, he traced the northbound and major southbound roads serving Glencoe down to Laura Studios on Lindsey Lane. This exercise only served to confirm that he had, indeed, memorized the roads and side roads where an ambush might be laid. But he wasn't entirely happy with another traffic stop and shootout. For one thing, she would be expecting something like that and would be accompanied by an armed guard or two. He didn't like even fights, and he especially refused fights where the odds were in the other guy's favor. So the traffic-follow-stop-shoot scheme was tossed aside.

That left an attack on her home or an attack on her workplace. As he soaked in hot water, there was a third possibility that came to him, and it included all the stores and malls and restaurants and wherever else that she might on a whim pull into and visit. Nothing would suit him more than following her into a crowd, getting close and firing point blank into her head, then disappearing into the crowd and casually joining traffic and driving away before the police could even arrive. Those were the best hits of all. The only drawback: she almost certainly would have one or two body-guards with her at those times. Usually, they worked in pairs, one leading her and one following her. The way to avoid them returning fire was to make sure it was a crowded place where the risk of shooting an innocent was higher than the reward of shooting him.

His mind roamed back over his call from Ignacio Velasquez early that morning.

"She killed Javier," were the first words uttered when Montague accepted the call.

"My woman did that?"

"She did. Cut his throat. He bled out on the beach."

Montague shut his eyes. Javier had sent him on this mission, and now, at least in Velasquez's eyes, he had failed. The prey had succeeded in killing one of their own and yet she was still above ground. That couldn't be allowed to continue.

'I am very disappointed in you, Ishmael," said the detached voice from Mexico. "Your failure cost Javier his life. Who's to say what else she might do?"

"She's just one woman."

"One you evidently cannot make heel. She outsmarts you and makes you seem a fool from where I'm sitting. You must prove to me you are capable of finishing her before returning to Mexico. And before any further payment is made to you, Ishmael. We go way back, and I have faith in you, but I'm losing my trust. You have until Friday. After that, I'm sending someone for you."

The line went dead.

His mind was racing. It was Tuesday. That left three days to kill the woman, or he would be killed without further discussion himself. Then they would go to Argentina and kill his wife and his children. He had no doubts about any of that.

He climbed up from the tub and began drying. He knew it would be the last time he bathed before arriving back in Buenos Aires. Last night would be the last night he would sleep in a bed until then. He would dress now and locate a safe vehicle, one without warrants or holds. Then he would go to Glencoe.

38

K endra McMann was working as the head of Chicago PD's Organized Crime Division, which included gangs such as the Mexican cartels. She had seen enough kidnappings, and horrible murders by professional killers sent north from Mexico and Latin America that she had almost personally undertaken the fight against them.

Because her name was associated with the Lisa Sellars kidnapping case, she received notice when the girl's father, Mark Sellars, was murdered and his ex-wife Melissa Sellars shot. That pushed a button inside of her, so she assigned the investigation of that homicide to herself as an organized crime incident.

While Melissa was hospitalized, McMann was the first detective to visit her. She found the mother in a coma and decided to wait until she could talk. They had talked after that, but Melissa had been very little help in identifying just who had attacked them. Once she was shot through the chest, she had passed out. That shooting was the second shot fired that day by the attackers and thus she was, for all intents and purposes, a non-witness to her own shooting. She had no memory of faces, descriptions, or any other scrap of information that might help McMann and her detectives solve the case.

But there was one common item which might be a connector between the kidnapping a dozen years earlier and the murder a dozen years later. That was the name of Ignacio Menendez. His name had originally been given to her by a dancer known back then as Nancy Callender, whose professional name was Hermione. She decided to track down Nancy and talk to her just for old time's sake. Actually, for more than that: McMann wanted to know whether Nancy had heard from Menendez again. Especially recently.

McMann hit the computers and had a current address on Callender within minutes. She was married now and living in Niles, Illinois, where she was teaching high school history. Which gave McMann pause. From stripper to teacher? It was usually the other way around--teachers going into stripping to pay school loan obligations. But McMann, who had seen everything under the sun, thought no more about it.

She drove to Niles on a Tuesday afternoon just as Ishmael Montague was drying off following his bath. At Niles High School she parked and went inside to the administration offices. She explained that she had an urgent need to talk with Nancy Callender, who still used her maiden name to teach. She was rewarded with a quick retrieval of the teacher from class and provided a private office in the administration annex.

Nancy remembered the detective. She was very grateful to

her but still knew the cop could still ruin her life if the detective decided to file charges against her for her part in the kidnapping. Instead of filing those charges on her back then, McMann had allowed her to work as a CI--confidential informant. Crime was rampant at the Kit-Kat Klub back then. When the two owners were finally indicted for tax crimes and interstate transportation of minors, Nancy's help in bringing those charges wasn't forgotten. McMann had cut her loose to go her own way free and clear.

Callender arrived in the conference room with a bead of sweat on her upper lip. She was frightened beyond anything she'd felt in a dozen years. Here was that the same detective from back in those dark days now wanting to speak with her again.

She entered the room and forced a crooked smile. Detective McMann stood up from the table and gave the teacher a firm handshake that said unmistakably who was in charge.

"Nancy, I need your help again."

"I haven't been involved in any--"

"This is old stuff. You provided us with the name of Ignacio Menendez years ago. He had contacted you through a contact at the club, and you had staked out the home of Melissa and Lisa Sellars for him. We later searched your apartment and found no evidence that the kidnapped girl had ever been there, so I cut you a deal. You fulfilled that deal, and we all went on with life. Well, we've now heard from Menendez again. So I need to ask you another question. I am warning you that if you give me anything besides a true answer, you will go to prison. Understand?"

"Yes."

"Have you been contacted by Ignacio Menendez at any time during the past six months?"

"Yes."

"When was that?"

"Noon, today."

"How did he contact you?"

"Somehow he got my phone number. I was in the lounge eating my lunch when he called. I went to the restroom to talk to him."

"Tell me exactly what he said."

"He ordered me to take my own car to Glencoe to an address he gave me. He ordered me to watch for Melissa Sellars. He gave me a number I was to call when I saw her leave the house with her daughter. I was told the daughter is sixteen now and blond. For some reason, he wanted to know when they were together."

"Good. All right, here's what we're going to do."

The talk continued for another half hour. When they were done, Nancy was relieved simply because none of it was about her. Sure, she said, she'd help the police. Absolutely she'd make the call when the police told her to make it. They left it at that.

Then McMann went to talk to Melissa Sellars.

Step two.

39

Montague was surprised at the youthfulness of the man who provided the C-4 explosive. He couldn't have been over eighteen, Montague figured. He wondered where Menendez had found the guy, but he knew better than to ask.

Montague had called Menendez and updated him.

"I need enough explosive to blow a door off its hinges."

"What would that be for?" Ignacio Menendez asked.

"The police are watching the woman's house. She has armed guards with her twenty-four-seven. She is never alone. But I think they're going to run a scheme on me."

"How do you know that?"

"They brought a van to the house and ran it right into the garage. I was unable to see what came out, but I'm guessing it was cops. I'm thinking a bait-and-switch."

"They're going to fool you into attacking her car, but it will be loaded with cops?"

"Sure. That's common enough."

"You're probably right. So what will you do?"

"I won't fall for it, that's what. Except they'll think I fell for it and that's when they'll let their guard down."

"Do you need help for this?"

"Yes, I need two reliable trigger men."

"What's their risk?"

"Very low. In fact, there should be zero risks for them if they do what I say."

"Good. My wife's brother works out of Cicero. I'll send him."

"That works for me. What's his name?"

"Edwardo."

The men ended the call after Montague was given directions for obtaining the explosive. He followed the steps given to him, met the explosives purveyor at a local Burger King and made payment. The detonator and explosive were handed over in a plain paper bag. In exchange, Montague paid the man five thousand dollars, no questions asked.

"Do you know how to fire this off?" the kid asked him in a whisper.

"I do. Used it many times."

"You can drop it, shoot it, light it on fire--none of that detonates it. You absolutely must use the detonator. It's in the bag."

"How big a blast am I buying?"

"Enough to knock a door off its hinges."

"Excellent," said Montague. "That works."

VISCOUNT HALEY WAS a tough street cop with sergeant stripes who supervised a West Chicago district, an area with the highest incidence of gang shootings in the city. McMann borrowed him for her team. Viscount was two weeks shy of retirement when he entered McMann's Director's Office Thursday morning.

McMann told him to sit down. Two other uniforms were already with her.

"All right," she told them, "this is the deal. We have a cartel chief in Tijuana who put a hit on a Glencoe resident. The underlying crime of kidnapping happened here in Chicago a dozen years ago, so we've retained jurisdiction. We are, of course, working the Glencoe portion with the GPD. Any questions so far?"

There were no questions.

"The hitman is probably of Mexican descent. We say that because this is a critical hit for the cartel and it cannot go wrong. So they've sent one of their own, a trusted, loyal gunman."

"When is this all going down?"

"We're arranging for it to happen Friday."

"What do you mean, 'arranging'?"

"Making that his best opportunity."

"What are we expecting?" asked Viscount Haley.

"They tried hitting our woman when she was stopped at an intersection. They did manage to kill her husband."

"Heard about that," said Haley. The other two cops were nodding. They'd heard too.

"It was a perfect hit except the bullets fired into our woman didn't kill her. Before she could be shot one last time, her ex-husband raised his arm and managed to squeeze off a shot at the killer on her side. Killed him dead instantly. We don't think that's how it's going to happen next time. But we're going to try to make it happen that way."

"How are we going to do that and what's our role?" Sergeant Haley asked.

"Trojan Horse."

The three uniformed officers nodded. Trojan Horse was a good tactic. It involved drawing the enemy in and then using overwhelming and unexpected force to kill him. They approved.

"So what's our role in this?"

"You three men will stay behind in our target's house. This is just in case he smells a rat and tries to outthink us."

"How would that happen?"

"I can see him sniffing us out and then let us go while he circles back and hits the house where our target has actually remained. In other words, we send two officers in her car made-up to look like her and her daughter. He follows them and attacks their car at a light. That's what we're hoping for. But what if he sees through this and instead circles back and tries to enter her house? That's going to be your job, the three of you. Protection at the house. Any questions?"

"Are we it? Are there other officers left behind?"

"No, we think that carries too much risk of tipping him off."

"Could be," said Sergeant Haley. "So where's the target during all this?"

"The smallest girl will be home from school. She'll be with the two older girls and the target inside the target's upstairs bedroom."

"Are they armed? I don't want to be shot accidentally," said a uniformed officer.

"She is armed. She has a shotgun and will shoot anyone who comes through the bedroom door without identifying themselves. So here are the ID words we'll use to let her know we're friendlies."

McMann then gave out the challenge-and-response words they would use. She explained that Melissa already had these and would be ready to use them.

"Questions?"

None.

"Okay, we're done here. You, gentlemen, find an empty conference room and lay out your defense. You'll come on duty in this house tonight, eighteen hundred hours. I'll already be there."

40

My head was spinning.

"Melissa," said McMann when she called me, "I need to meet with you. Be at the Cine-14 at the Mayfair Mall at two o'clock. Theater four. I'll find you."

"Isn't that dangerous to leave here?"

"I have four cars surrounding you. It's safe.

"What's up?"

"You're in danger. Two p.m."

Nothing more than that, just meet her.

We'd been warned this might happen, that Velasquez would send someone after me. We'd been warned there would be repercussions over my trip to Mexico and my killing of Javier. Now it was happening.

It was a jolt back to reality after I'd been spending so much time with my two older girls. We'd been sorting out their lives and were pretty much agreed on a plan. I'd located a

GED course in Chicago where Susannah and Lisa would obtain their GED's. Then we would find a junior college. I was thinking of the one in Palatine as it was known for offering remedial summer classes for students who'd been out of high school for a long time. That seemed to fit what my girls needed just right.

So when the call came from McMann, it shook me up. I was going full-steam with my new family and found myself jangled after hearing there might be trouble again. I wasn't ready for trouble; I was ready for living. Lisa, I had loved since forever. She was a done deal, and I was lavishing time and attention on her like no mother before me. But with Susannah, it was a little different. She wasn't my daughter-- at least not at first. But then a funny thing happened: she opened up to me. She responded and began calling me "Mom," and following me around the house like a puppy. The three of us would spend time with mani-pedi parties with the Chinese sisters who made house calls. We all got involved in cooking dinner every night. And we had movie time every weekend where we'd pig out on finger food and British mysteries on PBS. Through all this, they got to know me and my likes, and I got to know them.

James was fantastic through it all. He was still unhappy with me that I'd insisted on going to Mexico after my grand baby, but then a cool thing happened. Elena took to climbing up on James' lap in the evenings when he was watching the news and dragging her blanket behind her so she could curl up on his lap and doze while he watched TV. Then Gladys would want to be up there too. He floated off into Happy Land and all anger at me just dissipated. My Mexico trip was forgiven, and he was more of a caregiver for our grand-daughter and Gladys than anyone else. They had every conceivable toy and doll and dollhouse. But he also got her involved with Gladys riding sidewalk cars and scooters in the driveway whenever he was home. He took them to the Shedd Aquarium. He took them to Disney on Ice. Sometimes Lisa went along, sometimes it was only James and Elena and Gladys. Like I said, the twosome had so enhanced his life it was beautiful to watch. He even asked me if I'd like another child. He reminded me I wasn't too old, and I told him I'd think about it. The truth was, I felt like I already had my hands full, but I also wasn't kidding myself. The two older girls would be out the door and going to college and dating for the first time in their lives, and they would grow away from me. But another child--that sounded very attractive. Especially if this time it was a boy. I would name him James Mark Sellars. And I would call him James Mark.

Anyway, McMann called me Thursday morning and said she needed to meet me in the Cine-14 at the Mayfair Mall. I was to come inside alone. My bodyguards were to bring me in one of their cars.

At two o'clock I was in Theater 4 as instructed when McMann came in and sat down beside me. "Let's head for the exit up front. We can talk in there."

We snuck out the exit and found ourselves in the area behind the screen where cleaning and food supplies were kept in two rooms.

McMann drew near and spoke in very low tones.

"There's going to be an attempt on you and Lisa. We think in the next twenty-four hours."

Oh, my God, I first thought, please spare me from this. But there you were: she went on to explain exactly what they'd learned from Hermione and what they believed it meant. There was a counter-play the CPD would be running jointly with the GPD to intercept and take into custody Ishmael Montague.

"Custody?" I said. "Seriously?"

"That's the goal. If he gets shot and killed in the process, it will be a justified homicide. I'll make sure of that."

I took it all in. But I wondered how ready they were for this. So I asked.

"Did you follow me here today?"

"Me personally? No. But there were four cars running a grid on you the whole way. Heavily armed police officers and two SWATs in each car. We were ready."

That made me feel better.

"What about my house? What's in place there?"

"Well, you have your people inside and out, and I have mine on the streets. He can't get within two blocks that we don't know it."

"So what's our plan over the next twenty-four hours?"

"There's an official plan and an unofficial one. The official version is we take him into custody, put him on trial for Mark's murder, and lock him up for life plus one-hundred years. That's the official plan. The unofficial plan--"

"Wait. I think I already know the unofficial plan."

She smiled for the first time.

"I think you do, too. I think you do, too."

When I left there I was convinced of one thing: I was done with all this. All of the fear, the worry, the anticipation of an attack on me or my family—I couldn't walk another step with all that hanging over me.

So I began making calls. XFBI was at the top of my list. My contact there, Klamath, told me to come to their office, where we'd make our own plan. The other unofficial plan.

So I did. I went there and we discussed where Velasquez and his people were their weakest. We discussed the man coming to kill me.

I could hardly stand to say it. Kill me? Kill Lisa?

It wasn't going to happen.

41

Thursday night, James and I went to our bedroom early and closed the doors. We felt confident that with the police presence that our home was safe.

I switched on the big screen and undressed, hopping into bed with only a T-shirt that said LAURA! James crawled in beside me and pulled me next to him. We watched a movie, and toward the end, I knew James wanted to make love. He rolled up onto an elbow when the movie had ended.

"Tell me how you're holding up," he said.

I came up on my elbows. "Wow. We need to talk. I've been thinking about all this."

Then we were sitting in bed side-by-side, holding hands.

"Let me tell you what I need. Listen carefully, please. First of all, I need you to make love to me. Then I'll tell you my plan."

The first part was easy. James kissed my face, my chest, teased my breasts and moved his mouth between my legs.

For what seemed like hours I belonged to him and to no one. I was free in my own ecstasy and floating across the universe. Then it would pass and then start building again. A half-hour later I was one big orgasmic burnout, I swear. I pushed him away and drew him up onto me. He was very excited. Moving against me and filling me with his penis I could inhale the James I had fallen in love with: the man whose breath and mouth smelled of me, the man whose semen would travel with me even as I went out that night to end this thing. I became his and his alone. I wanted to spend the rest of my life with that gentle soul and with our children--all of them because even Susannah now belonged to us. Then we were finished, exhausted, and we lay there recovering from our spent bodies for a long time.

I came back to reality, realizing I was staring at the same clouds, in the same full sky I'd had painted on our ceiling after we moved into this house. But for the first time, I looked beyond them, beyond them to the black that appears after we leave the blue behind when we die. Inexorably I felt myself being drawn there, up through the clouds, into the blackness, hoping against hope there would come a light to draw me along.

Moments later, I was out of bed, dressing.

"Listen to me," I said to James as he lay sleeping. "I'm going out. You're not. You're staying here with the girls. I could be gone several hours, but I will be back, I promise."

His eyes opened, and he lifted his head. "What on God's green earth are you talking about, Melissa?"

I went over and touched the side of his face with the back of my hand.

"After Mexico, I came home to you, yes?"

"What on earth, Mel?"

"After tonight I will come home to you too. Probably before dawn. So please wait here. Say a prayer for me. Say a prayer for yourself and for the girls. Send me positive energy."

"Where are you going?"

"I'm going to buy peace. I'm going to put an end to our drama with the Tijuana Cartel and with Ignacio Velasquez. Trust me on this."

"Mel--"

He knew better. He knew better than to try and stop me. At the hall closet downstairs, I stuck my hand in and retrieved my bag. It was heavier than I remembered. It was the overnighter that said "Captain's Club" on its side. Something from some airline in some airport somewhere--I didn't remember or care.

"Evening Ms. Sellars," said Sam Antonio, the burly watchdog of the front door. "Is it time?"

"It's time, Sam. Are you ready?"

"I am."

We opened the front door and went to his truck in the circle drive in front of our home. It was a relatively new RAM with roof lights. It looked like it could handle just about anything we threw at it. So we climbed inside and fastened our belts.

Sam pulled on through the drive, and the security man at the gate rolled it open electronically. Then we were on the street and speeding up to the T-intersection just east of us.

Without stopping at the stop sign, Sam hung a sharp left and floored it. We saw the unmarked car's lights come up on our tail. We were still accelerating. I was watching side streets out of the side windows, looking for the unmarked cars that would be following on either side of our road.

The pace cars were still with us when we came to the Kennedy Expressway. We blasted westbound a good ten minutes and then finally took the off-ramp to Palatine. At the bottom of the ramp, just before the stop sign, Sam suddenly stopped, backed up, and pulled lengthwise across the ramp, blocking it off. At just that same moment, a dark sedan pulled up just beyond us and stopped. I jumped out and ran for the sedan. As I was jumping in, here came the unmarked cars up to Sam's truck. They turned on their red-and-blue lights and began angrily broadcasting over their loudspeakers for Sam to move his vehicle By then, my new driver and I were across the interchange and heading back eastbound down the on-ramp.

"Klamath," I said, "it's working."

"Sure it's working, Melissa. Just like I told you it would. XFBI at your service."

They were one of the best secret security agencies in the world. XFBI had contacts all across the U.S. And Interpol and Scotland Yard and into France and Germany. They also had an office in Buenos Aires. Klamath, my new driver, had been an FBI agent working counterterrorism until his retirement just two years ago. He still knew everyone, and his contacts could find a needle in any haystack in the world.

Which is exactly what he had done with Mr. Ishmael Montague. He had found him; he had talked with him; he had held a big gun to his head, and he had made a friend out of a sworn enemy.

Well, maybe not exactly a friend, but a man who knew what it would take to go on living. That was close enough.

When we hit the downtown Loop's turnoffs, we zipped off the freeway and headed north. Up six blocks and down into underground parking, then a long elevator ride up to the seventy-eighth floor. I knew the way myself. I had been there after my meeting with McMann that afternoon when something inside me had snapped. Some people call it the last straw, some people call it something else. But what it meant for me—after McMann told me about Montague's enlistment of Hermione in a plan to murder us—it meant that I was done running. I was done with all the killing. Besides, if McMann did manage to kill Montague as she had suggested she might, that would stop nothing. Velasquez would just send someone else after me and keep sending more until I was dead. Maybe he'd even go after the rest of my family; who could say?

How do you stop a crazy man? You go after the thing that matters most to him. Which is exactly what I did.

There is a universal currency that men fight to obtain. It's a currency that gets them happy families, gorgeous mistresses, golf club memberships, shiny black cars from Germany and Italy. It's a currency that no man can ever have enough of, that no man can ever stop pursuing. It's built into the male psyche, I'm convinced, and it can open any door in the world. As we rode the elevator skyward, I studied the Captain's Club bag on the elevator floor. This special currency was secured inside.

At last, the elevator stopped, and we stepped through the doors.

There, straight ahead, was the simple brass sign beside a simple steel door: XFBI.

Klamath and I went inside after he had entered a series of numbers into the keypad.

42

I was told by Klamath that Montague was being held in a back office. But I would get to look him in the eye before we were done there that night. That was my demand of the agents I'd hired.

Then the work of creating a crime scene began.

I was stretched out on the floor, and a forensic tech appeared overhead. Looking up, I thought his eyes looked familiar, but the rest of his face was covered by a surgeon's mask. So I shut my eyes and let him begin. I felt his brush smearing the liquid on my chest and on the side of my face, smelled the sickly smell of the chicken blood as it was applied. Then I was told to open my mouth, which I did. A smear of oatmeal was put there, leaking down the side of my face.

"Don't move now," said the man in charge.

The makeup artist then fixed to my forehead the bullet entry wound he had modeled out of paraffin and acrylic paint. There was no blood around the wound; entry wounds rarely bleed upward when a victim is on their back.

The forensic tech then arranged my arms and legs and looped a purse around my wrist. Clasped to my chest by my free arm were several file folders that looked like I had just turned away from a filing cabinet when shot. Sure enough, at my head, not a foot away was a filing cabinet. Now the scene was set.

My eyes were closed. My mouth looked like it was vomiting. A bullet hole sprouted up and out of my forehead. There was no doubt to anyone at the scene: I was dead.

Photography then ensued. Close-ups of my face, shots of the whole of me against the floor, shots from every angle but the same light that never changed. Which was when they brought Montague into the room and told him to sit down next to me. He did. Using Montague's own phone the forensic tech leaned in and snapped a selfie of Montague with me.

Then we were done, and Montague was lifted to his feet by two agents.

Next, I was cleaned up and told to change shirts. All remnants of my murder were wiped, removed, and scrubbed clean.

Which was when they took me into Montague's room. I had my Captain's Club bag with me containing the currency that no man could ever resist. Especially Latin men.

They sat me at a desk across from Montague. He was a small man, much younger than I had imagined, with thick black hair combed back from his forehead, full lips below a brushy mustache, and hands that forever rubbed back and forth as he sought some kind of inner peace to ease their restlessness. Immediately I knew him for what he was: a paid killer. There was no light in his eyes, no sign of fear, and neither was there a bemused expression like some men will put on when they're cornered and know the end is near.

I swung the bag up onto the desk and said to him, "Look inside."

He did as he was told. Looking inside, he saw something else and looked at it.

Then he turned as pale as a sheet of copy paper, I swear it. Immediately his face was covered in sweat, and his mouth opened and closed soundlessly.

"Si," he said.

That was the only word I ever heard him say.

Si--yes, he would pursue us no more. And with the pictures of me at my murder scene which he would deliver to Ignacio Velasquez, the cartel would pursue us no more either.

It was done.

How do I know Ishmael Montague was a man of his word and would keep his end of the bargain for the huge sum of money I paid him that night?

I didn't--I don't. But so far he has, and it's been five years.

43

Detective McMann and I arrived at O'Hare Airport at just after six the morning after I met Montague and paid him off. She had been alerted there were airport CCTV films of Montague boarding a plane before dawn and flying out of Chicago. Facial recognition software had identified him and flagged Detective Kendra McMann.

Together we walked inside the airport after leaving her car at the curb right in front of the main terminal.

She knew the way to security on the second floor. We hurried up the stairs together.

A jocular young man wearing a TSA uniform allowed us to enter the room once McMann had flashed her star.

"Ishmael Montague," she told the young man. "All video."

"Coming right up," the TSA officer said. "Watch screen four."

We did as we were told. I was amused when I saw a man carrying my Captain's Club bag into the airport, right through the main entrance. There was no doubt who it was;

McMann turned to me "Meet Ishmael Montague," she told me through tight lips.

"I see him," I said. "He does look like a killer."

Which made no sense. I still wouldn't know a killer from a carpet cleaner as far as she knew. I was still a TV producer, not a cop. And not the woman who had seen the man the night before.

We watched as the man moved through the focus of several cameras: standing in line at the ticket counter; walking down the TSA security line; walking back up the long corridor toward the waiting area. And then we watched as he boarded a plane bound for San Diego.

"She was wheels-up maybe an hour ago. ATC says there is nothing unusual, they are non-stop to San Diego."

McMann turned to me. I'd never seen the woman look more puzzled than right at that moment.

"I honestly don't know what to think, Melissa," she said to me. "We could have him arrested, but we have no proof he committed any crime. I just don't know what to think."

"Me neither," I said.

"But we'll never let our guard down," she promised me. "He won't get within fifty miles of my city without me knowing. It's a done deal."

"That makes me feel better," I said.

We left the airport that day, and she drove me home.

Except we did stop off for breakfast after she'd made a half-dozen calls on her radio.

She gave me the third degree. How did I explain him leaving? Had I done or said anything to him personally? Had someone else done something? This went on for a good thirty minutes while I suffered through eggs and bacon that had never been as tasteless as when a police officer was expressing her suspicions of me between the lines of what she was actually saying.

I had done something, and she knew it.

She just didn't know what.

44

I shmael Montague did fly to San Diego, where he walked out of the airport and jumped on the trolley to the U.S.-Mexico border. From there it was a forty-five-minute ride on the Imperial Way blue line. He relaxed during the ride, jumping off the trolley one time to run across the street and buy a pint of gin, which he tucked into the pocket of his coat and nipped at after he had hopped yet another trolley south.

After arriving in San Ysidro, he walked into a pawn shop across from the station and sold his .44 magnum. Hanging from his shoulder was the Captains Club bag Melissa had given him. Inside were two 8 x 10 pictures. One of them was a picture of Ignacio Velasquez and written across the bottom in red ink were the words: "¡Matar a este hombre!" Kill this man! The second picture was a picture of his own mother. It had been taken by XFBI in Buenos Aires just two days earlier. It was the reason why Montague had come to Tijuana instead of flying straight home to Buenos Aires.

Then there was also a group of smaller photographs bound with a single silver paperclip.

From the station, it was a short walk to the Mexican border. He moved toward the left of the central San Ysidro transit center building. There were signs in both English and Spanish that lead the way to the well-known—to him— swivel gates and Mexican custom lines that lead to Tijuana. Passing through immigration into Mexico was a simple process.

Once he had crossed the Mexican border and exited immigration, he had a choice. Downtown Tijuana was about a thirty-minute walk. There would be plenty of cantinas along the way where he could buy a beer to chase his gin. So he decided to walk. His appointment wasn't until 11 a.m., so there was plenty of time. Besides, he wanted to be fairly well-oiled by the time he got there. The meeting and the outcome were going to be much more dangerous than anything he'd ever done before. Alcohol was a must.

Usually, he worked without alcohol. But this wasn't normally. This was a once-in-a-lifetime meeting with the most powerful man in Mexico.

Two miles south of the border he ducked into a cantina named Oso Negro after the famous alcohol producer. Oso Negro was a household name in Mexico, and the familiarity beckoned to Montague as he stepped inside and pulled out a barstool with the toe of his boot. The stool squeaked as he dragged it several inches across the tile floor, causing the bartender to look up from his chores at the wet sink and walk toward the killer.

"Yes, sir?"

"Dos Equis, please," Montague replied in Spanish.

A minute later, his beer arrived. He pulled the gin bottle from his pocket, took a swallow, and chased it down with a drink of the beer. Much better, he thought, much better than swilling down straight gin. Someone might think I'm no better than a common drunk, drinking straight from the bottle. Well, I'm not. I'm just—I'm just—

He couldn't even think it. He couldn't even think that he was scared—no—terrified at what he was about to do.

Three more beers chased down three more shots of gin. He paid his tab with American dollars, walked toward the cantina entrance, and looked out into the brilliant sunshine. Then he walked across the street, dodging cars and taxis as he went, and ducked into a leather goods store. Trying on several leather hats, he finally found one with a silver belt encircling the crown. The hat fit him perfectly, so he paid twelve dollars to the owner. Then he hailed a taxicab.

"I need a gun," he told the driver.

The cab driver looked at him in the mirror.

"Are you the police?"

"Do I look like the fucking police, huh?"

The cab driver turned off the main drag, went up two stop signs, and began driving up a small hill.

"How much do you want to spend?" the driver said as he pulled up alongside a well-kept adobe.

"Price isn't important. I need a small gun. A two-inch barrel if possible."

"I'll go inside," said the cabbie, and he went up and entered the house without knocking. A few minutes later he stuck his head out the door. "Five hundred American?"

"Okay," Montague shouted back.

The cabbie came and collected five one-hundred dollar bills from his passenger. Then he disappeared inside the house.

He returned carrying a white handkerchief wrapped around a solid object. He stopped at the rear window and passed the package inside. Montague unfolded the handkerchief and saw the .38-caliber S&W pistol. He checked the cylinder. Fully loaded.

Then he did a funny thing. He removed his hat and studied it. Then he turned it over and began pulling at the knot at the inside rear of the hat. The knot was a strong leather thong that exited out the back of the hat and comprised the belt upon which the silver conchos of the belt were strung. Freeing up the knot inside, he placed the gun in the top of the hat where it lay upside-down in his lap. Then he threaded the leather thong through the trigger guard and tied it off.

He next tried it on. The hat fit his head perfectly; the gun was nowhere to be seen.

"All right," he told the cabbie, "take me to La Posada Rojo."

"This is going to cost you."

"Money is no object. Is one-hundred USD enough?"

"Yes, Señor, that is fair for the ride."

"And how much to keep you quiet?"

The cabbie studied him in the rearview mirror. It was like the killer had read his mind.

"One thousand U.S."

Ever so slowly Montague counted off eleven one-hundred dollar bills. He passed them forward to the driver.

For the next several minutes they threaded through creeping, late-morning traffic. Everyone was out by now, and the streets were clogged with cars and trucks and scooters, particularly in the traffic circles, where it was mayhem. Montague checked his watch.

He still had fifteen minutes.

The taxi pulled up in front of the cantina with the sign of the red inn, La Posada Rojo. Without exchanging another word with the driver, the passenger threw open the rear door, climbed out and disappeared inside the cantina. The taxi lurched ahead and began a run for the other end of town.

Montague entered the cantina and looked around for a table. Everything was taken even at ten forty-five in the morning. It was mostly tourists, so he stood at the bar and ordered a beer while he waited for a table to open. Halfway down the beer a man and woman got up from the table under the bullfight poster. The man threw a few bills on the table, and they were walking away when Montague hurried by them and claimed the table. He sat down and whistled to the bartender to bring him another beer.

While the killer waited, his eyes slowly passed across every other face in the cantina. He was looking for the telltale eyes of the cartel man, eyes that held no light and no love. But the men and women who were occupying the tables and dancing to the jukebox were for the most part gringos— tourists on a lark. He didn't feel threatened by any of them, which was a good thing. He just might make it out alive after all.

At 11:05 Montague was horrified that he might have been stood up. He had called the man last night and told him he had the pictures of the dead woman to give him. The man wanted the pictures. He wanted proof that the killer of Javier Menendez was in hell where she belonged.

At 11:07 everything changed. The man himself walked in. To the utter astonishment of Ishmael Montague, the man had but one other man with him. Montague wasn't about to lapse into a false sense of security just because the man was traveling with only one bodyguard. He figured there would be three or four outside on the sidewalk carefully watching everyone who came and went.

Montague stood up from his table and raised his arm over his head. The man's head turned. He had seen the killer.

Walking over with an expressionless mask that he wore when doing business, Ignacio Velasquez started for Montague's table. He roughly pushed his way through several dancers who were swinging and swaying to Elton John's *Saturday Night's Alright For Fighting.*

Coming up to the table, Velasquez took the far seat across from Montague, snugged up against the wall and the bull-fight poster. His bodyguard made Montague raise his arms out to the sides, and he patted him down. "Clean," he told his boss. Velasquez nodded. His bodyguard sat down next to him, blocking the narcotraficante with his bulk.

"What would you like?" the bodyguard asked his boss.

"We just wait," said Velasquez. "Someone is coming."

Sure enough, minutes later a woman wearing a peasant blouse and bright red lipstick on her full lips was bending forward, displaying her ample cleavage to the crime boss. She knew that he owned La Posada Rojo and knew he expected the best alcohol and service and whatever else he wanted when he came there.

"Bring me a Coke in a bottle," said Velasquez.

"American or Mexican?" asked the waitress, smiling beyond all reasonable smiles.

"Mexican Coke always," the boss answered.

"Anyone else?" she said to the bodyguard and Montague.

"I'm fine," said Montague.

"He don't drink on duty," Velasquez told the woman, smiling and showing his gold dental crowns. "And bring this other one another bottle of beer. He's running on empty over here."

Montague shrugged at the woman and smiled. Another beer would be just fine.

The woman sliced back across the dance floor effortlessly. While she was away, no words were exchanged. They would talk when it was time.

The drinks arrived. Velasquez watched as the woman opened the Coke with a bottle opener. The beer was already open when it arrived.

"To you," said Velasquez, holding the open Coke aloft. He

touched it to the beer bottle held by Montague. Then they both drank deeply.

"So. Do you have them?" Velasquez asked.

"I do."

Montague unzipped his Captains Club bag and looked inside. The photographs he wanted for the narco were clipped with a single paperclip. He pulled the photos from the bag and laid them before Velasquez, right side up. He removed the paperclip.

Velasquez slowly slid picture after picture to the side, studying the woman who had come to his home and played the gun game and won. It looked to him like she had finally lost.

He studied the close-up of the bullet hole in the center of her forehead.

"There's no blood," he said to Montague, an eyebrow raised.

Montague reached across the table and slid the picture aside. "Look at this next one. It's taken further away. Now, look at the blood on both sides of her head. The bullet blew out the back of her head, Iggy."

"I see, I see."

"I promise you, she is quite dead."

"Now I can see that. You have done well, Monti. A very nice piece of work. Now I don't get to kill you. Maybe some other time." The same smile with the same gold crowns was displayed, proof to Montague that the narco was only teasing. But Montague didn't take it as a tease. He took it in all seriousness.

"Well," said Montague. "I'm glad you're satisfied. Now I have to find the bathroom. Too many beers."

Velasquez's eyes were still studying the photos when Montague stood and pushed his chair away from the table. The bodyguard studied his every move.

"Please," said Montague, removing his hat, "please watch my hat while I'm gone." He went to lay it down but didn't. Instead, his hand swept inside and found the snub-nosed pistol, and he pointed the muzzle directly at the guard's forehead. With two quick shots, he killed the guard and Velasquez. It was short and over in a millisecond. Many in the cantina turned to look, but Montague was already leaving through the front door.

"Take me to the border," he told the cabbie waiting out front for a tourist. "¡Prisa!"

They flew through the streets back to the border while Montague pushed one-hundred-dollar-bills over the seat-back into the driver's lap. "How fast can you get me there? Faster!"

The American border agent would take no less than five-thousand dollars to let him pass through at the head of the long line. He waited on others while Montague counted out the bills then passed them through the window inside his American passport. The passport came back to him empty, and the gate opened to allow him through.

Rather than a trolley ride, this time he took a cab back to the airport. A flight was waiting to Lisbon, Portugal, where his wife and his mother and his son would already be waiting for him.

There was enough money in the bag that they would never want. The American woman had seen to that.

45

My beautiful family.

My adopted daughter Susannah got her GED and became a dental hygienist. She's happily married to a stockbroker on the Chicago Exchange. At first, she cleaned his teeth. Then they went out and were later engaged. They married at First Methodist in Evanston and now live in a suburban condo with its own back yard in which two English Sheepdogs play with the twin girls who come outside under Mommy's watchful eye. The yard is fenced, and there are video cameras all around.

Susannah herself is a happy, well-adjusted young woman who is confident and sometimes even a bit trusting of others around her. My relationship with her isn't perfect, mostly because her history with her birth parents wasn't what it needed to be. Hopefully, James and I have filled some of her empty places in her soul, and hopefully, she'll continue to drop by and see us every other day or so, with and without kids, with and without her husband, just because she likes us. We don't talk about Mexico--ever. She is satisfied with the work she did with the counselors we provided and the time we all spent together before she married. I wouldn't trade her for any of my kids; she is special in her own right, and she is loved.

Gladys is at that awkward stage between childhood and teenager when friends are the most important thing in the world, and there aren't enough hours in the day to send and receive all the texts one needs to make one's world a satisfactory place. She runs the sprints in track and has a trophy wall in her bedroom as she's now winning county-wide events. James and I attend all of her track meets, and we sometimes chaperone her school dances. When she grows up, she wants to be an environmental scientist specializing in community water supplies. She works and earns money by babysitting, and some of that goes to African water well exploration and drilling. We are repeatedly warned by her how foolish it is to buy bottled water; we use a relatively inexpensive filter on our taps that she researched and recommends.

James knows I miss Mark. He knows that in one way Mark was the love of my life and he knows that in an entirely different way he—James—is the love of my life. They are very different men, and they appealed to entirely different parts of me. I teach my girls that women are very different from men in how we see the world and family and mates but that we all have the same brain that can learn and excel at the same mental challenges in this life. I like to think that because of this my girls have never flinched from trying things in the world that a half century ago women weren't supposed to be doing. We're all equals now, and that's the one thing I have asked they seek in a mate--whether male or female--a partner. The reason I go into such depth on this stuff with my girls--especially Susannah and Lisa, is that they had so much of their personhood--read 'womanhood'-- all but extinguished by the men who once owned them and abused them. We talk a lot, all of us, about the value of the individual and the gift of equality we're all born with.

But I digress from James. He knows, more than anything else, that he's the man I chose--while there was the opportunity to have a choice--to spend the rest of my life with. He knows there were times I wavered, but I always came home to him, even when I loved my husband who was no longer my husband. Mark's parents participate in all of our girls' lives as well as the life of James Mark.

That's right, we did have another child. He's a happy, healthy, bouncy boy who climbed on top of the refrigerator at fifteen months and scooped out most of a chocolate cake for himself. We have a lot more teaching moments with James Mark about the physical world than we did with all the girls combined. Which is something I've learned about men: they are born to hold things, touch things, taste things, and disassemble things and then leave them in pieces for someone else to enjoy. This seems to be the story of their interaction with the physical world, as near as I can tell, and I love them for it. My little girls went inward--feelings, family, mothering, loving--while my little boy goes ever outward: like I said, hold, touch, taste, disassemble, move on. I am so glad we had another. I wouldn't have missed James Mark for anything. Here's the really crazy part about him: he is James' spitting image, as they say. But there are parts of his personality that are Mark all over again: the derring-do, the willingness to saw off the branch he's sitting on just to see what happens, the fearlessness of all things mechanical. But I know, these personality traits aren't derived from Mark, or are they? Maybe some part of me was so deeply touched by this man that I absorbed his genetics and now pass some of him on to my own son. Of course, that's impossible. Until science proves otherwise--which is where my money's riding.

My mothering of Lisa didn't change Lisa nearly so much as it changed me. I went from being a somewhat shy, socially inept person with a giant creative brain that translated well into producing hugely popular TV shows, to being a shy, socially inept person who would kill a man to save my grandchild's life. Do I regret that at all, that I killed Javier? Not for a minute. Not even for a second. I'm the woman in the courtroom who would jump over the rail and claw the eyes out of the man who raped my daughter. Or cut his throat with a jagged seashell and lie back thanking God while he bled to death in the sand next to me. Maybe I always was that person and just hadn't been challenged. Maybe we're all like that. I think mothers are, probably fathers too.

The other day I was waiting outside the freshman Sciences building of the University of Chicago Medical School where Lisa spends her days. It turned out she has a brain capable of absorbing and utilizing massive amounts of information, especially in the sciences and mathematics. She did college in three years at Loyola, maintaining a four-point GPA all the way through. UC Med School bent over backward trying to get her signature on their letter of intent. She says that she's going to become a trauma surgeon. Why? "Because," she says with a laugh, "My middle name is trauma."

She came out of the building at 4:05 p.m., carrying her brief-case and her unopened umbrella. Her raincoat was unbuttoned, and the light rain was quickly matting her blond hair to her head. I watched her through the wash of my windshield wipers as she strolled casually toward our car. She opened the door.

"Why didn't you use your umbrella?" I asked her. "You're soaked."

"Because of poor Mr. Durant."

"Who might that be?"

"He's the patient we lost this afternoon. I'm feeling the rain for him."

We then drove straight home. Elena was waiting for us at the kitchen door like she always does. When her mother entered the door first, the little girl's squeals were loud and long. She was so so happy to have her mom home with her again.

"Was she always with you in Mexico?" I asked Lisa later.

"No, there would be days when I would be with some man. Iggy passed me around. I would then come home to her, but I'd be too exhausted and too brain-dead to be any good for her. Thank God for Juanita, who was always there for her. She's another one who should be rescued."

I had no answer for that.

Our family has moved on from the horror. But there's one thing close friends continue to ask me. They whisper to me at parties and family gatherings, "Are you safe? Is the cartel done trying to hurt you?"

I cannot tell anyone the truth about what I paid XFBI to do for my family. It was very expensive. It involved their agents in Argentina taking immediate action to locate and confront certain people. Was it successful?

We're at five years and counting now.

Let me tell you why I think we'll make six years.

When a man comes home at night after a long day at work, he wants a hot meal and expressions of gratitude from his family for a job well done. It's never this clear cut, never this obvious, but if the signs and indicators are there, he will keep on coming home to that house at night, and he will stay loyal to the family living there.

With Latin American and South American families it's somewhat different than what North Americans might know. In those Latin cultures, there is an additional place at the table. That additional place many times will be the mother of the man of the house. In America, we put those women into nursing homes at the age where they have reached a particular disutility that we might think of as uselessness. Not so in Buenos Aires, Argentina, where Ishmael Montague hailed from.

In Buenos Aires, the custom is the man's mother at the table. She is revered by the man and sometimes by his wife--though not always--but she is second only to Mary, the Mother of our Lord in the man's pecking order. She is sacrosanct.

Imagine, then, Montague opening my Captain's Club bag and finding inside the one million dollars he had agreed to accept for leaving us alone. Now imagine how the bargain was sealed with that universal currency all men crave: a happy, healthy mother. A happy, healthy woman who repre-sents the first love of any man's life. Imagine how

Montague's heart jumped with joy when he saw his mother's picture in the bag.

Now imagine how he felt when he saw a loaded, cocked gun held against her head.

There's the empty place at the table no man wants to see.

THE END

ALSO BY JOHN ELLSWORTH

EMAIL SIGNUP

If you would like to be notified of new book publications, please sign up for my email list. You will receive news of new books, newsletters, and occasional drawings for Kindles.
— John Ellsworth

ABOUT JOHN ELLSWORTH

John Ellsworth 2016

USA TODAY Bestselling Author John Ellsworth practiced law while based in Chicago. As a criminal defense attorney John saw up close the devastation families of kidnap victims go through. Some of that experience and knowledge led to his writing this book, *The Empty Place at the Table*, which deals with the most terrifying challenges faced by a woman whose daughter is abducted.

Since 2014 John has been writing legal, crime, and psychological thrillers with huge success. He has been a Kindle All-Star (Amazon's selection) many times and he has made the *USA TODAY* bestsellers' list.

Reception to John's books has been phenomenal; more than 1,000,000 have been downloaded in 40 months. All are Amazon best-sellers.

John lives in Southern California where he makes his way around his small beach town on a yellow Vespa motorscooter and where he writes music and novels for fun.

ellsworthbooks.com
johnellsworthbooks@gmail.com

ABOUT JODE JURGENSEN

Jode Jurgensen received her undergraduate and master's degrees from San Diego State University and she taught English to college freshmen and seniors for thirty years before taking retirement with her husband and heading south of the border.

Before beginning her writing career, Jode and Ross traveled North America in their Dodge Ram and fifth wheel, developing an interest in lighthouses and serving as lighthouse keepers up and down the east and west coasts of the North American Continent.

Jode began writing in her teens and has written primarily poetry and professional papers on the life and writings of Emily Dickinson. She began writing fiction after retiring.

jodejurgensen@gmail.com

Cover design by Nathan Wampler.

Published by Subjudica Press, San Diego.

Amazon ASIN: B06XP4PS95

First edition

Ellsworth, John. *The Empty Place at the Table*. Subjudica House. Kindle Edition.

AFTERWORD

I make my living writing books and I'm very happy about that. The practice of law is difficult and will wear you out in a hurry. But because I make my living writing books, I would really like to ask your help. Book reviews are the lifeblood of what I do, and your review of my book would mean a lot to me. If you would take a moment or two and leave your review that would be wonderful. I honestly thank you.